"I wanted...you."

Baldly, Natasha played her one, desperate card.

It seemed at first that he wasn't going to respond. He might have been a wooden statue. Then, unexpectedly, he flung back his head and laughed.

"That's good," he said finally. "Try another one."

She said, almost whispering, "It's true."

His eyes narrowed on her, studying her for a long, long moment as if she were something wriggling on the end of a pin. "Prove it."

She could do nothing at first but stare at him, her heart hammering, her shocked eyes locked with his.

His cool gaze dropped to the front of her dress. "You could start," he suggested, "by undoing those buttons."

"No," she said, feeling her heart break within her. It couldn't possibly make things any better, not when he could look at her with nothing in his eyes but that angry, oddly cold lust.

She made to step back, but the coffee table allowed her only a few inches more. "I'm no sacrificial virgin, Ryder. I won't let you make love to me for some kind of revenge."

Weddings by De Wilde™

Weddings by DeWilde™

PREVIOUSLY AT DeWILDES

DeWildes Fifth Avenue is back on track...

- Chloe Durrant has managed to turn the ledger page of DeWildes Fifth Avenue back to black...with savvy marketing and design plans, and a little help from a newly reformed, newly enthusiastic, newly in love Sloan DeWilde.

- Investigator Nick Santos has been sniffing around New York for clues to the disappearance of the famed DeWilde jewels.

Now, it seems, the trail is leading down under, to Australia, and DeWildes, Sydney.

Daphne de Jong is acknowledged as the author of this work.

ISBN 0-373-82540-4

WILDE HEART

Copyright © 1996 by Harlequin Books S.A.

Wilde Heart
DAPHNE CLAIR

Harlequin Books

TORONTO • NEW YORK • LONDON
AMSTERDAM • PARIS • SYDNEY • HAMBURG
STOCKHOLM • ATHENS • TOKYO • MILAN
MADRID • WARSAW • BUDAPEST • AUCKLAND

DeWildes™
SYDNEY

Dear ~~Valued Customer~~ *Natasha,*

It is my pleasure to invite you to attend two very special pre-Christmas functions at DeWildes' Sydney store.

To climax our *First Birthday Celebration* we will be showing, to invited guests only, the latest of our exclusive designer fashions, including fabulous wedding gowns from our own

DeWILDES BRIDAL COLLECTION

accompanied by priceless items from the legendary

DeWILDES FAMILY JEWELLERY

This private collection of some of the most exquisite and valuable jewels in the world has not been publicly shown since 1948. And the first night of this exclusive, never-to-be-repeated showing will be marked with a cocktail party for specially invited guests.

Your personalized invitations for both these exciting events are enclosed. I look forward to seeing you there.

Ryder Blake
General Manager

RSVP

CHAPTER ONE

RYDER BLAKE SIPPED at the chardonnay the waiter had poured into his glass and nodded approval. The man moved around the table to fill Grace DeWilde's glass, and Ryder took the opportunity to covertly study his lunch companion.

A beige silk suit and discreet pearl earrings complemented Grace's mature beauty, and her pale blond hair was drawn into an elegant knot, highlighting the delicate bone structure of her face. But Ryder noted signs of strain in the newly disciplined mouth and a tautness about her eyes, the fine lines more pronounced than he remembered.

She smiled at the waiter before he left the table—a smile that brought back memories for Ryder—and then turned her attention to him. "Well?" Her husky voice held a note of gentle humor. "Do I pass?"

Caught staring, Ryder smiled back at her, turning the glass before him with long, lightly tanned fingers. "You look great," he said. The compliment was sincere, but he was aware of a tug of grief in his gut, because something was missing. Beneath Grace's surface serenity there had always been a glow of gaiety, a quicksilver vitality and an unfeigned candor about her emotions that attracted and held people, made them want to bask in the warmth of her personality. The serenity was still there, but now the glow seemed to have dimmed.

"You look great, too, Ryder," she told him. "It's good for my ego." At the quizzical lift of his brows, she laughed.

"*You* may think of me as an honorary aunt, but other people see me lunching with a tall, dark and handsome younger man. I've received envious glances from several women of my age." Her discreetly painted lips twisted ironically. "My self-esteem has taken a battering lately, and I'm grateful for their flattering assumptions, even if they are completely wrong."

"I couldn't believe it when Gabe phoned and told me about the breakup," Ryder said. He was thankful he hadn't had to learn the news first from the terse company memo that had been faxed to his office in Sydney the following day.

Grace's blue eyes became shadowed before she glanced down and reached out her hand to pick up her wine and sip at it. Replacing the glass carefully, she kept her gaze focused on the snowy starched tablecloth. "Gabriel blames me. It's hard on him and the other children—" her voice became even huskier "—but Jeffrey left me no choice."

"You don't mean he threw you out?" Ryder failed to keep the shocked disbelief from his voice.

"Nothing so crude. He just...made it clear that our marriage was over, that he had no interest in it anymore."

"I can't believe that—" Ryder broke off as their Dungeness crab and side salads arrived, accompanied by a basket filled with another San Francisco specialty—sourdough French bread.

"So," Grace said as though he hadn't spoken, "I decided to come back home. London is a cold and gloomy place, and I only bore with it because I—"

Because she had loved her husband and their family, Ryder guessed as she reached for a piece of bread. And she hadn't always hated London. He recalled her enthusiasm for its ancient streets and famous landmarks, even after she'd been living in England for years. She'd loved to take him and Gabe to Rule's, the city's oldest restaurant, and point out the names and portraits of the historical figures who had dined there, and she'd adored going to shows at Covent Garden.

Sometimes she'd taken Gabriel and Ryder with her. Jeffrey claimed to be tone deaf and was happy to see Grace escorted by her son and his friend. She had professed to disbelieve him. "It's an excuse. You just prefer being a couch potato," she'd teased once. "Staying home with your latest Robert Ludlum book and your video player. Are those blue movies that you've rented? Just as well I'm taking the boys away." The two teenagers were hovering in the doorway, ready to leave.

Jeffrey had raised his brows at that and said in a voice intended for her ears only, "Why would I need blue movies, my darling?" And then he'd smiled slowly, tenderly, his eyes never moving from hers.

Grace had blushed like a girl, and Ryder, overhearing, had experienced an odd, tight sensation in his chest, silently comparing his own parents' relationship with theirs.

Thanks to Grace, Ryder had learned to be at ease in the sophisticated world in which the DeWildes moved, and to appreciate music of all kinds. Grace had also taught him an appreciation of the world of business. He'd had all the normal teenage boy's abhorrence of shopping with a woman. But Grace didn't merely shop—she approached the retail trade with the mentality of a guerrilla leader gauging the strength of the opposition. The boys became adept at helping her check out DeWilde's competition—the Carnaby Street boutiques, the department stores on Oxford Street and, of course, their world-famous archrival, Harrods.

"Gabriel reckons your opening a store here is just to spite his father," Ryder said now. "Setting up in opposition to the house of DeWilde."

Grace's eyes flickered, and he thought he detected a wounded expression in them, but when she spoke, her voice was composed. "If I'd wanted to take business from DeWilde's, I'd have located my store in New York. Gabriel is . . . hurt, and lashing out. You know what he's like under-neath that cool, hard-headed manner he cultivates, trying to be like his father.''

Ryder smiled faintly. He did indeed know. He'd first met Gabriel DeWilde at their exclusive English boarding school when Gabe had taken on a couple of much bigger class-mates who'd been teasing him. His fists flying and face red with fury, the younger boy had obviously given no thought to the fact that he couldn't possibly win, and that discre-tion would definitely have been the safer, if not the better, part of valor in the circumstances.

Ryder had weighed in to even the odds, earning Gabe's reluctant thanks and scrupulous repayment of the debt in the form of an invitation to join Gabriel and his parents for afternoon tea on the next Parents' Day.

Neither boy had mentioned the reason for the invitation at the time, and Ryder had thought that Gabriel's father— a tall, spare man with a rather aloof air—was puzzled when Gabe declared, ''This is my friend Ryder.''

Ryder had been a big boy at the ungainly stage of adoles-cence. He had a chip on his shoulder that showed in his de-fiant disregard of the neatness the masters tried to impose on their uniformed charges, and he wore an expression of wary mistrust. Even his wayward dark hair refused to con-form to the regulation school haircut. But Grace had given him a dazzling, welcoming smile and kissed his cheek just as she had her son's. She smelled of flowers and had re-tained a coloring of her American accent, softer than the clipped upper-class English tones he heard every day. In half an hour she'd made Ryder her slave for life.

She'd drawn out of him the laconic information that his parents lived in Australia and that he didn't know where he would be spending the summer holidays. Seeing sympathy in her eyes, he'd been ready to add something aggressive and uncaring, when she bestowed another of her wonderful smiles on him and said firmly that of course he must come home with Gabriel in the holidays.

If Gabriel was dismayed, he had been far too well brought up to show it. During that holiday the two boys, different in background and temperament as they were, had forged a real friendship that lasted far beyond their school days.

"How is the Sydney store?" Grace asked as she put down her fork. He noticed that she'd hardly done justice to the crab, although it was deliciously moist and lightly flavored with a lemon butter sauce.

Ryder answered noncommittally. "It's early days, but the signs are good."

"With you in charge, I'm sure it's going to be one of DeWilde's most successful ventures."

"Plans are already getting under way for celebrating our first year in business. Do you have any ideas?"

"You'll want to make the most of it. Storewide promotions of special merchandise, a party atmosphere—make the public feel they're part of the celebration. A fashion show featuring DeWilde designs, of course... Have you fixed on an advertising budget?"

"It's being worked out now."

"Tell your advertising manager that we'll help—"

In the sudden silence Ryder heard the clink of glasses at the next table and the hum of private conversations about them seemed loud. Grace's eyes were wide with appalled realization at what she'd been about to say, and he reached out to place his right hand over her left one.

"I'm sorry," she whispered. Firming her voice, she went on, "I got carried away there, didn't I?"

"There's nothing you need to be sorry for," Ryder said, adding with force, "and Gabe is a bloody fool. Jeffrey, too." It felt disloyal saying that. Jeffrey and Grace had always been one entity; Grace so obviously adored her husband that Ryder had simply accepted him as a part of her. As he came to know the family better, Jeffrey's incisive intelligence, his quiet integrity and the deep, though reticent, love he felt for his wife had earned Ryder's respect and eventual affection.

Grace smiled sadly. "You don't need to take sides, Ryder dear. That's the last thing either of us wants. But thank you, anyway." Her hand turned under his and for a moment gripped before she drew it away. "You haven't told me what you're doing in San Francisco—or is it a trade secret?"

Beneath the determined lightness of the question, he heard the wry undercurrent but didn't comment on it. "A business seminar," he said. " 'Taking Trading in the Pacific Basin into the Twenty-first Century.' A mate of mine who was at business school with me told me about it." It had given him a legitimate excuse to visit the city and look up Grace.

"Mate," she teased, smiling gently at him. "I'm glad your years in England didn't manage to iron all the Aussie out of you."

"Or yours all the American out of you," Ryder retorted, just as gently. He felt unusually helpless, not knowing what to say. Where Gabriel had been perplexed and angry at his mother's inexplicable desertion of her husband and the worldwide retail business that defined the DeWildes as a family, Ryder had felt numbed. Now he too experienced a stirring of anger—against Jeffrey. Because it was plainly evident that Grace was hurt, that she had not chosen this course willingly but had been forced into it.

"I had a brochure about the seminar," Grace said. "I might have attended it myself, but I'm so busy right now, organizing the financing and staff for my store, and spending a lot of time arguing with the DeWilde lawyers." A bitterness touched her mouth.

"I heard that Jeffrey was fighting you about the name of your store." Gabriel had said in his last phone call to Ryder that the corporation was threatening an injunction to stop Grace from trading under the name DeWilde.

"The name's not the real issue," Grace said, her gaze momentarily bleak. "I'm calling the store Grace. What Jeffrey wants to do is prevent me from drawing on my thirty-two years' experience with DeWilde's to promote my own store. But everyone in the business knows who I am. I can't simply obliterate my past."

"Your leaving has made the DeWilde Corporation vulnerable," Ryder reminded her. "Jeffrey's trying to protect it."

"I have to survive!" Grace said tensely.

"Surely Jeffrey would see that you're financially secure—"

"This isn't just about money, about Jeffrey buying me off. He's trying to impose conditions that will stop me from running my own store. Sometimes I think he wants to punish me for...what he sees as my defection. I'm not ready to spend the rest of my life doing nothing. All I know is retailing bridal and women's wear, and I'm good at it—"

"Brilliant."

She gave him a strangely empty little smile. "Thank you." Her eyes focused on him as though she'd just been struck by a thought. "I should have realized when you asked for this meeting ... I suppose you're worried about what repercussions there might be on your own financial position."

Ryder felt his shoulders stiffening. His voice cool, he said, "That isn't why I wanted to see you."

A faint flush stained her pale cheeks. "I'm sorry, Ryder. Lately...even my own family have become strangers." She paused. "Did Gabriel ask you to...?"

"To contact you?" Ryder hesitated, wondering if a lie would be kinder, but he had never been able to lie to Grace. Resolutely he met the clear blue gaze. "No."

Her expression didn't alter. The waiter came and asked if she'd finished with the crab, took their plates and offered dessert.

Grace shook her head, and Ryder declined, too, although she urged him to have something more. "I ate far too much during the conference," he told her, and ordered coffee for them both.

When they parted outside the restaurant, she said, "Thank you, Ryder, it's been so good to see you. And . . . promise you won't fall out with Gabriel over this. He needs your friendship."

"I promise," he said, "for your sake." He bent to kiss her cheek. "Keep in touch."

CHAPTER TWO

"THAT NEW ZEALAND TV reporter from the Kiwi Connection is here," Ryder's secretary told him, opening the solid cedar door to his office. "Shall I send her in?"

"Yes, do." Seated at his restored Victorian desk, his dark suit jacket slung over the back of the leather executive chair, Ryder was reading his mail. Skimming through Grace's latest letter, handwritten on pale lavender paper with a stylized, embossed silver rose in one corner, he smiled at the P.S. in her looped and flowing script. *What do you think of my new perfumed stationery?*

Perfumed? As his secretary pushed the door wide, he lifted the sheet of paper to his nose and realized that the subtle floral aroma had been with him for some time, virtually unnoticed. "Mmm," he murmured appreciatively. "Very nice, Grace." It was typical of her elegant, understated femininity.

"Miss Pallas to see you, Mr. Blake."

The woman was already in the room, the secretary withdrawing. Ryder dropped Grace's letter onto its matching envelope and courteously rose to his feet. One thing English public schools instilled was a habit of good manners.

"Miss Pallas." He held out his hand to her, and she crossed the room and put hers into it.

"Good morning. Thank you for seeing me, Mr. Blake." Her hand felt warm and firm, the texture of her skin and the strength of her clasp bringing him unexpected pleasure.

She was about twenty-five. Her dark, wavy hair was fastened back from her face, allowing loosely curling tendrils to fall to the shoulders of an open-necked apricot shirt and bottle-green brocaded waistcoat. Her eyes were a warm, deep hazel flecked with brown, and her face escaped mere prettiness by dint of wide cheekbones and a square chin that hinted at determination. Easy-fitting oatmeal cotton trousers revealed a neatly defined waist, and the tan pumps she wore added a couple of inches to her average height. He found himself wondering what her legs were like.

Brushing the thought aside, he released her hand and indicated one of the comfortable chairs on the other side of the desk. "Please sit down." On impulse, instead of reseating himself in the big executive chair, he came round the desk and perched casually on it with one foot on the ground, his arms folded as he smiled at her. "What can I do for you?"

She looked slightly wary as her eyes met his, but after a moment she allowed the strap of her roomy leather bag to slide from her shoulder, and she smiled back at him. "Perhaps the Kiwi Connection can do something for you, Mr. Blake." Her voice was pitched at a pleasantly low level. "You'll remember our letter?"

He turned, brushing aside Grace's elegant notepaper and envelope to pick up the file his secretary had deposited on his desk. Opening it, he glanced at the contents, summarizing what he had read. "The Kiwi Connection is an independent TV company based in Sydney, making programs under contract mainly for New Zealand television channels. You don't have enough stories in your own country?" he inquired, looking up.

"We're interested in our neighbors, Mr. Blake. There's always a demand in New Zealand for news of Australia, particularly about Kiwis who've moved over here. It's cheaper for New Zealand TV channels to contract out work to us rather than send camera crews, researchers and reporters to cover stories here.''

''And you think New Zealanders will want to watch a program about an Australian department store?''

''Quite a number of people fly across the Tasman Sea two or three times a year for a few days' shopping in Sydney.''

''Including you?'' he queried.

The near-brown eyes widened. ''Heavens, no! I've never had that kind of money to spend.''

His eyes involuntarily went to her clothes in a quick assessment. The shirt might have passed for silk to the uninitiated eye. The trousers were well cut but probably came from a mass production line, and the tan leather shoes were cared for but certainly not new. Around one slender wrist she had fastened a cheap watch with a wide leather strap and large, practical dial; the other was circled by a simple, inexpensive gold chain.

When his gaze returned to her face, a slight color had risen in her cheeks and her eyes were indignant. ''As you can see,'' she added, a hint of acid touching the beautiful voice.

No use trying to gloss over his lapse of good manners. And a compliment, however sincere, would look like a sop. Ryder closed the folder and sat up straighter. ''Habit,'' he explained ruefully, ''being in the clothing business. I apologize.''

She thought it over for a second, then nodded. ''Accepted. I hoped that you'd had time to give some thought to our proposal.''

He had, but not much. His brief response, dictated to his secretary, had been cautious, leaving the door open but not promising anything. ''You're welcome to film any public events connected with the birthday celebrations,'' he said, ''provided that you don't inconvenience our customers.''

''Things that are open to all the news media? Yes, I know. But we'd like to do something more exclusive.''

''Did someone commission this?''

"Not yet. We need your agreement first. But I've talked to the producer of a New Zealand program called 'Inside Story,' and he's interested."

"So it's your own idea?"

"Sometimes we suggest stories to our clients. We were sent publicity material about the plans for DeWilde's birthday celebrations. I thought there'd be a good program in it, and that your store would welcome the exposure."

"My secretary said you were a reporter. Isn't this preliminary stuff work for a researcher?"

She smiled. "I do most of my own research and editing, and even directing. We're a small company. We can't afford a lot of staff."

"Just how much exposure do you expect to be able to give us?"

"An hour-long documentary would fit right into the format of 'Inside Story.' Their biggest viewing audience is in Auckland, which is also closest to Sydney."

"What's this program's target market?"

"Business and professional people interested in current affairs and commerce. Mainly in the twenty-five to forty-five age bracket. People likely to take holidays in Australia or even emigrate here."

"Current affairs and commerce?" His voice sharpened a little.

" 'Inside Story' has a bias toward business and industry, but last year the program profiled a charity organization, the coroner's court and the day-to-day routine of a maximum security prison."

Ryder raised his brows.

"That's just an example of the program's diversity," she said hastily. "It has a high profile and a good reputation. The Kiwi Connection supplies the bulk of its Australian material, but we also work for other programs and channels. We've done a number of stories on New Zealanders who've made it in Australia in the business or entertainment world."

"No scandals, no dirt-digging?"

Natasha Pallas hesitated, but her eyes didn't waver from his. "We've covered stories where everyone doesn't come up smelling of roses. Some of our assignments involve less savory subjects. As I said, we'll be targeting 'Inside Story' for this project. It isn't a good-news program, but it's not 'Hard Copy.'"

She looked engaging and earnest and transparently truthful, but he sensed a tension in her. Although she wasn't sitting on the edge of the comfortable visitor's chair, her back was held straight, her hands clasped tightly on top of the bag in her lap, almost as though she were secretly praying, and even her steadfast gaze betrayed suspense.

Her letter had seemed innocuous enough. But the strain she was doing her best to hide indicated something more was at stake than light entertainment.

"We may find a market for the program in Australia, too," she continued. "And our sales department might sell some clips to news programs here and overseas. That would bring you some good publicity. News has the highest viewer ratings of any show on TV."

She was trying to persuade him that the advantage would be entirely on his side—or the store's. Good marketing strategy, he acknowledged. But all Ryder's instincts were telling him that Natasha Pallas had a hidden agenda. And people with hidden agendas were dangerous.

He pushed himself off the desk and said dismissively, "I don't think that it's really our kind of thing, Miss Pallas. I'm sorry to disappoint you—"

As he'd expected, that brought a spontaneous reaction. She shot to her feet, dismay stripping her of her precarious composure. "Oh, no! Please—" she said breathlessly, and actually caught his arm. Through the sleeve of his white shirt he felt the warm grasp of her fingers and frowned, annoyed at himself because he was conscious again of the tug of sexual attraction.

Seeing the frown, she dropped her hand. "I'm sorry. But, please—it's important."

"Why?"

Dark lashes swept down, momentarily hiding her eyes. She must have realized how close to him she was—so close that he could see the rise and fall of deliciously rounded breasts under the apricot shirt as she took a deeper breath. She moved away a little and looked at him again. He knew before she opened her mouth that she was going to lie, and was surprised at his own sharp sense of disappointment. Her gaze was as steady as ever, but the limpid honesty had been replaced by a veiled caution. "It's a story with broad appeal," she told him. "A European corporation with branches in London, New York and Paris opening—"

"And Monaco."

"And Monaco," she repeated, "opening a store in the Pacific region. This must be the biggest, most glamorous retailing venture of the past year in our part of the world. We'd like to spend a week or two shooting the everyday workings of the store and build up to the birthday promotions. The fashion show should film really wonderfully."

It made perfect sense, Ryder knew, yet he still had that strong feeling of something not ringing true. He glanced deliberately at his watch. "I don't have much time right now," he said, although his next appointment wasn't for twenty minutes yet.

"Please don't turn me down without giving me a chance to convince you—"

"I was about to say," Ryder interrupted smoothly, "that the only free time I have today is my lunch hour." He paused, fighting an odd conviction that he was committing himself to some unknown risk. "If you'd like to join me then, we can discuss this over a meal. Say, twelve-thirty? I'll get my secretary to book us a table in the store's restaurant, unless you're busy...?"

She blinked in surprise, then a fleeting uncertainty crossed her face as her eyes assessed him. With faint amusement he deduced that she was wondering if he was a sexual predator.

Her gaze flickered momentarily away to his desk and then back to his face. His carefully noncommittal expression must have finally reassured her. "Thank you," she said, very crisp and businesslike. "I'll...rearrange my schedule and meet you here at twelve-thirty."

He saw her out, and when she'd gone he turned to his secretary. "Book a table for two in the Skyroom for twelve-thirty, would you?" he asked her. "And then see what information you can dig up about the Kiwi Connection and a New Zealand television program called 'Inside Story'—and Natasha Pallas. Before lunch. I know it's short notice, but get what you can."

Back at his desk, he found himself staring absently at its polished top, until his eyes focused on Grace's letter. He picked it up, returned it to the envelope and shoved it into a lower drawer.

There had been a letter from Jeffrey in the morning's mail, too. Marked Confidential and addressed to The General Manager, DeWilde's, Sydney, it dealt strictly with business matters and was signed by Jeffrey in his capacity as CEO of the corporation. Share prices were beginning to recover from the effects of the shake-up in the company after Grace's departure, and some positive new directions were being taken. Branch managers were invited to put forward ideas for changes in marketing strategies and warned that it was always wise to exercise caution with the media.

News of Grace's defection and her threat to sell her shares in order to launch her own company had inevitably brought reporters to the company doorstep looking for a juicy scandal. Doing his best to freeze them out, Jeffrey had issued terse and uninformative statements through the firm's public relations officer.

Some less scrupulous members of the Fourth Estate, frustrated in their quest for information, had resorted to printing lurid guesswork masquerading as facts. At the height of the furor, Jeffrey had dictated a directive forbidding DeWilde staff to give information to the press about corporate affairs. This latest memo seemed to be a cautious and perhaps reluctant relaxation of that prohibition.

Could an obscure, down-under TV reporter be trying to stir things up again? Ryder doubted that. The upheaval in the DeWilde Corporation was old news now, even in this corner of the world. So what was Natasha Pallas up to?

He meant to find out. And that, he told himself, was why he had invited her to lunch with him.

HE HAD A SHEAF OF FAXES in his hand when his secretary reported that Miss Pallas had returned. Glancing at his watch, he saw that it was one minute before twelve-thirty. Miss Pallas was a very punctual person, he thought, reaching for his jacket. Or very anxious to please.

How anxious? he wondered briefly, recalling the smooth skin revealed by the neckline of her shirt, the feel of her fingers closing confidently about his, the warmth of her smile. Irritated and slightly disgusted at the trend of his thoughts, he wrenched his mind back to the faxes before him. "Tell her I'll be there shortly."

When he went through to the outer office, she rose from the chair where she'd been sitting and gave him a tentative smile.

"Sorry to keep you waiting," he said, thinking she was even lovelier than he remembered.

"I was early." She really did have a delightful voice, clear as a crystal bell but not high-pitched. Listening to it saying even the most banal words was a distinct pleasure.

They rode the one floor up in silence, standing close in the elevator because there were half a dozen others sharing it. Slightly behind his guest, Ryder could detect the spicy fragrance of her perfume. Her hair looked so soft, brushing against the shoulder of his jacket, that he had to fight an urge to lift his hand and touch it. The clasp that held the dark curls in check was a simple crescent of polished wood. He'd known more glamorous women, even more beautiful ones, but there was something about her that appealed powerfully to his senses. He gave a passing, rather rueful thought to the random nature of sexual attraction.

The restaurant was called the Skyroom because the original builders had incorporated a series of domed skylights into the roof. For years this floor had been used only as a storage area, but Ryder had thought it a crying waste, and the architects he and the DeWilde Corporation had called in to redesign the four-story building had agreed.

Natasha Pallas stopped just inside the wide open double doors. "Oh, it's magnificent!"

Light spilled from the skylights onto tables covered in cream linen and set on a deep green carpet, making the cutlery gleam and the glassware sparkle as people lifted them. Climbing plants softened the classical lines of fluted cream columns, and the decorative moldings had been picked out in gold to highlight their beauty.

Ryder couldn't help but be pleased at her reaction. "You haven't been here before?"

"I don't get to eat out much. Generally lunch is a matter of snatching a sandwich between takes or racing from one interview to another."

Ryder nodded at the maître d' who was hurrying toward them. "My usual table, James? It's all right, I can show Miss Pallas to it. Just send a waiter over for our order."

He put a hand on her waist to guide her, noting the slender suppleness of it. At the end of the room the floor was raised slightly. A small table set in an alcove before an arched window gave a view of the street outside.

"Once you could see the harbor from here, I'm told," Ryder said. Now tall office blocks barred any hope of that.

She was looking about her. "It's a wonderful old building, isn't it?"

"I think so." He felt oddly pleased that she shared his appreciation.

The wine waiter came, and Ryder, after asking if Natasha had any preferences, ordered a Hunter Valley rosé. He handed a menu to her and she skimmed it.

Ryder didn't bother to open his. "How long have you been in Sydney?" he asked.

"Living here? About a year. Before that I was sent over on assignment a couple of times."

"So what were you doing before?"

"I worked on a news background program in New Zealand. Then they changed the format and my job became redundant. The Kiwi Connection was a subsidiary of the network then, and they moved me into that unit."

"It's independent now?"

She nodded. "They figured it was too expensive to run and were going to close us down. Two of the senior production people decided to form their own company and buy it out. They asked me to stay on and I agreed, although the staff's been cut to the bone and they can't afford high wages. It's hard work, but fun."

So the company was operating on a shoestring, as fledgling companies often did, and there was no certainty she would get another job if it folded. Maybe that was the reason for her tension.

"What makes the new management think they can make a go of it?" he asked skeptically.

"Since we've been free-lancing, we've been able to branch out and sell to a wider range of clients. As I said before, the

DeWilde project has potential here as well as in New Zealand." She returned her gaze to the menu.

What wasn't she telling him? No use pushing it now. A seasoned campaigner, Ryder knew when to press a point and when to lull the opposition into a sense of security. Watching her scan the glossy list of dishes, he said, "The chef does a great entrée of yabbie tails in a lemon sauce. Very light."

"Sounds good. I love seafood. Though yabbies are freshwater crayfish actually, aren't they?"

"A small point. If you're fond of seafood, how about a main course of Coffin Bay scallops or Bruny Island mussels with a platter of miniature vegetables?"

They shared the vegetables, a mouth-watering collection of golf-ball-size pumpkins, cauliflowers and red and green cabbages and bunches of tiny carrots and turnips, all served on a white oval plate.

"An Australian first," Ryder told her. "They've only been on the market for a few years."

"They're delicious, and so were the scallops. Do all DeWilde stores have restaurants?"

"Not all. This floor lends itself to one, though. It's a wonderful space, but there's too much strong light for a retail department. It would ruin the merchandise." He'd already told her something about the enormous task of converting the neglected building to a workable modern retailing space without sacrificing its character. "We've installed an express elevator from the lobby that bypasses the other floors, so when the store is closed, the Skyroom is still accessible. At weekends it's often used for wedding receptions. It fits perfectly with the DeWilde image."

"Isn't it a bit of a risk in this day and age, opening a shop specializing in bridal wear?" she asked.

"Weddings are still remarkably popular. And we're not so narrowly focused."

"Mmm. I noticed there's a huge range of clothing and accessories on the ground floor, and the cosmetic counters are pretty extensive. Are the shops in the arcade leading to the ground-floor departments independent?"

"They're leased out, but we ensure that all tenant businesses are in keeping with our reputation as a bridal specialist."

"Leather goods?"

"Honeymoon luggage."

Natasha nodded. "Of course. Sportswear—"

"Some people do like to indulge in strenuous pursuits on their honeymoon."

She looked at him with suspicion, and in the face of his deliberately bland stare went on. "Menswear, linen, kitchenware—I see the connections."

"We try to provide under one roof everything that a couple planning a wedding—or their family and guests—will want. Including gifts."

"Mmm," she said reflectively. She had put down her fork and was resting her chin on one hand. "You don't strike me as a romantic, Mr. Blake."

Ryder laughed. "There's good money in weddings. But as you noted, most of our merchandise is suited to other occasions, too. Not all of our customers are planning a marriage in the near future. The second floor, though, is almost entirely devoted to bridal and evening wear. You've seen it?"

"I haven't had occasion to shop for a wedding dress. Besides, I think your prices would be out of my range."

"I'll show you after lunch."

"Thank you." She picked up her fork and idly played with a leftover piece of fennel garnish on her plate, then lifted her eyes to his and lowered them again without saying anything.

"What?" he prompted her.

She looked at him frankly. "When I asked for an appointment, I expected to meet a PR person, not the store manager himself. I'm not complaining, of course," she added quickly. "But I just wondered why..."

Because the company was extrasensitive to the media right now, and he'd wanted to assess for himself the chance that she and her TV company were angling to do a story that might damage DeWilde's image—and, if necessary, choke them off. Ryder wasn't going to tell her that, though. "If I'm going to have a camera crew running around my store, I want to know what kind of people are involved."

"*Your* store?" Her smile was amused, with a hint of the quizzical. "A figure of speech, I take it. All the DeWilde stores are family-owned, aren't they?"

Ryder hesitated. *You're almost family.* He could hear Gabe saying it when he'd described the old, rundown building over dinner in London with Gabe and the other DeWildes. He'd expressed his disappointment that he was unable to raise the money to buy it, restore it and turn it into his dream—an arcade full of specialty shops instead of a dusty rabbit warren of empty rooms, flimsily partitioned offices and storage spaces. "You're almost family. We can lend you some capital to start you off—can't we?" Gabe had turned to his parents. Ryder, stiff with embarrassment and wishing he'd never mentioned the subject, kicked his old friend under the table.

"Shut up, Gabe," he'd said. "The last thing I want is a loan from your family." He owed them enough already without adding a monetary debt, and he had never been into asking favors of anyone.

Gabe had looked about to argue until his twin sister Megan, sitting next to him, hissed something in his ear and he subsided. Grace smiled at Ryder, then turned to her husband and delicately lifted her brows. Ryder hadn't been able to interpret the look that passed between them, and Jeffrey's expression didn't alter. But as Ryder left, he'd said casually, "Come and see me at the office, will you, Ryder? Can you make it tomorrow? And bring any figures you have on this old building of yours. I may be able to give you some advice."

Gratefully, Ryder had shown up at Jeffrey's office as requested. Jeffrey had been noncommittal, said he needed more information, which Ryder obtained. And a week later Jeffrey came up with an astounding offer. The DeWilde Corporation would buy the property and install Ryder as branch general manager.

He hadn't expected Ryder to turn his proposition down. But after the first moment of sheer elation, Ryder had done just that.

Regarding him thoughtfully, Jeffrey said in mild tones, "If you think this is charity, Ryder, you're wrong. My son and my wife might be willing to gamble millions of dollars for sentimental reasons. We owe you something, after all." At Ryder's surprised expression, he added, "Grace believes Gabriel would have been unmercifully bullied if you hadn't looked out for him at school."

"Gabe could look after himself perfectly well if the odds weren't stacked against him. He wasn't as big as me or some of the other boys because he was by far the youngest in our class, but he's a stubborn fighter and won't ever give in."

"I know that. But—you're his friend, and a very good one. We've all grown fond of you. However, I didn't bring DeWilde's to where it is today by giving away money. What I'm offering is a proposal that I think will ultimately benefit the corporation. You're young for the job, but your qualifications are excellent, you have some experience and, equally important, I know you have determination and ambition. Besides that, you know the family and I'm sure you could work well with us. I think you can do it."

Ryder had risen from the chair where he'd been sitting on the other side of Jeffrey's big mahogany desk. Taking a deep breath, he'd jammed his hands into his pockets and looked steadily into the other man's eyes. "The thing is, I don't want the job," he said. "I don't want to be anyone's manager in the place. I want it to be mine."

Jeffrey looked back at him, his shrewd, hazel brown eyes and thin, intelligent face giving nothing away. Then he'd unexpectedly thrown back his head and laughed.

When he stopped, the laughter still lighting his eyes, Ryder said woodenly, "I'm sorry. It's a generous offer and I don't mean to throw it in your face, but—"

Jeffrey held up a hand, waving away the apology. "I understand," he said, "you arrogant young sod." But the words were tempered with affection. "Get out of here. I have to think."

"DID I SAY SOMETHING funny?"

The low, melodic voice reminded Ryder that Natasha had asked him a question. He wiped the reminiscent grin from his mouth and said, "No, sorry. I was thinking of something else. DeWilde's is a family business, but the shares are publicly floated. I hold a large personal stake in the company."

Natasha stared at him thoughtfully. "I'd have thought the family would ensure they always had control."

Was she fishing? Ryder wondered, suddenly wary again. It had been Jeffrey's great fear after her departure that Grace would offer her shares in the DeWilde Corporation to other investors and tip the balance away from the family. Natasha was a business reporter—how much did she know? "They do," he said, "but as an inducement to take the job, I was offered an incentive package of stock options and a large measure of personal control over the direction as well as the day-to-day running of the Australian store." At that time, neither he nor Jeffrey, he was sure, had dreamed that in less than two years the family and the firm would be racked by division, bitterness and suspicion.

"You drive a hard bargain," Jeffrey had said to him when they'd finally agreed on the structure of DeWilde's, Sydney, "but I respect that." In return for the shares and a heavy investment from the DeWilde Corporation in the venture, Ryder had agreed to accept the DeWilde name and come under the DeWilde corporate umbrella. Instead of using his own savings as a deposit and raising the finance himself, he had put most of his savings into extra DeWilde stock on very favorable terms. He'd sacrificed a measure of independence but knew that he had Jeffrey's trust and would retain some autonomy. It wasn't an offer he'd have accepted from anyone else.

Natasha was looking thoughtful, poised for further questions. He might have told her more but for the lingering distrust of media people engendered by recent events. He raised a hand to signal the waiter, asking her, "Do you want dessert?"

"Just coffee, thanks." She didn't press the issue. Probably too experienced to do so, he thought. He hadn't missed the quick, penetrating glance she'd given him before he turned away. Natasha Pallas was no fool. And she liked to keep her wits about her. He'd been prepared to ply her with wine, but she'd made one glass last for the entire meal.

As they waited for the coffee, he said with apparent casualness, "You did a real job on Tazmanz Industries, didn't you?"

Her eyes swept up in surprise. "You know about that?"

As of about forty-five minutes ago, he did. "It was a pretty big scandal in New Zealand, wasn't it? Even made the Sydney papers." He didn't recall seeing it at the time, but one of the faxes his secretary had handed him was a copy culled from the financial pages of the *Sydney Morning Herald*. Tazmanz's managing director had ended up in jail after it was revealed that the firm was playing the markets with money it didn't have. "And it was your reporting that blew the whistle. Something of a coup for you, surely."

"It was a team effort."

"I guess it gave you a good deal of satisfaction. Got the adrenaline flowing?" He gave her a lazy smile.

The waiter brought the coffee, and she murmured thanks without taking her eyes from Ryder. She was on to him, and the knowledge gave him an odd little buzz. She wasn't easily fazed, this young woman, and she knew she was being checked out.

"We took on Tazmanz, yes, when we suspected they were cheating their shareholders—including pensioners who'd invested their life savings, and working people hoping for a decent retirement fund. Small investors who had trusted supposedly clever money men. And those men had just gambled it away on dicey investments. Honest businesses have nothing to fear from us."

He gave her the hard, cold stare that had brought a tearful confession from a fabric buyer who'd been creaming off stock and making herself a nice profit, the stare that had reduced the floor manager who'd been sexually harassing junior counter staff to stammering, red-faced bluster before he tendered his resignation as requested. "DeWilde's reputation," Ryder said icily, "will stand any amount of investigation."

Her gaze didn't falter. She even tried a small smile as she moved her hand toward her coffee cup. "Then," she said, the beautiful voice a trace huskier than before, "there's no reason why you shouldn't agree to let us do a program on the store and the anniversary of its opening, is there?"

She was challenging him. She'd closed her hand about the cup, but she didn't lift it, and her eyes hadn't shifted from his. Damn the woman, he thought, his feelings a confusing mixture of amusement, anger and reluctant attraction that was growing stronger by the minute. She was twisting him round her little finger. It wasn't something he was used to. "There's also no reason why I should," he told her.

She swallowed—he saw the small movement of her throat and had a stupid desire to place his finger over the pulse beat in the shallow hollow framed by the collar of her shirt. Wrenching his eyes upward to hers, he was surprised to see an expression of something like panic there before she looked hastily away and picked up her coffee cup, gulping down some of the hot liquid. "That's up to you," she said, replacing the cup on its saucer with a tiny clatter. "But it would be a pity to miss the opportunity for some great publicity."

"Can you guarantee," he asked her, his voice unusually harsh, "that it will be good publicity?"

"I can guarantee," she said slowly, "that I'm only expecting to present a positive image of DeWilde's. I can give you my word that I'm not setting out to dig up any dirt on this firm. Is that good enough for you, Mr. Blake?"

He looked back at her, his eyes as probing as he could make them. She didn't even blink. Finally he nodded. "I'll clear it with London and let you know. And the name," he added deliberately, "is Ryder."

CHAPTER THREE

NATASHA KNEW THAT RYDER Blake found her attractive. She ought to be pleased, she reflected as they rode down to the second floor in the elevator. Instead she found herself vaguely troubled. That she was aware of a mild, tingling pleasure when he placed a hand on her waist to usher her into the elevator only added to her unease.

Not that she didn't like the look of him, too. The dark hair that was expertly cut and groomed but waved down to his collar; the straight, slashing brows over eyes whose exact color she hadn't figured out yet—were they more green or gray? The way his mouth quirked when he smiled. They all added up to an undeniably attractive man.

The door slid back and she walked ahead of him into a large showroom. Here the columns and walls were white, the fine detailing picked out in silver, and among the columns stood thin, haughty, long-lashed mannequins draped fabulously in white silk, satin or brocade, lace or broderie anglaise, with clouds of veiling.

A strong hand took her arm in a light clasp. "This is the heart of DeWilde's, the most romantic part of our business."

"And the most expensive?" Natasha asked as he steered her across the burgundy carpet. There were other people about, quite a number of them, but the thick carpeting and the distance between the displays gave an illusion of spaciousness.

"That, too," Ryder answered her equably. "In the mezzanine boutiques above the ground floor, customers can buy cheaper but good quality special occasion wear—a lot of it by up-and-coming Australian designers."

"Mmm, I had a quick look round this morning." As well as the clothing boutiques, she'd noted a travel agent, a florist and even a photographer. As Ryder had said, everything that a bride or her family and friends might need was contained under this one substantial roof.

They passed from the almost exclusively white-clad brides to a bevy of attendants' dresses in all colors, from palest pastels to vibrant reds and purples. Another section held bolts of materials and long swathes of fabric draped on stands to show off sheen and texture.

"Very impressive," Natasha said, her eyes drawn to a dashing Edwardian-style gown with a hint of a bustle, teamed with a matching wide-brimmed hat trimmed with huge satin cabbage roses. "That's gorgeous!"

An auburn-haired woman—fortyish and warmly attractive, with a shapely, rounded figure—hurried toward them. "Mr. Blake, good afternoon. May I help at all?"

"I'm just showing Miss Pallas around, Violetta. We're fine, thanks."

A smile softened the dismissal, and the woman smiled back, cast a discreetly curious glance at Natasha and went to speak to a mother and daughter who were hesitating before a collection of bridal headdresses displayed on a silver-painted tree set in a silver tub.

"What a pretty name," Natasha said. "Is she Italian?"

"Her parents were immigrants, I believe," Ryder told her. "Violetta's in charge of our bridal wear department." He hadn't introduced them, and Natasha guessed that he didn't want her talking to the staff before he'd given the TV company the go-ahead.

Turning away from the Edwardian creation, Natasha said casually, "The jewelry department is on this floor, isn't it?"

"Over here." He guided her through a broad archway into a smaller space lined with glass counters and display cases filled with gold and silver and winking stones set against velvet and satin. About a dozen people browsed among the displays, and three staff members behind the counters were serving customers. A uniformed security guard stood unobtrusively in one corner.

Natasha stopped at a breathtaking array of rings, all gold and glitter beneath the smooth glass.

"You're interested in jewelry?" Ryder asked.

"I admire it," she said, "from a distance, like most people."

As she stepped back to gaze at a display of iridescent opals in a wall case above the rings, her shoulder came up against Ryder's chest, and she turned to murmur an apology, expecting him to move. Her mouth almost brushed his chin, and she had a quick glimpse of close-shaven skin and a high, jutting cheekbone before he looked down and she caught a flare of awareness in his eyes that turned them silvery like the underside of a blue-gum leaf.

She moved away immediately, steadying herself by placing a hand on the hard glass counter while she took a sharp little breath.

It wasn't the first time she'd been attracted to a man, and at least this was mutual. Of course, it might be put to good use....

She turned, deliberately smiling at him.

He didn't smile back, but with a hand on her arm he led her to a black marble plinth in the center of the floor that had been blocked from her view by a small knot of people. On the stand was a transparent dome, circled by a chrome bar that would prevent anyone easily reaching over to touch the glass. Inside the dome, glittering under a recessed ceiling light, an ornate bracelet of interwoven strands of diamonds, emeralds, rubies, sapphires and amethysts—all set in gold—reposed on a background of black velvet.

"The Boucheron bracelet," Natasha said, moving closer.

She was aware of Ryder's swift glance. "You know it?" he inquired.

Natasha turned her head. "I do my homework—Ryder. It was mentioned in my research about DeWilde's."

She was giving him her most guileless smile, but it was hard to maintain in the face of his probing gaze. The remarkable eyes now had the patina of stainless steel. Natasha risked raising her brows in puzzlement. "Every DeWilde store has a piece from the family collection on display. DeWilde's Sydney has a bracelet made by Boucheron of Paris for one of the Rothschilds, later purchased by Max DeWilde."

Ryder studied her for a moment longer, then he shifted his stance, his hand closing on the chrome bar, almost trapping her against it. "You're very thorough."

Trying to make the movement casual, she turned to clasp the railing with one hand herself before looking at him again.

He was still watching her. "Is this really your first visit to this floor?" he demanded.

"I didn't say that," she replied lightly. "I could hardly pass up the chance to be shown around by the general manager, could I?"

After a second or two he seemed to relax, and even smiled faintly. "I suppose not."

"Is it safe to display this here?" Natasha indicated the bracelet. "It's worth a lot of money, isn't it?"

"It's locked away every night. And there is an alarm system."

She looked down at the shining black column, then at the light above. Nothing was visible.

As if reading her thoughts, he said, "The second it's lifted, all hell breaks loose."

"If the bracelet's lifted?" she asked thoughtfully. "Or the glass?"

"Either. It's very well protected. Have you seen enough?" he asked rather abruptly.

"Here? Yes, thank you." He wasn't going to allow her to see any but the public areas, she deduced, or introduce her to anyone. "I'm sure I've taken up enough of your time," she said. "You've been very kind. I'd like to wander round the store a bit longer, pick up some ideas for the program. Perhaps I might phone you in a day or two?" She held out her hand.

He took it slowly in his. "If you don't hear from me before then." He didn't let go of her hand, and his brow crinkled a little. "Are you giving me the brush-off?" His eyes blatantly questioned her.

"Certainly not!" She tugged her hand from his. "I know you must be busy. I appreciate the trouble you've taken."

"My pleasure," he said, his voice deep and deliberate.

"If we're going to do the story, I need to start the preliminary preparations for filming fairly soon." She hoped he wasn't going to turn her down, after all. He had given himself an excuse—all he needed to say was that London had vetoed the idea.

"I'll let you know as soon as I'm sure." She thought he hesitated before adding, "Where can I contact you?"

He had her letter with the company letterhead and phone number in his office, but after a slight pause she took a business card from her shoulder bag and handed it to him. "This has both my business and after-hours numbers on it."

"Thank you." Ryder tucked the card into his breast pocket. "Enjoy your day." He looked at her as though contemplating saying something more, then seemed to change his mind.

She couldn't resist watching him as he made his way through the banks of wedding finery to the elevator. His dark suit was undoubtedly of good quality and it fitted his broad shoulders and lean hips well; it looked comfortable, not stiff and formal. He moved with a lithe, unhurried, easy stride. Altogether a very appealing, sexy man, and not at all what she'd thought the manager of DeWilde's would be like.

He was probably married, she thought cynically. Any man with his looks and advantages and high-powered job was bound to have been snapped up years ago.

In which case he'd had no business making that oblique but very deliberate query about contacting her outside office hours.

Anyway, she had other things to think about. *Her* main objective might be to gain inside entry to DeWilde's, but as far as her boss was concerned, it was equally important for her to keep this afternoon's appointment with the owner of an ostrich farm, contact an elusive expatriate Kiwi who was reported to be doing very well for herself designing and selling industrial laser-cutting equipment, and interview the Australian Minister for Trade about the impact of reciprocal agreements between Australian and New Zealand manufacturing interests.

All of which she would deliver on, she promised herself, plagued by irrational guilt at the knowledge that filming the store's anniversary was no more than a smoke screen.

She looked at the glass dome again. The alarm wires must be hidden inside the plinth, unless there was an electronic sensor system incorporated in the light above. She peered up at it.

"May I help you, madam?" A black-suited young man with smooth hair and pale butterfly hands, stood at her side. In twenty years' time he would exactly match her preconception of what the manager of DeWilde's should look like.

"I was admiring the bracelet," she told him, returning her gaze to the display. "The way the light falls on it . . ."

"Superb, isn't it? A number of customers have asked if they can buy it."

"You have customers who can afford jewelry like that?" Natasha asked.

"No price has been put on it. It's for display only, not for sale."

"How much is it insured for?" Natasha asked.

The man visibly froze. "I'm not at liberty to say."

Natasha wondered if he knew. She smiled at him. "But it is the real thing, isn't it? You'd think they'd use a replica or something."

"The DeWildes?" He was shocked. "They wouldn't dream of it. That is an original Boucheron with a guaranteed authenticated history. Security, of course, is very tight."

A customer appeared at his elbow, asking to see some watches, and as the young man excused himself, Natasha found herself being scrutinized by the security guard in the corner. He'd certainly be able to describe her if necessary, but his gaze held more curiosity than suspicion. He'd seen her come in with Ryder Blake. She smiled warmly at him, waited while he blinked and smiled uncertainly back, and then she left.

"OUR PR MANAGER THINKS it would be good for the store's image," Ryder said to Jeffrey DeWilde that evening when he called the London office from his apartment. Because of the time difference, much of his business with head office was conducted from his home phone after hours. He had discarded his tie and unbuttoned the collar of his shirt. "Lee was disappointed we didn't snap up the offer immediately when the Kiwi Connection first contacted us. I thought, since I received your latest memo this morning, that I'd run the idea by you. A bit of positive publicity wouldn't come amiss after the speculation in the financial pages of the newspapers over the past months. And it will help publicize the anniversary."

"Perhaps you're right," Jeffrey conceded. "I trust your judgment, Ryder. If you're quite certain this TV person doesn't have some ulterior motive..."

"Actually," Ryder said slowly, "I'm not certain of that at all."

"What?" Jeffrey's voice was sharp.

"I have a feeling she's keeping something back, but I'm fairly sure she isn't out to damage DeWilde's." And any grounds he had for that assertion, Ryder knew, were shaky indeed. Possibly he was being blinded by his strong attraction to Natasha Pallas. "But it will be easier to keep tabs on her and what she's doing if we offer cooperation. You know how the media are—"

"Indeed I do," Jeffrey said grimly.

"The more you try to choke them off, the more convinced they are that you're concealing something. I suggest we give them as much assistance as possible."

"Hmm, you may be right. Just don't expect me to appear on camera."

Ryder smiled to himself. Typical of Jeffrey to shun personal publicity. "I haven't even told her you'll be here."

After he'd said goodbye to Jeffrey, Ryder sat looking at the phone for a few seconds, then glanced at his watch. Just after ten. Natasha Pallas had a busy schedule. If he waited until he was in his office tomorrow morning she might miss his call. He poured himself a whisky, went into his bedroom and took her card from the pocket of his jacket. Sitting on the edge of the bed, he picked up the phone from the nightstand and dialed her number.

The phone rang at the other end until he'd almost decided she wasn't in. Then a breathless voice said, "Hello?"

Something hot and heavy curled in his gut. He was getting it bad, he thought, both appalled and amused at himself. "Natasha." He let the name flow from his lips, savoring the soft syllables. "Ryder Blake." Wondering if she'd been entertaining someone, he added, "You're busy? I was just about to hang up."

"No, I was in the shower."

He had an instant picture of her standing naked in a dim room, clutching a towel to a body glistening with water, her hair tumbling in damp curls about her face and shoulders. His own body was reacting to the drift of his imagination, and he lifted the glass in his hand and gulped down a shot of burning liquid. "Sorry to disturb you," he said, his voice deepening with the effort to keep it steady and relatively impersonal. "I thought you'd like to know I've just spoken to Jeffrey DeWilde in London and we've agreed to let you film in the store."

There was a surprised silence before she said fervently, "Oh, thank you! That's wonderful news! And thank you for letting me know. I really am grateful."

There'll never be a better moment, an interior voice jogged him. He hadn't even realized what he was going to do before he heard himself say, "Are you free tomorrow evening?"

"Yes . . . why?"

"I thought we might iron out some details over dinner. I expect you'll be tied up all day?"

"I do have a number of appointments."

"And I have a heavy schedule, too. So . . . dinner?"

He heard her hesitation, but when she spoke, her voice was firm. "That would be fine, thank you. Where would you like me to meet you?"

"I'll call for you, if you give me your address."

"No, really," she said. "I'd rather meet you."

"Perhaps we could have a drink first. Do you know the Kangaroo Court?" It was a trendy new bar in a well-known hotel in the city.

"Yes, I've been there."

"Good. How about seven o'clock?"

"Yes, sure. I'll see you in the lobby."

So he wasn't going to be invited into her home, Ryder thought as he replaced the receiver. Not before dinner, anyway.

Did he want to be? His body was telling him *yes* in no uncertain terms. But it was a long time since Ryder had been ruled by the sometimes inconvenient dictates of his body. He had only met this woman today. And she wasn't, he was convinced, telling him all that she wanted of him and DeWilde's. He should be extra cautious. His breath felt thick, his chest tight. He'd reacted to her voice even before she'd said, with unconscious provocation, "I was in the shower."

Ryder stood up and pushed a hand through his hair. Maybe he needed a shower, too. A cold one.

WHEN HE SAW HER COME through the door the following evening, he experienced a shock of pleasure. She was wearing a dress that skimmed her knees, and he couldn't help noticing with satisfaction that her legs were all a man could wish for, their length and shape flattered by a pair of high-heeled black pumps.

Over the simple black shift she wore a short-sleeved black lace jacket threaded with a hint of silver. One hand held a black beaded bag that was flat and oblong but large enough to hold a notebook and pen. He guessed she'd tried for businesslike elegance while making concessions to the hour and the nature of their meeting. But no clasp confined her hair this time, and it curled gently about her face, softening the strong bones and distracting attention from the determined chin and perceptive eyes.

Maybe that was deliberate, too, Ryder thought as he moved toward her. She hadn't yet seen him and was looking about her, seemingly oblivious to the attention she was garnering from several men lounging in chairs or standing around on the marble floor of the spacious lobby.

Her eyes found him, and he had the impression she was holding her breath. Then she smiled and started toward him.

Ryder curbed an impulse to open his arms and invite her into them, to claim her before all the men enviously watching. Instead he smiled back, casually said hello and contented himself with touching her arm on the pretext of guiding her in the direction of the bar.

They sat in deep chairs, facing each other across a tiny circular table, and a waitress hurried up for their order.

Natasha asked for a dry white wine, and Ryder said, "I'll have the same."

The waitress hurried away, and Ryder turned to Natasha. "You've been here before, you said?"

"We had a staff thing here one evening."

Not a date, then. "How do you like living in Sydney?"

"It's fun. Fast, exciting—I guess the novelty hasn't worn off yet. I'm still a wide-eyed Kiwi girl."

Maybe that was the image she hoped to project. But she was decisive, persistent and apparently very good at her job. Her job as an investigative reporter—something he mustn't lose sight of.

He wanted to reach out and touch her hair, or discover the texture of her warm, slightly olive skin. Instead he slid a bowl of mixed nuts toward her. She took a cashew and he watched her lips open for it, and found his heart pounding as he imagined them opening like that for his tongue....

Dragging his gaze away, he grabbed a handful of nuts at random, although he didn't really want them. He was relieved to see the waitress coming back with their drinks.

"I'm so glad we're going to be able to film DeWilde's," Natasha said. "Did you . . . was London sticky about it?"

Had he gone to bat for her, she meant. "They trust my judgment," he told her, *they* being Jeffrey, but there was no need to spell that out. "And I told them I want the publicity for the anniversary of our opening. I also told them—" he paused deliberately "—that I believed it would be favorable publicity."

"If you have nothing to hide . . ."

"We don't." He hadn't moved his eyes from her, and she met his gaze squarely, staring back at him.

It was on the tip of his tongue to ask what *she* was hiding, then she lifted her glass to him and smiled. "Here's to a great program that'll do us both good—DeWilde's and the Kiwi Connection."

Ryder smiled back and joined in the toast, and the moment passed.

He took her to dinner at the hotel's best restaurant, and she asked him questions about the store and the birthday promotions. When she unzipped her bag and removed a notebook, he laughed.

"I'm sorry...?" She looked up at him, ready to apologize. "Shouldn't I—"

"No problem." Ryder shook his head. "I had a small bet with myself that you'd stowed a notebook in there."

She grinned engagingly, not a professional smile, and he felt the pull of attraction intensify, creating a constriction in his chest. "I never go anywhere without it. When is the first in-store promotion planned for the birthday celebration?"

"I'll ask our PR guy to contact you tomorrow," Ryder promised. "He'll have everything at his fingertips, and I'll tell him to give you all the help he can."

"Thanks. We'd probably want to film the staff setting it up beforehand, along with their regular routines. The idea is to show the work that goes into the day-to-day running of this kind of store, as well as the special events."

Ryder nodded. "We do have security rules, of course. There'll be certain things you can't film."

"I understand." She had her head bent and was opening the notebook, poising a ballpoint pen over it.

She asked a few questions and scribbled down the answers. He noticed that her fingers were ringless. Which didn't necessarily mean she wasn't involved with anyone.

When the coffee came she put away her book, and he smiled at her and asked, "How did you get into this kind of work?"

"Journalism school and then a short course run by a television company. I always adored TV—my mother used to say I watched it too much. I'm really lucky to be doing what I am."

"Which is, exactly... ?"

"Practically running my own show, really, once I get approval for a project. Everything from researching to hosting the programs. I've learned heaps. What about you?"

"Me?"

"Was your childhood ambition to manage a bridal store?" she asked innocently, her eyes alight with amused curiosity.

Ryder grinned. "That was kind of accidental—or fortuitous. I studied business administration and was managing a textiles factory when what is now the DeWilde building came on the market. I'm interested in architecture and I saw the old place had possibilities. There was talk of tearing it down to build a car park. I thought that would be a crime."

"Yes, it would! So how did the DeWildes come into it?"

Ryder habitually downplayed his personal connection with the family. "My plan was to raise the money to buy and renovate the place, but I couldn't get enough backing. When I was in England for a few weeks, I presented the DeWildes with a proposition. The board looked it over and thought it would be a good idea to expand into a branch down under."

"You must have been very persuasive. Did you just walk in and ask for an appointment?"

"Not exactly." Ryder glanced up from placing his coffee cup on its saucer. "I went to school with Gabriel DeWilde for a while. He... introduced me to his father."

Natasha nodded, without apparent censure. "The old school tie." She had finished her coffee but still held the cup in both hands. "What are they like?" she asked him. "The DeWildes?"

Ryder felt the hair on the back of his neck prickle warningly, and he remembered again that she was a reporter. "Gabe was exceptionally bright at school—a class ahead of his age group. But the family keep a low profile. Do you want more coffee, or shall I ask for the bill?"

She shook her head, taking the hint.

In the lobby he asked her, "Did you bring a car?"

"No, I don't have one. But don't worry about me—"

"Wait a minute." He asked the doorman to get them a cab and over her mild protest urged her into it. "Where to?"

She gave him an address at Blackwattle Bay and sank back into a corner of the wide leather seat. "You didn't drive yourself?"

"I don't always feel like rationing my drinks when I eat out. This way is safer. Can you see the bay from your place?"

"No. We were lucky to find a cheap flat there. It isn't big but it's quite cozy."

"You're sharing?" He hoped it sounded like a casual inquiry.

"With one of the studio staff. We get along well."

"Isn't getting along with people part of your stock-in-trade?"

She looked at him for a second or two, the streetlights playing over her face as the cab passed beneath them. Perhaps she'd heard a note of cynicism, suspicion, in his voice. "Turning on the charm, you mean? There's more to it than that."

"Yes?" He allowed his skepticism to show, wanting to draw her out.

She glanced out of the window at the darkened street, then looked at him again. "It's a matter of being interested in people and what they do. Of finding out what they know, what they're passionate about."

"Passionate?"

"You know, everyone has something they care about, something they want to show the world. Even," she added dryly, "if it's only themselves."

Ryder laughed. "Are there many of those?"

"They make good TV. Don't knock it." She sounded ever so slightly cynical herself.

"Is that what you're passionate about? Good TV?"

She smiled. "I guess."

"Nothing else?" Ryder prompted.

"Well . . . my family."

"You're close?"

"I'm very close to my mother and grandmother."

"What about your father?"

"He drowned when I was eight. Trying to rescue someone who'd got caught in the surf. The lifeguards eventually saved the other person, but they couldn't reach my father. He was given a medal for bravery—posthumously."

"You must be proud of him."

"I suppose I am."

"You weren't there when it happened?"

"Yes, but I didn't realize what was going on at the time. I don't remember much except being kind of bewildered. Of course, when it hit me later what had happened . . ."

"I'm sorry." Ryder reached over and closed his hand about hers. "I didn't mean to upset you."

"I'm not upset. It was a long time ago." She didn't pull away, but after a few moments Ryder released his light clasp on her fingers.

Minutes later the cab drew up outside a two-story building that had a wrought-iron railing fronting a narrow veranda on the top floor. Ryder asked, "Am I going to be invited in?"

There was a moment's silence before she said, "It's late. I don't want to disturb my flatmate. Thank you for the dinner, and for bringing me home."

He told the driver to wait and walked with her up the path to the front door, which she opened with a key. Her hand still on the doorknob, she turned to him. "Thank you again."

He had his hands in his pockets, a faint smile on his lips. "Not at all. I enjoyed myself." He paused, then decided not to force the personal issue. "I'll tell my PR director to call you soon."

She pushed the door and stepped inside, turning to offer him her hand. "You've been very kind. Good night."

He took her hand briefly again in his, resisting the urge to pull her into his arms and kiss her. "Good night," he said formally. "I'll see you around the store."

He spent the ride home pleasurably reliving his evening with Natasha, recalling the feel of her hand in his, the smooth skin overlaying the fine bones, the way her hair fell on her shoulders, the luscious outline of her soft lips.

She'd smiled at him and answered all his questions with an expression of absolute candor. And he'd liked her. She was bright, capable, occasionally funny. Her sense of humor matched his—low-key but acute.

Perhaps he'd been wrong about her. Maybe the tension he'd detected at their first meeting had been nothing more than anxiety about her project, or—he'd been almost afraid to consider this possibility—maybe she too had been taken unawares by a powerful attraction to him. But she was being cautious, not sure of where it would lead them. Well, that was all right, Ryder thought, his lips curling slightly in anticipation. He didn't habitually rush into relationships, either. And he had always enjoyed a challenge.

CHAPTER FOUR

"AND THIS IS OUR SPECIAL pride and joy." Lee Bolton, DeWilde's publicity officer, waved a hand to encompass the bridal department. "The heart of DeWilde's."

Natasha smiled. It must be a catchphrase. "Mr. Blake said the same thing."

"Ah, yes." Lee covertly cast a curious glance at her. "Ryder showed you round himself?"

"Briefly, on our way back from lunch. It was the only time he could spare to talk to me."

Lee nodded his handsome, silver gray head. "He works hard."

"And plays hard?" Natasha was unable to stop herself. Curiosity got the better of her.

"If he does, he's entitled. Have you met Violetta Concetti?"

"We weren't introduced, but Mr. Blake mentioned she's the head of the department."

"Violetta is the one to talk to about the fashion show that's the climax of our birthday celebrations. She's expecting us."

They found the department head in a large, functional-looking workroom. Long tables lining the walls were strewn with pattern books, bolts of material, scissors and tape measures. Several mannequins in various stages of undress and minus the odd limb occupied one corner.

Violetta recalled seeing Natasha with Ryder and invited her and Lee into her small office adjacent to the work-

room. Friendly and knowledgeable, and obviously in love
with her work, she would come across well on screen, Natasha decided, and asked her if she'd agree to be interviewed on camera.

Violetta laughed. "Me, a TV star? My kids will love
that!"

"How old are they?" Natasha asked, smiling. If anything was calculated to open people up, it was the opportunity to talk about their children.

"Oh, they're all grown up. Two of them are married. I
have three boys, two girls."

"Quite a family."

"Italians tend toward big families. My husband was a
wonderful father."

"Violetta is widowed," Lee explained.

"Oh, I'm sorry to hear that."

Violetta smiled sadly, her natural vivacity momentarily
fading. "Ben died just over a year ago. I still miss him.
But," she added quickly, "you're not here to listen to my life
story."

Natasha asked a few questions and made rapid notes,
then thanked Violetta for her time. "I may come back with
more specific questions later."

"Anytime. I'm usually here."

As they left the office, Lee said, "I'll take you to the
jewelry department next. The family originally were diamond merchants and jewelers in Amsterdam. Later they
opened a store in Paris, the beginning of their bridal wear
business."

The top brass might have been initially reluctant, but the
staff were proud of their store and very willing to talk about
it. Natasha already had a folder full of publicity material
that Lee had pressed on her.

"And I've just been told," he said, almost rubbing his
hands, "that the DeWildes are sending some of their own

jewelry collection over for display during the final week of the celebrations.''

Natasha felt her heart skip a beat, her excitement at least equal to the publicity manager's. ''Here?'' she asked. ''In the store?''

''I believe so. Quite a coup for us. It's been many years since the collection was last shown. I wish we'd had more notice—it doesn't give us much time to publicize the event.''

''It must be priceless,'' Natasha commented.

''Oh, certainly. But we have some very valuable stones in our own store, you know, and you've seen the Boucheron bracelet?'' He was steering her toward the jewelry department.

''Yes, I have. I wondered if we could film it out of its case? The glass and bright overhead light would make it difficult for the cameras.''

''You'd need to talk to Ryder about that. He said to bring you along to his office before you go. Ask him about it then.''

After introducing her to the jewelry manager, Lee took her upstairs and told Ryder, ''Natasha wants to film the Boucheron bracelet out of its case.''

Ryder cast her a quick glance. ''We'll talk about it,'' he promised. ''I'll take over from here, Lee.''

When Lee had left, Ryder turned to Natasha. ''There are security requirements for insurance purposes, but I don't think there should be a problem.''

''Good. Lee tells me the DeWilde family has agreed to let you show their jewelry collection as part of your birthday bash.''

''Lee hasn't wasted any time, has he? Jeffrey DeWilde made the offer this morning. Naturally I was delighted to accept. Although it will mean extra security measures.''

''I hope we'll be able to film it.''

''Jeffrey seems keen on maximum publicity for the collection.''

"It's one of the best in the world, isn't it?"

"That's not generally known. The DeWildes have never flaunted their wealth."

"I told you I'd done my homework," Natasha said, detecting a questioning note in his tone. "It seems a pity that such beautiful jewels should be locked away when they were meant to be worn."

"Unfortunately in today's world it's not safe to wear things like that casually. Did Lee introduce you to the head of security and explain that you and your crew will need ID cards?"

"He was very thorough. I'll set up a couple of days with him to bring in a camera crew and film the store's normal activities, and then we'd like to come back for specific events. I may spend some time in the various departments beforehand, working out what shots I want."

"All that for an hour-long show?"

"There's a lot of preparation involved. A good deal of time is spent setting up cameras and lights and reshooting bits where something hasn't quite gone right. And then the footage will be edited."

"Sounds complicated. Would you like to have lunch with me again and tell me more?"

He smiled at her, in his eyes a question that she couldn't mistake. Smiling back at him, she asked, "You want to know about the mechanics of filming?"

"Among other things." His eyes deliberately held hers. Softly, he said, "So how about it, Natasha?"

"Lunch?" His gaze remained on her face as she thought about it, his mouth quirking farther at the corners. "I think that's an offer I can't refuse," she said, discarding caution. "Last time it was delicious."

"Good." He glanced at his watch. "I've already booked the table. We have time for a drink or two beforehand."

But he hadn't booked the table in the DeWilde restaurant this time, Natasha discovered. Instead he took her downstairs, ushered her into the street and said, "It's a three-minute walk. But we can take a cab if you'd rather...?"

Natasha shook her head. "I like walking."

They passed tall, brash new office buildings—all glass and polished marble—and old mellowed Victorian and Edwardian ones built of Sydney sandstone in varying shades of soft gold. The pavement was crowded with shoppers and businesspeople, the traffic noisy and loading the air with fumes, but the sense of bustle and purpose only added to Natasha's nearly euphoric mood.

She told herself her high spirits were the result of a successful morning of preparatory work for the program and the sense that she was beginning to see the way toward her real goal.

The restaurant was very different from DeWilde's Skyroom. Small and intimate, it boasted a modest lounge area where they had a leisurely drink before being shown to their table in a corner almost screened by a white-painted trellis and flowering indoor plants.

Over lunch Ryder checked on what she'd arranged with his publicity director, then moved on to questions about her job, and she regaled him with some of the more hair-raising and humorous assignments she'd encountered in her career.

Pushing away her empty plate, she said, "Hey, I'm supposed to be the interviewer here!"

Ryder grinned at her. "How does it feel having the tables turned?"

"Is that what you're doing?" It felt good, she might have told him. No woman could fail to be flattered by a man who took so much interest in her and her job. He seemed genuinely fascinated by the technical details. She asked lightly, "Do you have a yen to be a TV journalist?"

"I'm happy doing what I do—although at one time I wanted to be an architect. Are you having dessert?" When she shook her head, he offered her more wine, which she declined in favor of coffee.

As the waiter departed to fetch it, Natasha turned to Ryder again. "What made you decide on a business career instead of architecture?"

"Lack of talent," he replied promptly.

Natasha said nothing, waiting for him to explain.

"I studied architecture for a year," he said.

"And discovered you were no good at it?" The coffee came, and Natasha stirred a spoonful of sugar into hers.

"I might have made a reasonable career designing functional, unexciting public buildings, but I lacked the spark of creativity, originality, the instinctive feel for the possible. I would have been frustrated at not being as good as I wanted to be. On the other hand, I arranged the end-of-year exhibition of students' work and found my real métier—organization and management. That's when I decided to go to business school and learn how to do it properly."

"You must have learned pretty well."

He looked at her inquiringly, and she expanded on the thought, studying him with frank curiosity. "You persuaded the DeWildes to invest in a project no one else would touch, and to give you the job of general manager. Did you marry into the family or something?"

He carefully lowered his coffee cup to the table. "I was in the right place at the right time," he said, and added coolly, "and I'm not married. Did you think I was?"

Natasha took a sip of her own coffee and held the cup in both hands, looking down at it. When she raised her eyes again she said, "I didn't know. It's no concern of mine."

He was still looking at her, his eyes greener than before. "Do you go out with married men?"

"No. Only when it's business."

Their eyes clashed. Ryder's lips curved in a faint smile. "Business? Is that what you thought this was?"

"Isn't it coming out of your expense account?"

He laughed. Then, leaning back in his chair, his eyes gleaming under drooping lids, he asked her quietly, "Suppose I don't charge it to my expense account, Natasha?"

She looked away from him because her answer required thought, and as she caught sight of her watch, she realized how much time they'd spent here. She'd been enjoying herself too much. "I have another appointment," she said hurriedly. "You must excuse me, I'm afraid."

As she pushed back her chair and made to rise, he closed a hand about her wrist. "Don't run away."

The warmth of his fingers seemed to travel right up her arm and straight to her heart. "I told you—"

"You have another appointment, yes. When can I see you again?"

"Next week I'll be at the store with a camera crew—"

He studied her for a moment longer, then released her hand and stood. "I'll look forward to it," he said politely. "Now I have to get back to the office, too." He fished out his wallet and left some money on the table with the bill.

Afterward Natasha castigated herself for being gauche, and possibly stupid into the bargain. She should have been prepared for a personal approach from Ryder Blake and able to handle it with aplomb. A graceful refusal would have been more appropriate than coy equivocation.

The truth was her nerve had failed. She needed to find out something about the setup at DeWilde's, and surely there was no reason to feel guilty because Ryder Blake was attracted to her. She ought to be making use of the fact. Only the thought of doing so made her uncomfortable. She was unsure of the possible repercussions of becoming close to the manager of the store.

It seemed he hadn't taken offence, anyway. The following week she turned up with a camera crew and shot some scenes around the store. After they finished shooting, she found that Ryder had joined Lee Bolton, who had lurked unobtrusively nearby as she talked with Violetta about trends in bridal wear.

While the camera crew packed up their gear to move to another department, Natasha went over to the two men. Ryder smiled at her and asked, "How's it going?"

"Violetta's a natural. I'm glad you're here. I was going to ask Lee to set up an interview with you."

"With me?" Ryder looked a little taken aback.

"It will probably come down to only two or three minutes of screen time, but we'd need perhaps half an hour with you. We'd like to film you moving about the store rather than sitting behind a desk."

"Wouldn't Lee do?" he asked, turning to his publicity manager.

"We'll be giving Lee his few minutes of fame, too." She flashed a smile at the other man. "But I do need you—"

"Really?" A gleam of laughter lit Ryder's eyes for an instant.

"For an overall perspective."

"Ah."

"So...can I ask when it might suit you? We'll try to fit it in with shooting some of the special events, if that's okay with you."

"Come to my office after you're done here—I'll consult my appointment book and see what I can do."

When she presented herself a short while later, the secretary waved her right in, and she found Ryder bent over some papers on his desk, pen in hand. He looked up at her entrance and rose to his feet, coming round the desk to close the door behind her before waving her to a chair.

Then he lounged against the desk as he had at their first meeting and said, "So you want me...on camera?"

"Yes, please." She made her voice crisp. "We can't do an in-depth profile of the store without showing the manager managing it."

"Then," he said with a resigned smile, "I suppose I'd better do it. Can I ask you for something in return?"

"That depends on what it is."

"Nothing too onerous, I hope. I want to see you again—without the camera crew and the notebook. Strictly non-expense-account."

"Is this a condition?" she asked him.

He seemed to go still, his eyes darkening, and he said finally, "I said I was asking. I'm not into sexual extortion."

"I'm sorry," she said quickly. She'd offended him, although his temper was well under control. "You did say 'in return.'"

"I guess I expressed myself badly." He waited a second, then stood abruptly. "Obviously you're not interested. My apologies—"

"I didn't say that!" Natasha heard herself protest without even thinking. "I don't know why you should apologize," she added. "It isn't an insult, exactly, to be asked out by... by a man like you."

"Then...?"

Natasha swallowed, wondering if she was being sensible or extremely stupid. "Thank you," she said quietly. "I'd very much like to go out with you. What did you have in mind?"

"Do you fancy a show at the Opera House?" he asked her. "I can get tickets to the musical that's playing now. But perhaps you've seen it?"

"That sounds wonderful, and I haven't seen it." Tickets were expensive and not easy to come by, but he seemed confident. No doubt he had contacts.

"We could have dinner there first," he suggested, "and admire the sunset on the harbor."

A FEW EVENINGS LATER, Natasha, wearing a new bronze chiffon dress with tiny bronze beads sewn into the gathered bodice, sat at a small outdoor table of a harborside restaurant opposite Ryder Blake, who looked breathtakingly handsome in evening clothes.

Across the water a cruise ship was berthed, and as the golden sheen of a gorgeous sunset faded and the sea darkened, festoons of lights illuminated the liner, while other lights sprang up along the foreshore, their reflections shimmering in the water.

The air had cooled a little but was still pleasant. Looking about at the other diners, the elegant tables and the soaring windows of the Opera House reflecting the harbor, Natasha smiled and shook her head slightly. This was the stuff dreams were made of.

"What is it?" Ryder asked. And when she looked at him inquiringly, he said, "What are you thinking?"

"That this is all too romantic. It's unreal."

He glanced about them. "It's real," he said. "And so am I. Are you?"

She twirled the tall glass of sparkling champagne in front of her on the table. "I was last time I checked."

"May I check for myself?" he asked, and held out a hand to her.

She gave him her left one, and he folded his fingers lightly about it, turning it over. "No rings," he commented. "No ties?" His eyes met hers.

"Only my job," she told him. "And my family."

He released her hand as the waiter came along and placed their first course before them. "You haven't said much about them."

"You're surely not that interested." She picked up her fork.

"Why should you think that? Do you have brothers, sisters?"

She hesitated only for a second. "Two half brothers from my father's first marriage. My father's first wife died young. He was quite a lot older than my mother. After the boys moved out, my mother and I went to live with my grandparents. They were getting on and had a big house to maintain.''

''You didn't mention your grandfather before.''

''We lost him last year.''

''I'm sorry. Were you fond of him?''

''Very.'' Her mouth curved sadly. ''He had the most wonderful way with words. He used to tell me stories. I think it's because of him that I became a journalist.''

''Are you admitting that journalism is telling stories?''

''A story is a story, whether it's truth or fiction.''

''Some people have trouble defining the difference,'' Ryder commented. ''And that includes journalists.''

''Not the good ones.'' She smiled. ''I think Grandpa had that problem sometimes. A few of his stories would have given a giraffe a run for its money.''

Ryder grinned. ''How did you get on with your half brothers?'' he asked.

''They spoiled me,'' she said simply. ''One lives in Queensland—I've been to visit twice since I moved to Australia. He and his wife made me very welcome. He still thinks of me as his baby sister.''

''Nice for you.''

She looked at the odd twist to his mouth and said, ''Yes, it is. But actually I'm all grown up now.''

His smile changed as his eyes slipped over the snug-fitting bodice of her dress. ''I can see that.''

''What about *your* family?'' she asked him. ''Were they English?''

''Why do you ask that?''

Natasha shrugged. ''Your accent. You don't sound quite Australian.''

''We don't all talk like Crocodile Dundee.''

''I know. I just wondered.''

''My parents came out to Australia in the sixties. I was born here but got sent back to my father's old public school in England for my secondary education.''

"And that's how you met Gabriel DeWilde."

His gaze seemed to sharpen, and he took a second to reply. "You don't forget a thing, do you."

"It's part of my job to have a good memory."

"Tonight," he said, "you're not working, are you?"

It was a very calculated question and she could see he expected an answer. Recklessly, she looked straight into his eyes and said softly, curling her fingers about her wineglass, "No, tonight I'm not working."

From then on the evening took on a magical quality. Pushing all other considerations aside, Natasha relaxed, determined to enjoy the moment. They talked about all kinds of things and discovered mutual interests in music, reading and politics, and divergent opinions on all of them. She made him laugh with her tales of TV disasters, and he returned the favor with stories of quirky customers and surly suppliers.

Later he roused her to a passionate defense of the media's role in shaping opinion and had her leaning forward, spoon in hand, while her dessert melted in its glass dish. She challenged him on the role he played in the consumer society and listened thoughtfully to his analysis of the relationship between commerce and national prosperity.

If she didn't always agree with his opinions, she had to respect them, because there was nothing superficial about them. Nor had he rubbished hers. He was a good listener as well as a persuasive advocate for his own views.

When their meal was over and they left the dining area, Ryder took her hand, and she let him hold it throughout the show, enjoying the feel of his long, strong fingers curved about hers. When his thumb began to move over the back of her hand, she kept her eyes glued to the spectacle on the stage, but every nerve ending was conscious of that tiny, unseen caress.

Afterward he offered her coffee before they left the building and she said no, then yes, because she didn't want the evening to end. But as she sat opposite him again, talking about the show, she saw the look in his eyes and wrenched her gaze away, finding her hand not quite steady as she spooned sugar into her cup. Hoping he hadn't noticed it, she said, "It was a good show, wasn't it."

"Yes," he answered. And then added, "Actually, I have no idea."

She looked up at him and down again swiftly when she read the message in his eyes. She felt dazed herself. She knew what sexual attraction was—a couple of times she'd even thought herself in love—but this was something different, a fire in her blood, a sensation that made her feel as if she were standing on the very edge of some precipice, where a leap in the dark might lead to unknown ecstasy or total disaster.

Maybe it was the atmosphere, the wine, the glamour, she tried to tell herself. But she knew it wasn't true.

No, it was the man. And there was more than physical attraction at work, powerful though that was.

There was a ruefulness in her smile as she met his eyes. Oh Lord, but he was beautiful! And he was staring at *her* as though he thought her the most stunning creature on earth.

"Don't!" she said involuntarily, her voice husky.

"Don't look?" His brows rose.

"That kind of look could go to a girl's head!" She tried to sound light, teasing.

"Dare I hope so?" he answered, his voice deep and slow. "Would you like to come back to my place with me?"

The direct invitation had the effect of steadying her a little. Natasha distrusted instant passion. A surprising number of men assumed that any woman working in the media must have a casual approach to sex; her profession seemed to have inherited the reputation an earlier age had assigned to actresses and dancers, but it wasn't her way to plunge blindly into a relationship with a man she barely knew. Reminding herself of that, she said, "I think you had better take me home, thank you."

His smile was crooked. "Sure?"

He must know how he made her feel. He couldn't have looked so confident, so damned pleased with himself otherwise. She wondered if he habitually reduced adult, usually competent career women to stammering, simpering jellies. Maybe it was a special talent he had. "I'm sure," she said firmly, clearing her throat.

He looked at her a moment longer, his face giving nothing away now. "Right," he said finally. "Whenever you're ready."

He took her back to his car, and after they'd left the car park and joined the stream of traffic, he said, "I should have used a taxi tonight."

"You haven't had anything to drink since dinner."

She saw his mouth twitch. "I wasn't thinking of that. In a cab," he said, "I could have been kissing you by now."

"You think I would have let you?"

He gave a small laugh. "Wouldn't you?"

Just the thought of it was making her tingle all over. "Maybe," she murmured. She wanted to know what it would be like, being kissed by Ryder Blake.

He shot out a hand and grasped one of hers, lifting it to his lips. She felt the warmth of his mouth against her fingers, then the gentle nip of his teeth on her skin before he let her go. "Maybe," he repeated, as if he knew she would be hard put to resist him.

He knew altogether too much, she decided, trying to rally her normal caution. After all, apart from the fact that he was madly attractive and good company, just how much did she know about Ryder Blake? She had never treated sex lightly, as something to be casually indulged in, and was wary of men who thought it no more important than a glass of wine or a game of cards. Ryder was attracted to her, but if they had wildly different expectations, divergent values, sleeping with him could leave her with a load of regrets and even more serious consequences.

"Have you ever been married?" she asked him.

"Never." He glanced at her as though the question might have surprised him.

It had surprised *her*. She hadn't intended to ask it.

"You must be over thirty."

"Thirty-one," he confirmed. "Are you thinking of proposing to me?" He sounded amused.

"Not likely!" A first date was a bit soon to be entertaining thoughts of wedlock. Natasha wasn't against marriage, but it was some vague future prospect. Meantime her life was full and interesting enough. "You spend your life running a bridal store," she said, recalling the sumptuous gowns that graced DeWilde's bridal department, the emphasis on weddings that permeated their publicity. "I just wondered..."

"How I've managed to evade matrimony for so long? Maybe it's like running a chocolate factory. After a while you become immune to the temptation to sample the product."

For some reason Natasha felt suddenly depressed.

CHAPTER FIVE

BY THE TIME THEY STOPPED outside her flat, Natasha had decided that discretion was in order.

"Thank you, it was a great evening," she said. Leaning across the space between them, she brushed her lips briefly against his and added, "Good night."

She had her fingers on the door handle when Ryder's hands closed on her shoulders and turned her firmly to face him.

"Good night?" He drew in a breath and said, "Playing games, Natasha?"

She put her hands against his chest, holding him away as he leaned closer. "I don't play games, but..."

"Maybe you think I do?" he asked quietly.

Silently she tilted her head to look at him, trying to see his eyes in the dim light.

He shook his head but released her shoulders, only to close his hands over hers where they still pressed against his white shirt between the edges of his dinner jacket. "Did you really have a great evening?"

Natasha nodded, suddenly deprived of speech because he had begun moving her hands over the front of his shirt, slowly. She could feel the warmth of his skin beneath the fabric, the rise and fall of his breathing, the curve of his ribs.

She didn't resist, feeling only a peculiarly helpless pleasure and anticipation.

He leaned forward and his breath stirred the hair at her temple as he whispered, "So did I. You have lovely hands."

His lips were light as a feather against the skin of her forehead, and yet they scorched. "Do you know how they're making me feel?"

Natasha swallowed. She wasn't a schoolgirl, for heaven's sake! "I have a fair idea." If it was anything like the way the teasing touch of his lips wandering from her forehead to her cheek and chin made her feel, he must be burning up.

Her hands, imprisoned by his, reached his belt, and she made a slight movement to withdraw them.

Instantly he lifted them away, pressing his mouth to each palm in turn, and Natasha fought the desire to close her eyes in sheer enjoyment.

Then his lips settled against hers, questing for an answer. He placed her hands on his shoulders, and only when she slid her arms of her own accord around to the back of his neck did he gently part her lips with his own and smooth his hands down her back, drawing her closer.

The fire in her veins had turned liquid, and her mouth yielded under his urging, allowing him to deepen the kiss until they were both breathing heavily and the world seemed to spin away into the darkness around the car.

His hands came up to tip her head back, and his lips grazed the taut skin of her throat, tracing a line down to the edge of the low bodice of her dress. His open mouth was hot and moist, and when she felt the passionate pressure of it, she gave a small, wordless murmur of content.

He lifted his head and looked at her. "Did I hurt you?"

Natasha was trying hard to retain some shred of common sense. "No," she said, "but don't..."

One hand stroked down her neck to her back, the other cupped her cheek. "Don't?" His voice was amused but not quite steady. "I can't help it. I've been wanting this ever since the day you first walked into my office. This...and more."

His hand still caressed her back, sending shivers of delight along her spine. Before she could put her feelings into words, he said, "But this isn't the best place for what I have in mind."

"It isn't the best time, either," Natasha managed to say. "It's too soon, Ryder."

He moved back a little. "I'm rushing you."

"Just a bit," she said ruefully. "I don't usually..."

"Go to bed on a first date?" he asked bluntly.

She didn't even kiss like this on a first date. Maybe it was just as well he'd reminded her. "Can we just... slow down a bit?"

He laid his forehead against hers. "Sure. Don't worry, I can wait. I think."

She smiled at the wryness in his voice as she moved away from him. "I don't mean to be a tease...."

"I haven't accused you of that. You're entitled to be cautious."

The way he was smiling at her, chiding and tender and amused all at the same time, made her want to fling herself back into his arms and let him do whatever he wanted. Whatever she wanted, too, she acknowledged to herself. But she didn't quite dare. "I'd better go in."

"Is your flatmate home?"

"I don't know," Natasha admitted, but didn't invite him in. "Thank you again. Don't come with me." She was afraid that if she let him accompany her as far as the door, all her resolve would crumble.

Seconds later she had shut the door of the flat behind her, her knees so weak that she had to lean on it for a while. Her feelings hovered between elation and apprehension. Would a relationship with Ryder complicate things unbearably? Or make them blessedly simple? She was, in a sense, deceiving him. But, she promised herself, he need never find that out.

NATASHA AIMED to become a familiar sight around De-Wilde's. She carried a clipboard and pen wherever she went, and the staff became accustomed to her standing about making notes, asking the occasional question. She was careful to ask Lee's permission before entering any of the staff-only areas and never stayed long.

Ryder found her elusive. Once or twice he left his office when he heard she was about, only to discover that she'd gone by the time he reached the department she had been studying. She was out on assignments when he phoned her at the studio, and in the evenings he got her answering machine at home and stubbornly refused to leave a message. Supposing she didn't call him back? That would only confirm his growing suspicion that she was deliberately avoiding him.

RYDER WASN'T ENTIRELY wrong. Natasha wouldn't have said she was consciously avoiding him, but an affair with Ryder would be rather like entering a mine field. She would have to watch her step every inch of the way. She ought to forget the whole idea. At least until her task was accomplished. Then, maybe...

Although she managed to keep physically out of his way, she found herself living in his world. She learned a lot about him from the way his staff talked of him. He was known to the senior members by his first name, although in public they called him Mr. Blake. Violetta spoke warmly of the way he'd reacted when she'd applied for the position as manager of bridal wear, almost breaking down in his office as she explained that she'd recently lost her husband. "Ryder wasn't annoyed or embarrassed. He apologized for upsetting me and told me to take my time. And later he phoned me himself to tell me I had the job, and asked if I needed an advance on my salary, because he guessed I'd had unexpected expenses lately."

But, Natasha guessed, it wasn't compassion that had led him to offer the position to Violetta. He hired good people, and he inspired their loyalty and demanded their best work. She had talked to dozens of employees from senior management to cleaners, and she didn't meet one who had not had some personal contact with the general manager. It seemed he knew all of them by name and was aware of their level of performance. And if it wasn't good enough, he made sure something was done about it.

"He can't stand slackers," one department head told her, "but if you work hard, you can get on in this place. What's more, you get personally thanked, too. Which is a lot more than I can say for the last people I worked for."

When the day came to film Ryder acting out his managerial role, Natasha had plenty of background material to start from and knew the right questions to ask.

Trailed by her camera crew, she talked to Ryder first in his office, and then at three different locations around the store.

The camera operator was Terry Drinnan, a lanky, good-humored Australian whose laid-back style concealed a considerable talent. Natasha had specially asked for him because of his expertise and the fact that they were friends and she trusted him.

On the second floor Terry's eyes lit up as he looked about. "I'll set up at the end of this aisle," he suggested, "and you two can walk toward me, between the bridal displays."

Ryder watched him lope off down the carpet with his equipment, then quirked an eyebrow at Natasha.

"Okay," Terry called. "Take it slowly."

The line of brides on either side smiled glassily at them as they passed. White dresses shimmered and gleamed, misty veils softened perfect plastic faces graced with impossible eyelashes and demure smiles. All wholly artificial, Natasha reminded herself, yet she was assailed by an unexpected yearning as she pictured herself in a drifting white dress and delicate veil, her hand resting on Ryder's arm, their friends smiling at them from either side....

Not since she was an adolescent had she pored over pictures of brides, daydreamed about the shadowy but stunningly handsome man who would be waiting for her at the altar as she glided down the aisle toward him, swathed in white veiling and trailing lace and satin. Now she could almost see the candles, smell the flowers, hear the murmur of voices as she left the church on her new husband's arm.

"Shouldn't we be talking?" Ryder asked her.

"Yes." They'd been fitted with radio microphones and she should ask him something, but her mind was blank. She dragged her eyes away from a lace gown with medieval sleeves and a flowing train. "Tell me... tell me, what proportion of the store's profit comes from the bridal department?"

She hardly heard his reply, even though part of her brain automatically registered the figure.

"As much as that?" she said, forcing herself to concentrate. "What about the jewelry?"

"In recessive times, jewelry sales drop. At the moment they're showing a slight rise, perhaps an indicator of economic upturn."

She dredged up another question as they neared the camera and came to a halt. After Ryder made his reply, Terry straightened and said, "Okay, that's fine."

Natasha had left her bag in Ryder's office for safety and convenience. While the crew packed up, Ryder accompanied her there and handed it to her.

"Thanks." She slipped the strap over her shoulder. "I think we've done all we can for today. When is the jewelry collection due to arrive?" she asked casually.

"In a few days. It'll go on show in the jewelry department for the last two weeks of the celebrations."

"Yes, Lee gave me the dates," she said. "Will we be able to get some shots of the jewels before they're put away behind glass?"

"I think so. Did Lee tell you we plan to have a preview party for selected customers and business contacts?"

"No, he didn't mention it."

"I'll make sure you get an invitation."

She nodded. "Thank you."

As she turned toward the door, he put out a hand to detain her. "Natasha, I've been invited to spend Saturday with some friends who have a yacht up at Pittwater. Will you come with me?"

Natasha made up her mind immediately. She wanted to go, wanted to spend time with him. There couldn't be any harm in getting to know him better. "It sounds like fun. What sort of yacht do your friends have? If I'm supposed to help sail the thing, I'm afraid I won't know what ropes to pull."

He laughed. "Nothing like that. A nice, pleasant cruise up the coast—you won't even get your feet wet if you don't want to. And there'll be three other people who know what ropes to pull. All you need to do is relax and have a good time."

RYDER PICKED HER UP early on Saturday and they drove for about an hour to reach Pittwater, a popular marina where many Sydney "yachties" moored their pleasure craft.

Mac and Kerry McKenzie, a married couple in their late thirties, welcomed them aboard, treating Natasha with a casual camaraderie that made her feel instantly at ease. Mac, wiry and tanned, sported a sun-bleached mop of hair, and Kerry was a curvy blonde with a freckled nose and a wide, friendly smile.

At first the water was dotted with other yachts, but soon the little boat was on its own, a snappy breeze pushing it briskly along. Ryder seemed to know about ropes and sails, and for the most part Natasha concentrated on keeping out of the way, watching him help the others, captivated by the masculine grace and economy of his movements, the sureness with which he handled the rigging, the way he lifted his head to check the sails, his dark hair falling back from his face to reveal his strong, handsome profile.

The banter he exchanged with the skipper and his wife indicated an easy, long-standing friendship. But all of them were careful to include Natasha and not make her feel like an outsider. Now and then Ryder looked at her and smiled questioningly or raised his brows, waiting for her response, making sure she was having as good a time as they were.

When their hosts had gone below to prepare lunch, he beckoned Natasha and stood behind her, showing her how to steer the boat, keeping one arm hooked about her midriff as she carefully followed his instructions.

As the craft responded to her direction, the sails billowing from the mast, Natasha felt a thrill of elation.

"Enjoying yourself?" Ryder asked.

"It's great!"

"Good." She felt his lips brush the side of her neck, then he straightened as Kerry emerged from the narrow companionway.

They anchored in a small, deserted bay with a banana curve of sand lapped by clear water. Lunch on deck was accompanied by a bottle of bubbling white wine. Natasha discovered that her hostess was a painter, her husband a boat designer. Ryder, apparently relaxed and looking almost sleepy, his eyes half closed in the brilliant sunshine, said very little. But Natasha was acutely conscious of his hand casually resting on the back of her chair, and she was sure he was listening intently to every word.

"What do you do, Natasha?" Kerry eventually asked. Like most people, she and Mac were fascinated when Natasha disclosed her job.

"I thought there was something familiar about you!" Kerry exclaimed. "I've seen you on television! In a news clip about New Zealand shearers? Oh—and didn't you host a program about a professional burglar a while ago?"

For a brief second Natasha went blank. Then she told herself not to be so silly and nodded. "Yes, that's right."

Ryder turned his head. "You interviewed a burglar?"

"It was really interesting," Kerry said enthusiastically. "But sort of chilling, too. It was amazing the things he told Natasha. Like he was confiding in someone he knew."

"Friend of yours?" Ryder murmured. His eyes were lit by amusement, and a teasing smile curved his mouth.

Relieved, Natasha drew a quiet breath and deliberately relaxed. "He claimed he wanted to warn people how to look after their property, prevent themselves from being robbed, but I think he just wanted everyone to know how clever he was."

"He was, too," Kerry conceded. "We all know about getting lawns mowed and mailboxes cleared when we're away from home, but in future I'll be asking the neighbors to brush away cobwebs from the gate, too."

"Giving away his trade secrets?" Ryder asked.

"He says he's going straight now," Natasha informed him. "Retiring. He wants to write a book about his former life."

"He was pretty high-class, wasn't he?" Kerry said.

"What," her husband demanded, "makes a high-class burglar?"

"Selective," Kerry explained. "He only took easily carried valuables. Not the usual TV, stereo, electronic stuff. He specialized in small antiques and jewelry. He studied the market and had a good idea of what things were worth."

"There's a strong market for laptop computers," Natasha added.

"Sometimes he stole to order." Kerry turned to her husband. "I'm sure I mentioned the program to you. Remember I said we should upgrade our security system?"

"You're always saying we should upgrade our security system," Mac grumbled. "Why don't we just buy a dog?"

NATASHA ACCOMPANIED Kerry to the galley below and helped her wash up. By the time they were back on deck, the two men had stowed away the folding table and chairs and were ready, they said, for a swim. Mac hauled off his shirt and dived in, and his wife dropped the skirt she had been wearing over a bikini and followed him.

Ryder stripped to a pair of dark blue swim briefs. He looked magnificent, and Natasha wondered how he kept his body so lean and fit when his job was basically sedentary. If he went yachting often, that might account for it. "Coming?" he asked her.

Natasha hesitated. "I suppose it's safe?"

"Safe?" He looked at the inviting blue water, then lifted an eyebrow at her. "The *Jaws* syndrome?"

"I guess Kiwis are a bit paranoid," she allowed.

Ryder didn't laugh. "There are sharks in New Zealand waters, too."

"There have been isolated attacks," Natasha admitted fairly. "It's just that every time I've swum in Australia before, there've been shark nets."

"There could be the odd white pointer about," Ryder conceded. "We won't force you, but if no one's bleeding or cleaning fish, it's usually safe. I promise to come to your rescue if necessary."

"My hero!" she murmured, looking doubtfully at the blue water. It was tempting. "Well . . . you go first."

He grinned at her, turned and dived cleanly into the water. Natasha nerved herself, quickly stripped off the loose shirt and cotton trousers she wore over her swimsuit and followed with a slightly less graceful dive of her own.

When she came up, Ryder was close by, his hair sleek over his forehead. He pushed it back and grinned at her. "Brave girl. Okay?"

"Great." The first shock of water was cold but refreshing. She swam a few gentle strokes away from him and flipped onto her back, gazing up at white wisps of cloud floating against a blue sky. The other two were splashing energetically some distance away. She felt suddenly very happy.

"What are you smiling at?" Ryder asked.

Without looking at him, she said, "The day. It's so beautiful, isn't it?"

"Yes, it is." He sounded content, too. She turned her head and smiled at him, finding him closer than she'd realized. His hand grasped her chin, and then his lips were salty and wet on hers.

They sank under the water into a silent world, and she felt his limbs tangle with hers before he let her go and she surfaced, gasping, into the dazzle of sunlight.

It had lasted only a second, and he was laughing at her now, as though he'd only been teasing. But despite the coolness of the water she felt hot all over, the blood racing in her veins.

A shout came across the water. "Hey, you two! We're going ashore!"

Ryder waved acknowledgment, then looked back at Natasha. "Race you?"

She nodded and broke into a fast crawl, streaking for the white strip of sand.

She was good, but he was bigger and faster. He got there before her and stood up in the shallows, dragging her to her feet as they waded out of the water and walked toward the other couple, who were already sprawled on the sand in the meagre shade of a few scrubby plants growing on the sheer cliff that bounded the little cove.

Ryder didn't let go of her hand when they sat down, and after a halfhearted effort to withdraw it, Natasha gave up. She didn't want to make an issue of it in front of his friends, and besides, she liked the feel of his lean, strong fingers curled about hers as they lay side by side on the sand.

The conversation was desultory, and after a while Natasha dozed off, waking to find Ryder still holding her hand, smiling down at her.

"I was about to kiss you awake, Sleeping Beauty," he said regretfully. "You're going to get burned if we don't move soon."

The shade had shifted, and sun glinted off the sand that dusted her bare legs. Realizing she was alone with Ryder, Natasha started to sit up. "Are they waiting for us?"

"They said to take our time. Either they wanted to be by themselves for a while, or they figured that we did."

Natasha tugged her hand from his, shuffled back into what remained of the dappled shadow and began brushing the sand from her legs, trying not to wish that she'd slept a few minutes longer and been wakened by his kiss. "I hope they didn't think I was rude, dropping off like that."

"Not a bit. They're very easygoing. They did suggest it was my fault you were tired, though." He grinned sideways at her. "Don't I wish . . ."

Natasha grinned back at him. "I hope you set them straight."

"What, and sully my reputation?" he teased.

"Do you have a reputation?"

His grin faded. "Not that I know of. If I have, I assure you it's undeserved."

"You must have had girlfriends."

"Some," he acknowledged. "You want to know all about them?"

"It's none of my business. Sorry."

"You're entitled to ask." He paused. "I don't make notches on the bedpost. There wouldn't be that many if I did. And I'm not one of those idiots who don't believe in protection."

Natasha studied her knees. "Thank you." She appreciated his frankness. "But even so, there are risks." Other risks, too, she thought. The risk of heartbreak, for one thing. And the risk of him finding out things she didn't want him to know. . . .

"I won't say, 'Trust me,'" Ryder told her softly. "That's up to you."

She had a mad desire to trust him with everything, to allow her feelings for him to overpower discretion. But some secrets were not hers to divulge. And although she felt they were friends, perhaps future lovers, maybe her attraction to him was making her want to see safety where none existed. She swallowed and looked blindly toward the boat that gently bobbed on the water. There was no sign of its owners on the deck.

Ryder said with a faint grin, "I told Mac and Kerry that if you had a heavy date last night, it wasn't with me."

Natasha laughed. "I had a heavy week, workwise. I actually went to bed quite early. The sea air and sun have made me sleepy, that's all."

"You take your work very seriously, don't you? Lee and Violetta are both impressed with the amount of information you're asking for. More than you could ever use."

"I don't know before I start a project what information I may need to put it together. So at the beginning it's a scattergun approach," Natasha admitted. *Not to mention a camouflage operation,* her conscience added. Pushing the thought aside, she said, "I hope they don't mind answering all my questions."

"We want as much positive publicity for the birthday bash as we can get. I think you'll find the staff are all keen to cooperate."

"Except for the security people," she said involuntarily. The head of security had met her questions with a stolid stare and told her he had no information to give about his department's operations.

"Their job is quite different," Ryder said mildly. "They can hardly divulge details to the media."

"I suppose not," Natasha murmured. "You'll be hiring extra security staff while the collection is in the store, I guess."

"A few. We already have security staff on duty twenty-four hours a day. The collection will be stored in the jewelry department's safe, and the department itself is locked every night with a metal grille."

Natasha nodded. "But in the daytime the collection will be on public display."

"The minute a display case is moved or lifted, alarms will go off all over the place."

"So there's no chance of anyone... interfering with the exhibits?" Natasha said thoughtfully.

"None."

None. Scrub that idea, Natasha decided with reluctant resignation.

"How do you like sailing?" Ryder asked.

With good grace she dropped the subject of the jewels. "I think maybe I could take to it."

"I'm surprised you haven't tried before. I thought New Zealanders were born sailors."

"Not all of us. Owning a boat is expensive."

"Your family wasn't well off?"

"We did all right. It wasn't easy after my father died, but there was some insurance money to tide us over the first year or so. My grandparents helped when my mother let them. She's pretty independent."

"I never knew my grandparents on either side."

"That's sad."

"Tell me more about yours."

A little nonplussed, she said slowly, "Well, Grandpa was a gentleman of the old-fashioned sort. He had a rather natty mustache and a wicked twinkle in his eye. I think when he was young he'd been a bit of a lad with the ladies. He still was, even at eighty-odd."

"Did his wife mind?"

"I don't think so. She was very proud of him. He was better-looking than any other eighty-year-old around, and though he never stopped flirting with younger women, he always treated her as if she were special. He was devoted to her, and I'm sure he was faithful, even if..."

"If—?" Ryder looked at her curiously.

"Well..." There couldn't be any risk in this. "I don't think she was his first love. When he married my grandmother he was in his forties."

"And how old was she?"

"In her mid-thirties, I think. She'd been engaged during the war to an American serviceman who was killed in the Pacific, and I don't think she ever looked at another man until Grandpa came along."

"So they both had other loves."

"Yes, but they were happy together, I think. Although my grandmother was always nervous about what Grandpa might get up to next."

Ryder grinned. "With the ladies?"

"Oh, no. As I said, she tolerated that. But he was a bit of an adventurer. He celebrated his eightieth birthday by taking a trip in a hot-air balloon. Mum and I arranged it for him as a birthday surprise. Poor Gran nearly had kittens at the idea, but he loved it!"

"I hope I'm that spry at eighty."

"That was nothing compared to what he got up to in his younger days. He had a few hair-raising stories about the time he was opal-mining in the outback, only..."

"What?"

"Oh, I don't know. Sometimes he'd stop in the middle of a story, as if he'd stirred up memories that he didn't want to think about."

"He was Australian?"

"English, according to Gran's marriage license, but I'm not sure it was true. He spoke French like a native, and some German and Italian. When I was at high school he used to help me with my French homework. He had traveled a lot, and I think he served in the American forces during World War II. After he died I made some inquiries through a military historian in America, but he couldn't find any record of Derrick Freeman at all.''

"Bit of a mystery man, your grandfather."

Natasha sighed. "Yes, and . . ."

"And what?"

Natasha closed her lips. Ryder's questions had drawn out her memories, made her relax her guard. Had she already talked too much?

Surely he wasn't really that interested in her family history? "Never mind. There's Kerry waving to us from the boat. I guess we'd better get back."

HOURS LATER, slightly sunburned and decidedly tousled and salt-stained, Natasha said as Ryder slid into his car alongside her, "Thank you, that was a great day!"

"For me, too. What do you say we stop along the way and eat before I take you home?"

She looked down at her rumpled trousers and shirt, touched a hand to her tangled hair and said, "I don't think anyone would let me into a respectable establishment." Ryder, despite having worked far harder than she had, still looked sleek and fresh in khaki cotton slacks and a striped shirt. Probably, she thought resignedly, because his clothes were designer casual rather than chain-store cheap.

"Maybe I don't have a respectable establishment in mind."

Suspicious of his teasing tone, she looked at him warily. "What does that mean?"

"We could go to my place," he suggested. "Buy food on the way."

Natasha shook her head. "I'd like to change my clothes. But . . . if you like, we can eat at my place."

"Done." Looking pleased, he started the car.

Natasha found her flatmate using the shower when they arrived, and while she waited her turn, she fished in the kitchen for glasses to pour the wine that Ryder had bought.

Ryder sat on the secondhand sofa in the small living room and looked about at the ornate colonial fireplace, the mismatched but comfortable furniture, and the one note of luxury in the room—a real Bukhara rug.

"Not what you're accustomed to," Natasha commented, handing him one of the glasses.

Roberta, a towel wrapped about her body and another encasing her hair, peeked around the doorway. "All yours," she announced.

"Thanks." Natasha put her glass on the mantelpiece. "Will you excuse me? I'd like to shower before we eat."

"Sure." He lifted his glass to her.

She showered quickly, then dried her hair to barely damp with a hand dryer before slipping into a loose cotton dress with a buttoned bodice and a pair of Brazilian leather flats.

She heard voices from the living room and was glad Roberta was entertaining Ryder, but as she reentered the room the doorbell rang and Roberta said hastily, "That's my date. See you guys later."

"Nice meeting you," Ryder told her as she made her way past him to the door. He was standing, his empty glass in his hand, and as they heard the front door open and close again, his gaze slipped over Natasha, warming her from head to toe.

She had to drag her eyes away from him. "If you want to use the bathroom, it's free."

"I'll wash my hands," he said after a moment. "Thanks."

She placed cutlery and chopsticks on the table in the kitchen-dining alcove, then opened the foil containers and spooned out the fragrant Thai food onto plates. She was just putting the plates on the table when Ryder came back. "We've bought far too much," she said. "If I'd known Roberta was going out..."

He gave her a rather enigmatic glance, then turned his attention to his plate, picking up a set of chopsticks. "We'll do our best."

He had two helpings, but there were still plenty of leftovers. Ryder helped Natasha tidy up, then they carried their coffee into the living room. Ryder headed back to the sofa, and Natasha chose the big old velvet-covered armchair, curling her legs beneath her.

Ryder cast her a quizzical glance and laughed softly.

"What's funny?" she asked him.

"You look like a teenager, huddled into that chair. Is it a defense mechanism?" he suggested. "To discourage me from pouncing on you?"

"I don't think you'd pounce on anyone who didn't want you to."

"Now there's an interesting thought."

"Strike that," she said. "I didn't mean it to sound..."

"Like an invitation? No such luck, I suppose."

Smiling, she shook her head. "Tell me about your family. Do you have any brothers or sisters?"

Nothing seemed to change in his expression, yet Natasha had the clear impression that he'd shut something off inside. "Not really. I was an only child until I went off to boarding school in England."

"When you were... what, twelve, thirteen? It must have been pretty traumatic, being sent to the other side of the world at that age." She tried not to sound judgmental, but it seemed to her that loving parents could not have borne it.

He shrugged. "It's the way the British upper classes have operated for generations. My parents just happened to be farther away than most, and..."

"And...?"

"They were in the process of splitting up. My father had been seeing another woman—she was pregnant with his child, I realized later—and my parents' marriage was finished. They felt it was better all round for me to be out of the way until the whole mess was finally over. I was packed off to my father's old school, and when I finished there, they'd both married new partners and had other children, much younger than me. I didn't fit into either family. Not that it mattered. By that time my parents were strangers, anyway, and I went back to England to attend university. My father was glad to provide the money to get rid of me again."

"That's appalling!"

He put down his cup, laughing at her. "It wasn't so terrible. No one ever beat or starved me, and maybe I was better off in a stable, if slightly impersonal, environment in England than caught in the middle of my parents' screaming matches. Sending me there was probably the best thing they ever did for me. I made some useful contacts in those years."

Natasha didn't think any number of useful contacts made up for a lack of love, of a family life, but she didn't say so. "Like the DeWildes?" she asked.

"Yes, like the DeWildes. I was lucky there. No one knows more about retailing. It's in their blood."

"The DeWilde family are still firmly in power, aren't they?" she asked thoughtfully. "Even though it's a public company."

"When you've had a family enterprise for generations, you don't give up control easily. Jeffrey is a traditionalist, and an extremely efficient corporation head."

"A bit of an autocrat?"

"Not overtly. But I wouldn't want to cross him without good reason," Ryder admitted. A shadow darkened his eyes. "He can be fairly ruthless."

"In business?"

"Even in his personal relationships, when they impinge on what he sees as the good of the company."

Jeffrey DeWilde didn't sound very nice, Natasha thought, her heart sinking. "The kind of man who'd sell his grandmother for a buck?" she inquired lightly.

"I didn't mean to imply that. If anything, I'd say Jeffrey has a rather rigid code of ethics. Maybe that's why he can be hard on others who don't—in his eyes—live up to his standards."

That was no comfort, either.

"He's coming out to Sydney soon, anyway," Ryder told her. "You'll be able to meet him yourself."

Natasha's ears pricked up. "You never mentioned this before!"

"Jeffrey isn't one to court publicity. He'll be speaking at a staff dinner and meeting with the Australian shareholders, but he doesn't want a high public profile."

"An interview would be interesting." She couldn't pass up the chance to talk to the man, meet him in person. It was more than she'd hoped for.

"I don't think he'll agree. You can ask Lee to try to persuade him if you like."

"Couldn't you . . ." She stopped there. "I suppose not."

"For you?" he asked, giving her a slightly ironical smile.

"I'm sorry." It was tricky, this tightrope walking.

He nodded. "Maybe I will ask him . . . for you."

"He's bringing the jewels, isn't he?"

Ryder's gaze sharpened. "How did you know that?"

"I didn't. It seems logical for him to bring them . . . a member of the family. I suppose they'll be in a strongbox or something?"

"The security arrangements are top secret," he said rather curtly. "I'm sure you understand that."

"Yes, of course. But . . ."

"But?"

Natasha rapidly changed her mind. He was already a bit prickly. She didn't want to arouse his suspicions. At the thought, guilt wormed its way into her consciousness. "No, leave it. This isn't the time."

He looked at her pensively, then got up and came over to her chair, reaching down to pull her to her feet with one hand while the other removed her cup from her fingers and placed it on the mantelpiece. Possessing himself of her other hand, he said, "You're right. It's time for . . . other things."

A smile curved his mouth, but something momentarily disquieting flickered in his eyes. Natasha made a conscious effort to dispel her discomfort, telling herself she had nothing to feel guilty about—yet. Instinctively she moved closer to him, and raised her face in anticipation of his kiss.

There was a tiny moment when she thought he had changed his mind, when his eyes narrowed slightly and seemed to cool. Then he bent his head and kissed her eager mouth, kissed her thoroughly and completely, his arms holding her against him, his mouth moving over hers in unsparing passion.

When he broke the kiss, he swung her off her feet, took a couple of steps and lowered her to the sofa, settling himself beside her. He looked down, his eyes glittering with desire, and lifted a tumbled wave of hair back from her face. "You are beautiful," he said.

She touched his hair in turn, and let her hand slip down his neck and inside his collar, and he gave a throaty grunt and captured her mouth again. His hand roamed from her shoulder to skim her breast, and then swept down to trace the line of her hip. Her skirt was riding up, and he found the smooth skin of her thigh, stroked it until she was trembling. But when his fingers reached the edge of her panties she stiffened, making a sound of protest against his mouth.

He lifted his head a little. "Sh." But he moved his hand, bringing it instead to rest on her breast, while he kissed her neck, nuzzled the warm indentation below her ear, touched his tongue, like fire, to the hollow at the base of her throat.

He began to undo the buttons at the front of her dress, exposing the lace of her bra.

She raised her hand and slid it behind his head, her lips parting in invitation, and he took her mouth with his, fiercely, his body pressing her against the yielding softness of the sofa while his hand returned to her breast.

The blood in her veins was singing, her whole body hot and longing. She felt consumed by him, by their mutual need, their mouths clinging in an almost desperate union.

Then he pulled away, breathing hard. "Natasha," he said, "are you going to invite me into your bed?"

She had to swallow twice. She shook her head, her heart jumping about like a mouse in a cage.

"You still feel you don't know me well enough?"

It was much more complicated than that. That strange look he had given her just before he'd kissed her had chilled her a little. It was as if he didn't quite trust her, and maybe he was right. Trust was important in a relationship. Lamely, she grabbed at the feeble excuse. "It hasn't been very long, has it—since we met?" Sitting up, she began buttoning her dress, avoiding his eyes.

Ryder moved his head a little as if to clear it and stood up. "Do you want to get to know me better?"

Fitting the last button into its hole, she looked up, directly at him. "Yes."

He nodded in a satisfied way and turned toward the door.

Slightly flushed, Natasha got up and followed, and when he'd opened the door he turned, stretched out his hand and trailed a finger down her cheek. Natasha had to clamp her teeth together to stem a shiver of pleasure.

"When can I see you again?" he asked.

She'd been afraid he wouldn't ask. "Soon," she said, "please."

His finger was finding its leisurely way down the line of her throat, pausing at its base. "Good," he said, and moved his hand up again to tip her chin. He bent forward and lightly kissed her lips. "I'll phone you." He kissed her again, lingeringly this time, as though he couldn't quite bear to leave, and she found herself swaying toward him.

Ryder drew back at last and cocked a hopeful, teasing eyebrow at her. "Unless you want to change your mind, after all, and go to bed with me."

"I don't do that."

"You don't change your mind, or you don't go to bed with men?" He grinned down at her.

"Occasionally," she admitted enigmatically, daring to tease.

He was staring back at her, his eyes gleaming. Then he laughed. "But not tonight?"

It was an effort, but she managed to shake her head regretfully. "Not tonight."

CHAPTER SIX

RYDER DROVE TO the airport himself to meet Jeffrey. The company head was accompanied by a security guard in plainclothes, and a younger man with a metal case handcuffed to his wrist. "This is Nick Santos," Jeffrey told Ryder, "from New York."

That surprised Ryder. When the request had arrived for him to book three rooms, he'd assumed Jeffrey was bringing security people from London.

Santos looked as though he'd be a good man in a fight—and as if he might have had his fair share of them. But his Latin good looks had not been impaired too much. He topped Ryder's six feet one by an inch or so, and the well-cut suit he wore didn't disguise his broad shoulders and tautly muscled frame. His handshake reinforced the impression of physical power held in check, and his dark gaze swept the concourse as though he were searching out trouble and prepared to meet it head on. It wasn't until they were walking to the car outside that Ryder noticed the slight unevenness of his gait.

Ryder took the three men first to the DeWilde store. As they waited for an elevator to the second floor, Jeffrey told him, "There was an article in our flight magazine about the anniversary. Your PR people are doing their job well."

"Yes, they are. I hope there'll be news coverage of some of the birthday events here in Australia. The Kiwi Connection, as I told you, is filming an hour-long documentary that will be shown in New Zealand, and they're hoping to sell clips to news services, as well. They'd like to interview you."

"No," Jeffrey said. "You can do that very adequately."

"I'm not the president of the corporation."

"And I am," Jeffrey said with unconscious arrogance, "so no one can force me to appear on television."

"I wouldn't dream of trying to force you," Ryder said, adding with a grin, "and much good it would do me if I did. I warned Natasha you'd say no, but she wanted me to ask."

"Natasha?"

"Natasha Pallas, the reporter I mentioned on the phone. She'll be disappointed."

"Is she pretty?" Jeffrey asked dryly.

After a moment, Ryder laughed. "How did you guess? She's . . . lovely."

Nick Santos, who had been alternately glancing at the flickering numbers over the elevator doors and watching everyone who entered the lobby, turned his head, his gaze sharpening as it briefly collided with Ryder's.

"Hmm." Jeffrey looked thoughtful. "I've never known you to ask a favor for anyone before."

Ryder shrugged. "I'd like the publicity for the store."

Jeffrey shoved a hand into his pocket, rocking on his heels. "Grace would have...." He scowled impatiently. "But it's not my forte—"

"It could be a good idea," Nick Santos interjected.

Ryder turned in surprise. The American was looking at Jeffrey, and Jeffrey returned his gaze for a long moment before he said to Ryder, "Well, if you think it'll help, I'll do my best."

Then the sliding doors opened before them and two people alighted. Santos stepped back to allow Jeffrey and Ryder to precede him and the other guard.

In the jewelry department they deposited the metal case in the strong room in the manager's office, and afterward Ryder took the three men to their hotel.

Santos and the security guard shared one suite, with Jeffrey occupying the adjoining one. Ryder followed Jeffrey into his room and shut the door behind him. "So," he asked, "who is Nick Santos?"

Jeffrey was swinging a flight bag onto the baggage rack. "A private investigator...now. He used to be in the San Francisco police force until he got shot in the line of duty and was left with a damaged leg."

Ryder recalled the slight limp he'd noticed. An old injury would almost certainly stiffen up with the enforced inactivity of the long plane trip. "You couldn't find someone in England capable of guarding the jewels on the journey?"

Jeffrey turned to him. "Nick is...a specialist."

"He must be good."

"Damn good," Jeffrey agreed with unusual vehemence. "He'll be responsible for the security of the collection while it's in Australia."

Ryder said mildly, "We have excellent security staff of our own."

"I know you do. He'll liaise with your head of security, of course. And I hope you'll tell your people to cooperate with him. It's rather important—" Jeffrey broke off and rubbed his eyes with fingers and thumb, looking suddenly tired.

"Of course," Ryder said quickly as Jeffrey dropped his hand. "I understand that. Do you want to rest? Or would you like me to ask room service to send you something to eat?"

"Thanks, but I just need a few minutes to freshen up and then we'll raid the mini bar and do some catching up," Jeffrey decided. "Or," he suggested, glancing at the suite's kitchenette, "you could make coffee while you're waiting, if you like."

In the end they both settled for coffee.

Two armchairs flanked a small table by the window that gave a view of the harbor and a glimpse of the distinctive arch of its famous bridge. Jeffrey leaned back in one of the chairs, stretching his long legs as he cradled the steaming cup. His face looked thinner, Ryder thought, almost gaunt.

Hazel brown eyes met his, and Jeffrey gave him a slightly weary smile. "How are you, Ryder?" he asked.

"I'm fine. The store is doing well—you know that from the quarterly figures."

"I do. You're to be congratulated. Not that I'm surprised."

"Thank you," Ryder said. "And you—are you okay?"

"My doctor tells me I'm overstressed and need a break. So I thought a few weeks in a warmer climate..."

"I figured it wasn't my persuasion that induced you to take time off from head office. I suppose he suggested a proper holiday, and you refused point-blank."

"Compromised," Jeffrey argued. "I wouldn't know what to do on a holiday without—well, on my own." His voice held a hint of testiness.

Ryder spared a sympathetic thought for the doctor. "I saw Grace a few months ago," he said.

Jeffrey visibly stiffened. "Grace was here?"

"I was in San Francisco."

"I had no idea you'd been out of Sydney." Jeffrey's eyes had lost the glaze of fatigue and were alert and almost censorious.

"I didn't think I had to check with you every time I left the store," Ryder said evenly. "I was only away for a few days, attending a management seminar."

"And visiting Grace."

"We had lunch together."

Jeffrey's eyes flared briefly before he said unemotionally, "Oh, yes?" and, after a nearly infinitesimal pause, asked, "How was she?"

"She seemed well, and said she was fine. Looking forward to opening her new business. But...I don't think she's happy."

Jeffrey put his half-empty cup on its saucer and straightened. "I'm sorry about that," he said, as though it had nothing to do with him. "Happiness is something few people manage to attain for any length of time—and happiness based on illusion can't last."

"Illusion?"

"I hope you're not setting out to take on the role of marriage counselor, Ryder." Jeffrey's mild voice was laced with steel.

"I wouldn't presume—"

"I'm glad to hear it."

Feeling almost like a fourteen-year-old schoolboy again, Ryder said, "It's just that I have a great regard for you both. It was something of a shock to hear of the breakup."

"Thank you for your concern. I trust you didn't allow it to lead you into confiding company affairs to my... to an outsider. Was she hoping to head-hunt you?"

Shock held Ryder silent for a moment. Then he said, "Our meeting was a personal one. Grace has been good to me, as you well know. Surely you don't expect me to cut her out of my life?"

"That would be unreasonable." But Jeffrey was looking extremely austere. "Who you see in a personal capacity is, of course, your own business." He picked up his spoon and unnecessarily stirred his coffee again, then replaced the spoon in the saucer and lifted the cup. "Loyalty is admirable, and I certainly value that quality." A fleeting expression of something like pain crossed his face. "Only you won't lose sight of the fact that in terms of your career, your future is bound up with DeWilde's, will you?"

"I'm not likely to forget it," Ryder said quietly. His jaw ached with the effort of keeping his temper. With *Jeffrey*, for God's sake. He swallowed hard.

"Good. I'm glad you understand." Jeffrey hesitated as though debating whether to say more. Then he seemed to relax. "Now, can you bring me up to speed on the program for the celebration?"

NATASHA STOOD BY her desk, shrugging out of her jacket as she dialed DeWilde's number. She had just spent two hours on a windy headland talking to a bird-watcher who had earned his fifteen minutes of fame by discovering a rare albatross nesting on the clifftop.

Ryder's secretary put her straight through to him. "You left a message on my answering machine this morning?" she asked, trying to sound strictly businesslike. She hadn't heard from him for a couple of days. This was a busy time for him, with the birthday celebrations merging into the Christmas rush.

"Yes, I did." His voice induced a warm, shivery sensation in her midriff, and her hand tightened on the telephone receiver. Her jacket dropped to the floor. "Jeffrey says he'll give you an interview at the store. But not in a public space."

Concentrate, Natasha told herself sternly. She couldn't remember when just the sound of a man's voice had made her feel this way, if ever. "Thank you!" she said warmly. "I don't see a problem with that. Lee has a list of times when we'll be filming at the store. Do you think he could fit in with one of those?"

"I have the list, too. Jeffrey will do whatever suits you. He suggested I invite you to dine with us at his hotel tonight—if you're free?"

Surprised, Natasha said, "That's very kind of him. Yes, I'm free."

"I'll pick you up."

"There's no need, really—"

"Natasha."

The way he said her name stopped her. He made it sound so intimate, so special.

Into the silence he said, "I want to come and fetch you. I'll see you about seven."

NATASHA REVIEWED her wardrobe before settling on a classic-style dress in deep green with short sleeves, a wide neckline and a slim skirt. She had worn it a lot but it suited her and always looked right. Combing her hair neatly back, she fastened it with a silver filigree clasp that her grandmother had given her last Christmas.

When she opened the door to Ryder, he cast an approving glance over her and smiled. "You look wonderful. Gorgeous, in fact."

Her smile held a hint of disbelief. She was aware she wasn't plain when she took the trouble to look her best, but gorgeous? Her cheekbones were too broad, her jaw too strong. And although she'd been blessed with a fine, clear complexion, there was nothing remarkable about her features. She shook her head slightly but said, "Thank you. I'm ready." She had picked up her bag when she heard the doorbell.

"Are you always so punctual?" Ryder queried as he led her to his car.

Sliding into the passenger's seat, she said, "I didn't want to keep you waiting."

The look he gave her was a teasing challenge. "I wish I could count on you meaning that."

Natasha refused to rise to the bait. In the cold light of morning she'd told herself she ought to make good use of her friendship with Ryder. But that very thought made her balk at the idea of becoming his lover. It seemed too calculating, and too fraught with all kinds of risks, both practical and emotional.

When they arrived at the hotel, the car was whisked away by a uniformed bellman and the door held wide by another.

They crossed a marble-floored lobby to a carpeted lounge bar, and a tall, fiftyish man with a thin, intelligent face and disciplined brown hair rose from one of the deep leather chairs to greet them. Shrewd hazel eyes surveyed Natasha as she put her hand into Jeffrey DeWilde's firm clasp. His voice was quiet, but she guessed it could ring with authority when necessary. "Ryder told me you were lovely," he said. "The boy is quite right."

Boy? Natasha couldn't resist a laughing glance at Ryder. He gave her an answering grin but didn't seem bothered.

Another man, good-looking in a dark, brooding sort of way, had been sitting opposite Jeffrey DeWilde. He put down an empty shot glass and stood up, saying to Jeffrey, "I'll see you later."

"Sure you won't join us, Nick?" Jeffrey asked. "Miss Pallas, this is Nick Santos."

"Hi." A smoky but almost uncomfortably perceptive gaze rested momentarily on Natasha. She gave him a polite smile and murmured hello. He hesitated as if he might change his mind, then flicked a glance at Ryder standing beside her, and his mouth lifted at one corner. "Thanks," he said, "but I've got things to do. Nice to meet you, Miss Pallas." He gave a tight, controlled smile in her direction and then was gone, weaving his way among the tables toward the exit.

Jeffrey ordered drinks, and as Natasha sipped at a cocktail, he said, "I thought it would be a good idea to discuss beforehand just what form this interview will take. What exactly are you aiming for?"

Natasha studied him with cautious respect. Obviously he liked to be thoroughly prepared. "I want an entertaining, informative interview for the viewers. I would like to ask you about the reasons for DeWilde's opening a store in Australia, and something about the background and history of the firm, and then about new directions you might see for the future. Any more branches down under, or thoughts of expansion into other parts of the world.''

Jeffrey exchanged a glance with Ryder.

"I told you," the younger man said, "she's very thorough." He gave Natasha a slight grin of appreciation bordering on pride.

"Perhaps you'd let me have a list of the questions," Jeffrey said.

"I will if you insist," she replied pleasantly, "but the essence of a good interview is spontaneity. Sometimes your answers will suggest another slant that I might not have thought of, and that makes it more interesting. I prefer not to be tied to a script.''

Jeffrey appeared to be weighing her answer. "I should warn you, I will refuse to answer any personal questions. My private life is strictly off limits."

"That isn't the subject of this program, Mr. DeWilde. I could give you some idea over dinner of the kind of questions I'd like to ask."

Ryder interjected. "A list wouldn't help much if an interviewer wanted to catch you off guard. I don't suppose they'd forewarn you, in any case."

"I'm not planning to do that," Natasha protested. "Truly."

After a moment Jeffrey nodded. "Very well. I gather it won't be shown until after the birthday celebrations are over? And it's aimed at the New Zealand audience?"

"Initially, but there could be a wider market. We have had a nibble from an Australian channel that's interested in showing it here. And we're selling clips to news programs, but those often depend on a visual hook.''

His interest quickened. "Is the DeWilde jewelry collection what you'd call a visual hook?"

"Definitely." Despite the urbane expression on his face, the tranquillity of his voice, she detected an indefinable echo of her own tension in Jeffrey DeWilde. It was in his very stillness, in the concentration of his eyes as they met hers. She almost imagined some ethereal connection between them, an unspoken communication. "Will tomorrow morning suit you?" she asked.

Jeffrey turned to Ryder. "If that's okay with you?"

"No problem, but we'll have to alert security. You could use the jewelry manager's office, perhaps," he offered.

"That sounds okay."

"I'll look forward to it." Jeffrey smiled, and the rather stern lines of his face relaxed into an expression of surprising warmth. Natasha was startled at this new side of him, and at her own reaction. Suddenly she liked him very much.

As soon as he'd signed the chit for their meal, Jeffrey said he needed to catch up on some sleep after his long flight. "You two have a nightcap if you like," he suggested. "I'll tell them to charge it to my room account."

When they had settled into a couple of chairs, Natasha said, "You told me he wouldn't want to go on TV. Did you talk him into it?"

"No. I must admit I hadn't expected him to agree so readily." Ryder frowned slightly, as if something bothered him.

"He doesn't seem a shy man."

"Jeffrey has no craving for fame. He rather avoids attention. Especially since..." Ryder looked down into his brandy snifter, gently twirling it.

"Since...?" Natasha echoed inquiringly.

"You know he's recently separated from his wife?"

Natasha nodded. "I read about it."

"The two of them have run the firm ever since their marriage. It's hard to believe...." Ryder shrugged. "I don't understand what happened to them. Anyway," he went on, "the split had an effect on the business and there were reporters everywhere for a while. Jeffrey's even more reluctant to give interviews now than before the breakup. Grace was good at that sort of thing, so he used to let her do it."

Watching his bleak expression, Natasha asked softly, "If DeWilde's goes down, will that affect you very badly?"

"DeWilde's is in no danger of going down. There was a temporary dip in the shares while things got sorted out, and of course I was concerned, but—" he paused "—it's their own business, as Jeffrey made very clear to me earlier."

So Ryder had shown his concern and been rebuffed. That didn't surprise Natasha; Jeffrey struck her as a man who wouldn't readily discuss his feelings. But Ryder's offhand manner hid something stronger than business worries.

She had expected a professional relationship, cordial but distant. Instead, although there had been an uneasy undercurrent between the two men, she'd sensed that both of them had been trying to ease it, that their relationship was important to them. "You're really quite close to the DeWildes, aren't you?" she asked directly. "On a personal level."

Ryder looked at her with a hint of reserve in his expression. "Gabriel DeWilde," he said slowly, "is my best friend. His parents took me in during the school holidays every year I was in England, and treated me like one of their own. Those were the happiest times of my life. I'm closer to Grace and Jeffrey than I am to my own parents. I don't spread that about much—I guess I'm sensitive on the subject."

"Because people may think your position as manager is due to influence rather than merit?"

"Something like that. It's true in a way. Our friendship led to me getting the managership."

"A firm like DeWilde's surely can't afford to appoint people who aren't up to the job, just for personal reasons."

"No, they can't. And Jeffrey certainly wouldn't. But not everyone would see it that way."

"Some people are probably plain jealous."

He smiled at her. "Thanks. I'd appreciate it if you didn't tell the world, though."

Of course she wouldn't. This was a private conversation. *But,* a small voice whispered, *it could be useful....*

"Do you...see much of the family now?"

A shadow seemed to darken his eyes. "I haven't seen Gabe for quite a while, though we've talked briefly on the phone, mostly about business. I was planning to attend his wedding earlier in the year—it was supposed to be a big event—but it was called off when he and Lianne eloped. I last saw Grace in San Francisco a few months ago."

They lingered for a while, talking quietly, both reluctant to end the evening, but Natasha turned down a second brandy and Ryder figured he'd had enough to drink if he was to drive her home. He asked for his car and saw Natasha into the passenger seat.

She was rubbing her bare arms as he got in beside her.

"Are you cold?" he asked her.

"It's just the night air after being inside. It's quite warm in here." But all the way home she experienced little shivery feelings of anticipation. She clenched her hands in her lap, trying for a measure of control.

There was a light on in the flat. Natasha unconsciously let out a breath as Ryder stopped the car, her feelings a strange mixture of relief and disappointment. When he turned to her and his arm encircled her shoulders, the release of tension was so immediate that she let out a long, shuddering breath and leaned into him, her head resting against his shoulder.

"Natasha!" His voice was low and vibrant in her ear. "Look at me."

She sighed gently and did as he asked, her face taut with desire, and she knew he saw it, he drew his breath in sharply before he lowered his head and accurately found her mouth with his.

It was a sweet, fiery onslaught, passion without restraint, but even as her mouth flowered under his in instinctive response, he checked himself for an instant, seemingly aware of the soft vulnerability of her lips, the tender flesh of her arm where he gripped her. She realized he was holding back, careful not to bruise or crush her, and perversely it made her want to incite him, force him to forget caution, consideration. Recklessly she let her head tip farther back, opened her mouth and slid a hand into his hair.

He made a husky sound of satisfaction and took advantage of the implicit invitation, sending heated waves of sensation cascading through her.

She moaned in his arms, and he lifted his head, cursed under his breath and moved away from her. She saw him drag air into his lungs, then let it out again, and his hand rubbed briefly at his forehead. "Unless you're going to invite me inside," he said, "we'd better stop now."

One part of her thoroughly agreed, while another perversely felt rejected. She sighed, wishing her life was less complicated. If she'd had no ulterior motive the day she walked into his office and asked if she could film DeWilde's birthday celebrations, would she have been torn by doubts this way?

Remembering the immediate impact he'd had on her, she recalled something else, too. He'd looked up from sniffing appreciatively at a page of feminine-looking notepaper, smiling with tender amusement as he murmured something she hadn't been able to catch. That the letter had been from a woman and that it was personal was perfectly obvious.

Without intending to, she blurted out, "Whose letter were you reading the morning I came into your office for the first time?"

"Letter?" he repeated. "I get a dozen or so letters every morning."

"This one was perfumed." No use backing out now. "Lavender paper, matching envelope."

He stared at her, then began to laugh. "Darling, are you jealous?" As she stiffened and drew away from him, he reached for her hand. "It was from Grace," he said.

"Grace DeWilde?" Relief flared and died. It was a reminder of his closeness to the family.

"That's right." He grimaced. "You haven't been worrying over that all this time?"

Natasha shook her head. "No," she said truthfully. "I just remembered it and wondered.... It looked so... feminine, and personal. Not a business letter. So I...sort of noticed it."

He grinned. "Grace usually writes to me at home, but she knew I was moving and she didn't have my new address."

"It's really none of my business."

"I'm glad you asked, all the same. What else do you want to know about me? I'm not Bluebeard."

"I didn't think so," she assured him hastily—too hastily, perhaps. "But what do we really know about each other?" she asked, out of some obscure sense of obligation to warn him somehow that she had secrets she couldn't share.

"I know that I want you," he said. "And I know you want me."

She couldn't deny that. As she cast about for something to say, he said, "I told you I can wait. It's just damned hard when you kiss me the way you did tonight."

Natasha bit her lip. "I could," she offered, "promise not to kiss you."

The tension eased. He laughed and gave her hair a small tug. "Watch it!" he said in a soft growl. "I," he added deliberately, "am making no promises."

He walked her to the door and, before she went in, turned her to him and kissed her briefly on the lips. "I'll see you," he said. "I hope you sleep better than I will."

CHAPTER SEVEN

NATASHA SAT AT ONE SIDE of a low table in a corner of the room, Jeffrey at the other, both facing the camera and with lapel microphones unobtrusively pinned to their clothes. Between them rested a sturdy metal case.

The roomy office of the jewelry department seemed crowded. Besides Natasha and the TV crew and of course Jeffrey himself, the department manager was hovering in a corner, and Nick Santos had stationed himself near the door, standing with arms folded across his chest.

The camera operator nodded and Natasha rattled off her prepared introduction, then turned to Jeffrey and launched into her questions. When she got to "And you've brought some of the DeWilde collection to Australia with you?" the camera focused on the table.

Jeffrey unfastened the case, laying the two sides flat on the table, and two hinged trays covered with black velvet lids opened out, making a display box.

Jeffrey removed one of the lids to reveal velvet-lined, custom-designed compartments, each holding a piece of jewelry.

He took out a necklace that shimmered with diamonds and sapphires, thickly intertwined.

"This one is called Dancing Waters."

He held it up so that it looked like a sparkling cascade, and the camera operator suggested, "Zoom on that, Nat?" Natasha nodded.

There was an art deco brooch in a stunning mixture of stones—rubies, diamonds, emeralds and black onyx—then a graceful swan pendant fashioned of sapphires and yellow diamonds, and magnificent earrings dripping with diamonds and what Jeffrey said were Burmese rubies.

Natasha made admiring comments and asked the questions that she thought viewers would want answered.

Jeffrey held a glittering diamond tiara with six perfectly symmetrical teardrop pearls adorning its dainty arches. "This is said to have been worn by the Empress Eugénie on the occasion of her wedding to Louis-Napoléon. Perhaps," he suggested to Natasha, "we could show your viewers how it should look."

He reached up to place it on her head. "And this," Jeffrey said, removing the cover from the other side of the case, "is one of my favorites. An emerald, pink pearl and diamond bracelet featuring a particularly fine pink baroque pearl known as the DeWilde Heart."

Natasha caught her breath, totally forgetting to comment for the camera which whirred on in the silence.

"Why don't you try it on?" Jeffrey suggested.

She couldn't speak, her eyes riveted to the lustrous ribbon of gems draped across Jeffrey DeWilde's long, well-manicured fingers. He took her hand and she felt the cool, slight weight of the bracelet against her wrist while Jeffrey deftly fastened the hidden catch. She stared down at the heart-shaped pearl and the seed-pearl florets with their subtle pink glow, each centred with a pink diamond brilliant. The leaf-shaped emeralds between the florets gave off sparks of light. *This can't be real,* she thought.

"Nat?" Terry was saying. "You'll want a close-up of the bracelet, won't you? Hold it up a bit so I can get a decent shot, okay?" The sound operator was looking anxious.

She held her hand up for the camera, feeling as if she were moving through water.

"And a full shot, the tiara and the bracelet?" Terry asked.

"Yeah, okay," she said, scarcely hearing him. She lifted her head and gazed glassily at the camera.

Forcing her mind back to her job, she glanced at the folder in her lap, trying to focus on her notes. She turned to Jeffrey. "And this is the first time in almost fifty years that the DeWilde collection has been on show to the public?"

"The last time was when they were shown in all our stores around the world in 1948," Jeffrey confirmed. "Of course, the Australian branch didn't exist then."

The slight weight of the bracelet seemed heavy against her skin. "And they are all genuine, one-of-a-kind pieces?" she heard herself ask, as if some other person were asking the question.

Jeffrey smiled. "Jewelry like this is never mass-produced. Each is a unique creation designed for particular stones."

"This bracelet—it's worth thousands of dollars?" She stared at it, wanting to examine it link by link, stone by stone.

"Several hundred thousand," Jeffrey said almost casually. "It isn't a major piece."

"How did it come into the collection?"

"Max DeWilde, my grandfather, had it made for my grandmother, to mark the first anniversary of their marriage."

"So... it's a DeWilde design?"

"Oh, yes, like many pieces in the collection. This one, for instance." He turned to pick out another piece of jewelry.

As she wound up the interview, Natasha had a wayward thought that perhaps she needn't give the bracelet back. If there were some way...

She raised her arms and removed the tiara, placing it in Jeffrey's outstretched hand, and as he fitted it back in its place, she quickly undid the catch of the bracelet and took the lovely thing off. "I'm reluctant to let it go," she said truthfully. It made a surprisingly small glowing heap in Jeffrey's palm.

"Watch her, Mr. DeWilde," Terry said as he folded his tripod. "She's taken a shine to it."

Jeffrey smiled, replacing the bracelet in its box and locking up the case. "It's not the right piece for her. Miss Pallas should wear stronger, deeper colors—garnets perhaps, or the darker type of opals."

"I don't think she's fussy," Terry said.

Natasha laughed, as he expected, and shook her head. "I'm not the jewelry type."

Terry grinned. "Can't afford it, you mean. You coming back with us?"

"I wanted to talk to Violetta," she said, "about filming the rehearsal for the fashion show. I'll see you guys later."

She watched as the jewelry was deposited back in the safe. They were certainly taking no chances. To film the Boucheron bracelet, the camera crew had been asked to arrive before the store opened, and the head of security had been present, as well as two guards at the locked and grille-protected doors of the department.

Natasha found Violetta in the workroom of the bridal department, surrounded by racks of clothing and poring over a large table spread with fabric samples and fashion sketches and photographs.

"Are these for the fashion show?" Natasha asked.

"Some of them. I'm having trouble deciding just which garments to use."

"You're spoiled for choice, aren't you? I was wondering if we could film the dress rehearsal."

"As well as the show?"

"At the rehearsal we can go between backstage and the catwalk without distracting the audience, and maybe ask for another chance at a shot if it doesn't go right."

"I see. Well, clear it with security—I don't suppose there'll be any problem."

"Have you made any decisions at all?"

"That rack there," Violetta indicated. "Those are almost certain to be in."

"May I look?"

"Sure. I still have to choose accessories for them, and jewelry to go with the evening wear."

Natasha's interest quickened, distracting her from her survey of the clothes on the rack. "DeWilde jewelry, of course?"

"Oh, yes. Not from the collection, though—from the shop."

"Why not from the collection?" Natasha's voice was oddly hoarse. "Surely you'd like to use it?"

"Well, I'd like to, but..." Violetta paused. "You're right," she said. "Why not? When we started planning this we didn't know they'd be here, but as they are..." She trailed off thoughtfully. "I'm not sure it would be allowed."

Someone rapped gently on the open door, and Jeffrey DeWilde strolled into the big room. "Am I interrupting?"

Violetta turned, a welcoming smile on her face. "Mr. DeWilde! Not at all. What can I do for you?"

He smiled back at her and ambled across the room. "Jeffrey," he said. "And it can wait, if you're busy."

Violetta glanced from him to Natasha. "You know Jeffrey DeWilde, don't you?"

"We've just spent half an hour together," Jeffrey told her. "Natasha has been interviewing me about the DeWilde jewels."

"Jeffrey," Violetta began hesitantly, "could I ask you something?" At his encouraging expression, she went on, "I know they're frightfully valuable, and maybe it's too much to expect, but I wondered if we could use some of the DeWilde collection in the fashion show. We're already borrowing jewels from the shop."

Jeffrey stared at her for a moment, and she added hastily, "I shouldn't have mentioned it."

"But of course you should!" he said. "It's so obvious I ought to have thought of it myself. My wi— A woman would have suggested it in the first place. I'll have to contact the insurance people, and Ryder will need to see to extra security measures, but I think it's a splendid idea."

Violetta's face lit up. "Thank you! We have some absolutely fabulous gowns, and to team them with the DeWilde jewels would be really special."

"I actually came to invite you to have lunch with Ryder and me in the Skyroom," Jeffrey told her. "We can talk it over with him. Perhaps Natasha would like to join us?"

"That's kind of you," Natasha said, "but you needn't feel obliged—"

"Not at all. I'm sure you would find the discussion of interest for your program, and Ryder certainly won't object."

His dry tone and the knowing look in his eyes made her flush slightly. "Thank you," she said. "I'd like to hear more about the history of the jewels."

"Good." He glanced at his watch. "Shall we go?"

Ryder greeted both women with obvious pleasure. The waiter quickly set two extra places at the table.

Jeffrey seemed more mellow and approachable than Natasha had seen him, and he regaled them with stories about the DeWilde collection while they ate. A matched sapphire and diamond set, he said, had been part of the settlement of a debt of honor. There was the Empress Eugénie's tiara, and the flawless diamond smuggled out of Africa in the nineteenth century to become the center of an exquisite necklace that had been Genevieve DeWilde's favorite.

"She would have been your grandmother?" Violetta asked.

"Yes," Jeffrey confirmed. "That's right."

Violetta leaned toward him, her face glowing with inspiration. "Jeffrey, would you tell some of these stories during the show? It would be wonderful to have a member of the family commenting on the jewels."

Clearly taken aback, Jeffrey said flatly, "I don't think so."

Disappointed, Violetta urged, "Please give it some thought? We could have two microphones—one for you and one for me—"

"You're doing the commentary on the clothes yourself?" Jeffrey asked.

"Yes, I know them best. And Natasha tells me I have a good microphone voice." She smiled briefly in Natasha's direction. "But *you* know the jewelry better than anyone. Ryder—" Violetta turned to him, appealing "—don't you think it would work well?"

"Splendidly, I should think. She's right, Jeffrey."

But the older man was shaking his head. "It's not my sort of thing. I prefer to keep out of the limelight."

Violetta laughed, a pleasant, warm sound. "Heavens, Jeffrey! You don't think anyone will be looking at you? With a dozen gorgeous young models in fabulous gowns and priceless jewelry parading in front of them, who's going to notice you except as a disembodied voice in the background?" Her lips curved in a gentle, amused and slightly mischievous smile.

For a moment Jeffrey looked mildly astonished, and then he laughed and said ruefully, "You make me sound very precious."

"I didn't mean it like that, but..." Violetta smiled at him coaxingly. "I do wish you'd consider it. No one else could do it the same way. When you talk about the jewels, it's almost as if they're part of your family."

She was right, Natasha thought. Although his appearance and manners gave an impression of containment, he'd handled and spoken of the jewels with something approaching tenderness.

Jeffrey appeared almost embarrassed. "They are part of the family heritage, and I have a protective instinct about them." His face resumed its stern lines. "I'd defend the collection almost to the death."

Natasha had no trouble believing it. There was an intensity about the statement that was chillingly convincing.

"Has it ever been under threat?" Ryder was looking at Jeffrey rather curiously; perhaps he too had noticed the sudden stone-cold hardness in the other man's eyes.

"What happened in New York?" Natasha asked.

If she hadn't been watching him so closely, she might have missed the quick shock on Jeffrey's face before he masked it. He took a moment to reply but didn't quite manage to erase the note of sharp inquiry from his voice. "What do you know about New York?"

"The last time the collection was exhibited, back in the forties, didn't someone try to steal some of the jewels?"

Ryder and Violetta both looked surprised. "Is that true?" Ryder asked.

Jeffrey's voice was now perfectly neutral. "Where did you get your information from?"

"Old newspapers. Well, not directly. I did a computer search on the Internet for information on the DeWildes as part of my research for the TV program. A data base I tapped into turned up an old item from newspaper archives about a smash-and-grab raid on the DeWilde collection when it was exhibited in the New York store in 1948."

"Did they get away with anything?" Ryder asked.

Jeffrey, who had been holding himself stiff, a fork poised in his hand, seemed to relax. He even smiled slightly as he dug the fork into a piece of sautéed beef. "I'd forgotten about that old bit of family gossip. But don't believe everything you read in the newspapers," he advised Natasha.

"You mean there was no raid?" Natasha sounded skeptical. "The papers said a man had been charged."

"Did your research tell you what happened to him after that?" Jeffrey asked.

"The charges were dropped. I wondered why."

Jeffrey swallowed the piece of beef and lowered his fork to his plate again. "The whole thing was a storm in a teacup. A rather hot-tempered family acquaintance had an argument with my uncle, who was running DeWilde's in New York at the time, and a glass case was smashed, probably accidentally."

"There was a fight?" Ryder queried.

"It was a long time ago, and who knows what the truth might have been? I expect Uncle Dirk was pleased enough to have the police haul the chap off to jail to cool his heels— and his temper."

"So there was no robbery?" Ryder asked.

"As far as I know, the incident took place in broad daylight with dozens of people about. Almost certainly there was no intention of theft on Villeneuve's part. For one thing, his family wasn't at all short of money."

"I thought *Henry* DeWilde was in charge in New York back then," Ryder said, looking puzzled.

Jeffrey shook his head. "Dirk actually founded the New York branch. Henry took over a few years after the war."

"Why would this Villeneuve man have attacked your uncle?" Violetta asked.

"I can only guess. Possibly he blamed the family for breaking up his engagement to my Aunt Marie-Claire."

"Ah, a broken engagement! Romeo and Juliet?" Violetta guessed, obviously entranced.

"You could say that, I suppose." Jeffrey smiled at her, amused. "The Villeneuves and DeWildes were always rivals in business, but when Marie-Claire and Armand became engaged, for a time both families saw possible advantages in the marriage and a merging of interests.

Now...Armand is a bitter man, and he seems to have devoted his life to trying to ruin the DeWildes—fortunately without success.''

"He sounds like Heathcliff in *Wuthering Heights,*" Violetta said.

Jeffrey laughed. "I don't think he's cut in the same heroic mold as Heathcliff. According to my father, my aunt broke off the engagement because she discovered her fiancée was having a sordid little affair with some dancer from the Paris opera."

"This was when the family were still living in France?" Ryder interjected.

"Yes, before the Second World War."

"Was it an arranged marriage?" Natasha asked.

"No, not at all. Marie-Claire was brokenhearted when she found out about the other woman. Her brothers never forgave Villeneuve. Uncle Henry, although he would only have been young at the time, got into a fistfight with him, and right up until he died, my father never missed an opportunity to best the Villeneuves in business."

Ryder's brows rose "After all those years?"

"DeWildes defend their own." Jeffrey sounded grim. "And they never forget a betrayal."

"I wanted to do business with the Villeneuves in Hong Kong when we first started the store here," Ryder recalled. "I wondered why you vetoed it so promptly."

Jeffrey looked at him, a slight smile on his lips. "Well, now you know. My father would have turned in his grave. I heard the story from him when I suggested the same thing." He paused, glancing at the two women. "I must be boring you, dragging out family skeletons."

"No!" Violetta's eyes sparkled. "I'm riveted, honestly. A family feud!"

Natasha said, "Isn't it rather extreme, conducting a vendetta against the whole Villeneuve family?"

"Perhaps," Jeffrey acknowledged. "But it seems his family saw nothing particularly reprehensible in Armand's conduct, except a certain carelessness in allowing his fiancée to find out. Even his mother thought Marie-Claire was a naive little goose to call off the marriage. I believe Villeneuve senior had kept a mistress for many years while his wife turned a blind eye."

He paused. "No doubt they were right about Marie-Claire being naive. But you see—" Jeffrey's eyes darkened, and Natasha saw his hold on his wineglass tighten "—she thought she was loved, and in reality she was being married for expediency, because she was a good match. And that," he finished, looking down into the shimmering red depths of his wine, "was unforgivable."

THE SALES REP FROM THE Kiwi Connection let no grass grow under her feet. Natasha's interview with Jeffrey DeWilde was shown that evening on two channels in Australia. Thinking the item might be picked up in New Zealand, too, Natasha phoned home.

"How's Gran?" she asked when her mother answered.

"Better than when you talked to us last, but still fretting a bit. I keep telling her we have to be patient, give you a chance to work on the problem."

"I told her I'd take care of it, and I will," Natasha said, more positively than she felt. "But there are complications."

"Are you in trouble?" her mother asked anxiously.

Not yet. Keeping that thought to herself, Natasha said, "No, I'm not in trouble, only...something unexpected happened. I interviewed Jeffrey DeWilde this afternoon on camera. Don't be surprised if you see a news clip of me wearing...wearing a one-of-a-kind, guaranteed unique, genuine emerald, pink pearl and diamond bracelet that Mr. DeWilde has brought with him from England."

"Brought with him...?"

"Uh-huh," Natasha confirmed dryly. "As he just told the whole of Australia, it's been part of the DeWilde collection since it was specially designed and made for his grandmother."

"Pink pearls, diamonds and emeralds?" her mother reiterated.

"Centred with a heart-shaped baroque pearl."

"But . . . ? Natasha, how can that be? You told us—"

"There's only one explanation," Natasha said. "It's got to be a fake."

CHAPTER EIGHT

THE FIRST RULE of journalism, Natasha reminded herself, was to check your facts, and then check again. The following day found her being ushered into the proprietor's office of a plush, carpeted jeweler's shop off Castlereagh Street.

The man who rose from behind the big polished desk, her card in his hand, was balding and slightly paunchy. Wearing an expensive three-piece pin-striped suit over a white shirt and dark tie, he was the epitome of respectability, and he didn't look at all pleased to see her.

"Ms. Pallas," he said, reluctantly waving her to a chair. "What can I do for you this time?"

Natasha came straight to the point. "Good morning, Mr. Dancey. Were you watching TV last night, by any chance?"

Burt Dancey had subsided into his chair. "Yes, I saw the...item you are referring to," he said, stirring uneasily. "I don't know what you're playing at, but if it was some kind of test, I have to say your tactics were—questionable. I'm surprised that the DeWildes allowed it."

"If you saw the program," Natasha said, "you know that Mr. DeWilde brought the collection out from England just a couple of days ago."

His eyes hardened on her. "What are you saying?" He looked positively belligerent.

"Just that possibly you made a mistake."

Offended, he drew himself up in his chair. "Mistake? I know my trade, Ms. Pallas. I do not make that kind of mistake, I give you my word on it."

"But Mr. Dancey," Natasha said softly, "how do I know I can trust your word?"

He flushed. "What possible reason could I have had for lying? It would have been of no advantage to me."

That was true, she supposed. Still... "Perhaps I ought to get a second opinion."

"You can if you want to," the jeweler said huffily. Then, giving her a shrewd stare, he added, "But if, as you impressed on me most strongly at the time, you want a *confidential* opinion, I would advise against it." The slight sneer in his voice wasn't lost on Natasha. "I should remind you that the usual procedure in these cases is to contact the police. The only reason I didn't do so was that you came to me through a mutual ... friend. Who, I might add, assured me that as a journalist you would never reveal the source of any information."

And who had equally assured her that Burt Dancey was the best in the business. "Your name will never cross my lips," she told him, resisting the temptation to laugh at his claim that he would ever have contacted the police. This shop and its proprietor were certainly not her idea of the seedy underside of the jewelry trade, but the burglar she had filmed had given her Dancey's name. The jeweler was, he'd told her, "an honest fence." In the skewed world in which they moved, a crooked jeweler who gave a fair cut to the thief was apparently held in high regard.

"And you stand by your opinion?" she pressed him.

"It was not mere opinion," he said flatly. "I examined the piece most carefully, even more so since I couldn't imagine how it came to be here in Australia. There is absolutely no doubt in my mind."

Natasha thanked him and left the shop, pausing outside to gather her thoughts. Glancing around while people passed to and fro in front of her, she found her eye caught by a sign across the street and a little farther along. Another jeweler's shop.

A second opinion, she'd suggested to Burt Dancey. But he'd been certain of his own judgment, and as he'd warned her, anyone else might contact the police.

A man who had been walking along the street opposite stopped in front of the shop she'd been looking at. Something about him seemed familiar, and she hesitated until he turned his head for an instant and she saw his profile. Nick Santos, Jeffrey DeWilde's underling. A bus rattled by, obscuring him from her view, and when it had moved on he was gone.

Natasha turned and walked rapidly toward the busy thoroughfare of George Street.

WHEN IN DOUBT, choose the simplest way out, Natasha said to herself. The simplest way would be to go straight to Jeffrey DeWilde....

He didn't like media attention, that was a point in her favor. But she couldn't break her solemn promise, especially since she wasn't sure how Jeffrey might react. Even Ryder, who was fond of him, admitted Jeffrey had a ruthless streak. She remembered his declaration that he would defend the DeWilde collection "almost to the death." And he'd told them that story about his aunt Marie-Claire and the Villeneuves. It must have happened almost sixty years ago, but *"DeWildes defend their own... they never forget."* His father had taken every chance to avenge Marie-Claire's humiliation, and only months ago Jeffrey himself had prevented Ryder from doing business with the firm of Villeneuve. Forgive and forget apparently wasn't in their vocabulary.

. She would have to think again.

NATASHA HAD ASKED to film the preview party for the DeWilde collection and Ryder had said yes, but he wanted her to stay on after the team had finished.

They filmed for about thirty minutes, and when the others left, Ryder took her arm. "You're not working now," he said. "Let me get you a glass of wine and something to eat."

"Shouldn't you be looking after your guests?" she asked him. The jewelry department was crammed with people admiring the collection, which had been placed in specially designed showcases along one wall, and the crowd had spilled out into the bridal wear section. Natasha recognized several faces that regularly appeared in the social columns of Sydney newspapers and national magazines.

"They're being adequately fed and watered," he said, glancing about him. Red-jacketed waiters circulated with trays of hors d'oeuvres and drinks among the formally dressed, chattering groups. "And I've introduced Jeffrey all round. He's the one people want to meet."

Jeffrey looked distinguished and at ease, talking to a high-profile politician and his wife. Violetta passed him holding a wineglass, and he reached out, bringing her to his side with a hand on her arm to introduce her.

Following Natasha's gaze, Ryder frowned slightly. Then he took her elbow and said, "Come on, what can I get you?"

"White wine," she said. "And if there are any oyster patties left, I'd love one."

"Coming right up," he promised.

He was as good as his word, but as she bit into the patty, Ryder's chief of security discreetly approached through the crowd and murmured something in his ear.

"Sorry," Ryder said, "I'll be back. Don't go away."

With her mouth full of crisp pastry and creamy, pungent oyster, Natasha could only shake her head. She didn't want to go anywhere, unless it was with him. While they'd been filming, she'd watched him moving among his guests and exchanging brief words with his staff members, occasionally catching the smile in his eyes when they met hers. He was friendly but not deferential to the politicians and business tycoons, and with the workers he was equally friendly and yet commanded their respect, which required a considerable balancing act. But for all his ease in social situations, he carried an indefinable air of aloneness. She guessed that few people would be really close to Ryder Blake, and those few would value that closeness.

Jeffrey DeWilde was one of them. She wanted to be another, she admitted to herself, her gaze resting idly on the wide doorway through which the still tableaux of bridal splendor glowed under the lights. With a sense of déjà vu she recalled that odd yearning she'd felt when Ryder had walked at her side between the rows of mannequins in their white gowns. Again the ghosts of girlhood dreams tugged at the edges of her consciousness.

Shaking herself mentally, she washed down the patty with a mouthful of deliciously cool sparkling wine. She was wondering if the crush about the exhibits was thinning enough to make it worthwhile trying to get another look at them, when a deep voice said, "All alone, Miss Pallas?"

"Mr. Santos." She glanced up at the American. "I didn't know you were here." He looked handsome and sleek in a tuxedo, but she had a feeling the polish was all on the surface.

His eyes were hooded and lazy-looking, but with a lambent curiosity in their dark depths. "The name's Nick."

"Natasha," she reciprocated.

He cocked his head, then nodded.

"You're security, aren't you?" Natasha asked, guessing at the obvious. "You work for the New York branch of DeWilde's?"

"No."

"Oh, I'm assuming on the basis of your accent," she confessed.

Briefly he showed his white teeth in a grin. "That's San Francisco, not New York."

"Sorry." She could no more distinguish between regional North American accents than most Americans could between Australians and New Zealanders. "Are you with the London branch?"

He seemed to debate whether—or how—to answer her, saying finally, "I'm a free-lancer, on special assignment."

"I see." He was giving nothing away. She tried a different tack, enquiring sociably, "Is this your first visit to Australia?"

"No." He moved slightly so that he almost stood beside her, enabling him to cast a quick but searching glance about the room, particularly at the people gathered near the display cases holding the DeWilde collection.

"The jewels are well protected," she said. Guards stood with their backs to the showcases at either end of the row, and two more were at the door. Others were stationed at the elevators and the stairs.

"They're extremely valuable."

"Are they?" Natasha muttered to herself.

"Sorry?" Nick bent his head toward her inquiringly.

"I said, they are, aren't they? I wonder if they were as well guarded the last time they went on display."

Nick was scanning the room again. "So do I." He bit off the remark abruptly, as though he had thought better of making it.

"I'm sure you won't let anyone smash any cases."

"Jeffrey told me you knew about that." His eyes, returning to hers, were suddenly piercing.

"He did?"

"Found it in your research." It wasn't a question, but she detected a note of query in his voice.

"That's right."

"Which data base were you in?"

She told him, and he nodded. "What others did you try?"

As she listed them, she wondered why he was so interested.

"They're all public domain," he commented. "Don't you journos sometimes hack into restricted areas?"

"I'm not a hacker." She wasn't going to tell him that she'd enlisted the help of a computer-whiz friend with exactly that in mind but had met with scant success. "Are you responsible for DeWilde's computer security?" she asked.

"I'm responsible for the collection."

She could see he wasn't going to give her a direct answer. "I suppose all this publicity is making things difficult for you."

"Why do you say that?"

"It can attract all sorts of people."

Nick had turned his head slightly as he made another visual circuit of the room. His eyes arrowed briefly back to her, black and penetrating. "That's right," he said, resuming his survey of the crowd.

Talking to this man was like opening oysters with her fingernails. "Ryder said Jeffrey's publicity shy, but he's bending over backward to make sure this birthday celebration's a success."

"Yeah," Nick Santos agreed. "Sure."

She gave him a puzzled look, and he said, "Jeffrey DeWilde is a very thorough man. When he takes on something, he gives it all he's got and follows through to the very end, no matter what it costs him."

"That's a pretty comprehensive character analysis. It sounds as if you know him quite well."

"We've spent a lot of time together lately. He's not a guy who's easy to read, but some things are obvious." He spoke almost absently, renewing his surveillance.

"I wouldn't have thought there's much about Jeffrey DeWilde that's obvious."

He withdrew his attention from the room at large and once again focused on her wide, candid gaze. "Everyone has hidden depths."

Including you, Natasha thought. "And you know Jeffrey's?"

"I didn't say that. He runs a successful international business, and I've seen the way he operates. Think about it."

Natasha thought about it, wondered if she was being given an oblique warning, and concluded that Nick was evading her question. "You're very discreet," she told him, and smiled as nicely as she knew how.

He gave her a tight, rather tigerish grin in return.

Ryder had threaded his way back to her, nodding at Nick as he joined them. "Sorry," he said to Natasha. "Security are just doing their job."

"Problems?" Nick inquired tersely.

"No problem. Some late arrivals who'd left their invitations behind. I was needed to vouch for them."

"You know them personally?"

"Yes, I know them," Ryder answered. "Our security is watertight, believe me."

Natasha, looking at Nick, saw a very odd expression cross his face. Ryder touched her arm, saying to the other man, "Will you excuse us?" Then, "Mac and Kerry are here, Natasha."

She was glad to see the couple again, the first time since the day she and Ryder had spent with them on their boat, and when, sometime later, Ryder suggested they all go back to his place for coffee after the function, she hardly hesitated before accepting.

"Jeffrey's coming, too," he told Natasha as they left, the security staff lowering the grille over the jewelry department behind them. "Violetta's going to bring him in her car."

His face was perfectly neutral, but there was a note of reserve in his voice. Natasha glanced at him. "They know each other well?'' she asked as he ushered her into an elevator.

''Jeffrey always talks to the department heads when he's here. They're not close.''

He could be wrong about that, Natasha thought. ''Does he visit often?''

''He was here for the opening of the store last year, and he's made a couple of visits since.''

After negotiating a narrow hillside street, Ryder parked the car in the underground garage. Jeffrey and Violetta were waiting outside Ryder's apartment building, standing close together in the doorway, intent on their conversation. They seemed quite startled when Ryder spoke.

''Sorry to keep you waiting,'' he said tersely, and strode past them to put his key into the lock. ''I see you found it all right.''

As he stood aside to let them into the carpeted lobby of the building, Mac and Kerry arrived, and they all crowded into an elevator.

''Is this a converted warehouse?'' Natasha asked him as they were carried up to the top floor. The exterior had been refurbished, but she'd noted the solid walls and decorative features of Victorian times.

''Yes, you're right. There are six apartments, two on each floor.''

He let them into his and switched on the lights to reveal a long, high-ceilinged room with a bank of windows that gave a view of winking city lights across a darkened bay.

''Why don't you all sit down and I'll put the coffee on.''

''Can I help?'' Violetta offered.

''Sure,'' he said after a moment. ''Thanks.''

She followed Ryder into the kitchen, and Natasha joined Jeffrey on a long, rich red leather couch facing the window, while Mac and Kerry shared an identical set at right angles to it. A third completed a U-shape around a large polished wooden coffee table.

The floor had been sanded back to its original wood and covered with scatter rugs in different patterns, with black and gold predominating. Near the kitchen, a small round dining table and four chairs sat on a circular rug. An antique cabinet set against the wall held chinaware.

Seeing her interested gaze, Jeffrey said, "You haven't been here before, either?"

Natasha shook her head. "Haven't *you?*"

"Ryder's moved since my last visit to Sydney. He used to have a house on the North Shore. When he told me he'd got sick of joining the traffic over the bridge every morning and bought a one-bedroom warehouse apartment, I didn't envisage anything this spacious."

Kerry said, "I love what he's done with it."

While they chatted, Natasha covertly watched Jeffrey. He conversed easily, and even smiled once or twice, yet he gave nothing away of himself, she decided. But she saw his eyes soften a little when Violetta came into the room carrying a tray, Ryder close behind her.

Over coffee they talked about the success of the evening, then drifted on to other matters. Natasha answered when she was spoken to, but the rest of the time she concentrated on Jeffrey, trying to discover any chink in his armor of urbane courtesy.

When Violetta rose to go, Jeffrey followed. Natasha wasn't surprised that he turned down Ryder's offer to take him back to his hotel if he wanted to stay longer.

Violetta volunteered to give Natasha a lift, too, but she scarcely hesitated before saying, "Thank you, but it's out of your way. I'll be fine."

Violetta looked from her to Ryder and didn't press the point.

Kerry and Mac didn't stay long after that, and when Ryder closed the door behind them, Natasha stood up, murmuring that she should be going, too.

Ryder didn't move from the door. "Not yet. I'll take you home—whenever you want," he added, looking straight into her eyes. "Come here."

She walked slowly toward him, and he reached out a hand, drawing her closer, leaning back against the door as he folded her into his arms.

Natasha returned his kiss, locking her own arms about his neck, her body curved into his, her lips parted and welcoming.

He lifted his head, rubbed his cheek against hers and let out a long sigh. "I've been dying to do that for hours."

Natasha rested her head against his shoulder. So had she, but she'd tried to hide it.

His lips nuzzled her ear. "We've hardly spoken all evening—I was almost jealous of Jeffrey."

"Jealous?" She stared up at him.

"You sat beside him and scarcely took your eyes off him the whole time he was here."

"He's an interesting man."

"He's too old for you," Ryder said, almost seriously. "And anyway, he's—"

When he stopped there, Natasha said laughingly, "And anyway, he's interested in Violetta, right?"

Ryder's arms slackened, allowing her to step back. "Violetta?" he said sharply. "Nonsense."

"I don't think so, Ryder. I was watching him."

"You're imagining things. Just because she gave him a lift—"

"It's more than that. You didn't notice?"

"Notice what?"

"He likes her—a lot." Hadn't Ryder seen the rare warmth that lit Jeffrey's eyes when Violetta was near? Natasha walked over to the table and began gathering up the coffee cups.

Ryder followed her. "Everyone likes Violetta. I do, myself."

"Yes, I know, but—" He knew what she meant, but for some reason he didn't want to admit it. "Well, perhaps I was mistaken." The fact that Jeffrey recognized an attractive woman when he met one didn't mean they were having an affair or even heading for one. Seeing the hint of a scowl on Ryder's brow, she abandoned the subject and turned to pick up another cup, balancing it on the pile she held.

"Leave those." Ryder took the stack of crockery from her hands and put it on the table. Then he drew her down with him onto one of the sofas and began kissing her again.

His mouth was insistent on hers, seductive. She let him coax her lips apart, and his hand found her breast.

Natasha tried to remember all the reasons why this was not a good idea, only it was difficult to call them to mind when his fingers were playing tantalizing little games— stroking, exploring, cupping and gently kneading—so that her breath suddenly caught and her spine went rigid.

"What?" he murmured, drawing away a little. "I didn't hurt you, did I?"

"No." She lifted her eyes to his. "Oh, no!" Not yet, an inner voice whispered, reminding her that she was in danger of setting herself up for hurt that she could barely imagine, telling her that this hadn't been in the game plan, that she ought to leave before it was too late.

But Ryder was smiling at her, the tenderness in his eyes melting every barrier she'd tried to set between them, making all the reasons that she shouldn't get too close to him seem trivial, irrelevant. And his hand was moving over her, touching her as if she were precious, breakable, beloved. His eyes were heavy-lidded with appreciation, and the faint curve of his lips made her want to touch them with her own.

He lifted his eyes and found her watching him, and his smile widened, pleased but almost diffidently so, as though her naked desire for him were an unexpected compliment, as if he'd expected her to reject him, after all.

Behind the successful, polished exterior that Ryder presented to the world, she glimpsed the lonely, scared boy who had been sent halfway around the globe by seemingly uncaring parents. And whose second family—the people he'd felt closest to in all the world—was breaking apart, Jeffrey and Grace separated, their children perhaps taking sides, straining his relationship with all of them.

In that moment she stopped fighting her emotions, stopped considering consequences or trying to weigh possible advantages against probable risks.

He wasn't asking, and he'd never force the issue. If she got up and walked away he'd take her home without a word of protest or disappointment.

But he needed her, needed to be close to someone. His relationship with Jeffrey had changed, and that was hurting him. The disintegration of the DeWildes' marriage, of the perfect family, was hard for him. Maybe even his friendship with Gabe was threatened. And anyway, Gabe was far away in England.

But Natasha was here. She could at least give him the comfort of knowing that she cared. She could love him.

He touched her cheek with his thumb. "What is it?" he asked quietly. "What are you thinking?"

"I was thinking about you."

"I like that."

She laughed at him, then lifted a forefinger to trace the small quirk at the side of his mouth. "What else would you like?"

She felt him go still, and the spark of desire in his eyes deepened to a dark, intense fire. He said slowly, "What are you offering, Natasha?"

Everything, she thought. *Me... Love...*

I love you. The revelation hit her with a rush of adrenaline that made her dizzy. This was no temporary buzz of hormones. This was real, irrevocable. Forever. She knew it in her bones.

Maybe Ryder wasn't ready for that; he had never mentioned love. Possibly he never would. It was a risk she had to take—one more risk among the many she was taking tonight.

She leaned across the few inches of space between them and laid her lips against his, slid her arms about his neck, and gave him an invitation so explicit no man could have mistaken it.

He hauled her closer, kissing her senseless, and when at last he lifted his mouth they were both flushed and breathing hard. Her dress was undone and her bra loose. Somehow Ryder's hand had found its way underneath it.

"I have a perfectly good bed in the other room," he told her. "Shall we see if we can make it that far?"

She looked over his shoulder, measuring the distance, and shifted a little, experimentally, her thigh rubbing against his. Her expression was thoughtful as she pretended to gauge the odds. "It's a long way. Are you a betting man?"

Ryder laughed. He got up, pulling her with him, then swung her into his arms. "Come on, let's do this properly."

The bedroom was in darkness, but he left the door ajar and light filtered through from the lamps in the other room, throwing a wide swath across the double bed.

Ryder set her on her feet and threw back the covers, then eased the dress and bra down.

"Unfair," Natasha complained as her clothes slid to the floor and she reached up to tug his bow tie undone. He linked his arms loosely about her waist, above the bikini panties she wore, and patiently waited while she undid the pearlized buttons and pulled his shirt out of his pants, hooking her own arms around him as she parted the material.

He wrapped her close, and she gasped as her deliciously sensitized breasts met his bared chest. Her head went back under his kiss, and he lowered himself to the edge of the bed, bringing her with him, her knees gliding to each side of him as he settled her in his lap with her legs snug against his hips.

His hands drifted up her back, then down along the smooth skin of her thighs. They were still kissing, enjoying the heady taste of each other, when he touched her breasts again and she flung her head back with a low cry of pleasure.

Holding her securely, Ryder encouraged her to lean back against his arms so his mouth could take up what his sensitive, clever fingers had begun. Just before it became too sweetly unbearable, he returned his lips to hers, his hands tangling in her hair as he fell back with her onto the sheets. Then his hands were everywhere—on her shoulders, her arms, her hips, tugging away her bikini briefs, while she fumbled at his belt. He shucked off his trousers and underpants, and then his arms came round her again, his lips nuzzling at her ear, her throat.

"If you want me to wait," he said, his voice ragged, "it's okay. Only don't—" he sucked in a breath as her hands moved down his body, found how smooth and hard he was "—do *that!*" he finished through clenched teeth.

"Don't wait!" she said tensely. His hand traversed her inner thigh and she shifted her body, allowing him to assure himself that she was as ready as he was. He lingered a little while, gently stroking the soft, slick folds, and she gave a sigh of contentment, because it was so good.

"You feel wonderful," he told her quietly. "Like warm, wet satin." When he took his fingers away, she felt a mixture of disappointment and anticipation, and then he was with her again, filling her completely, and the pleasure and the anticipation built and flowed and engulfed them both, sweeping them into that other world where there was nothing but the two of them, complete in each other.

He held her for a long time afterward, and then started over again, this time slow and sweet and languorously. "I want to cover all the areas we missed the first time,'' he told her.

"I didn't think you'd missed much," she said.

"Toes." He was sliding down in the bed, his hands following the shape of her legs, her ankles, her feet.

"Toes?"

He lifted her foot and started kissing her toes one by one, making her laugh. When he arrived at the arch of her foot and ran his tongue along the delicate curve, she stopped laughing and her eyes glazed. By the time he reached her knees and pushed them apart to run his tongue along her inner thigh, she was breathing faster, and he never did get as far as her waist.

AT DAWN NATASHA got up, gathered her clothes and found the shower. When she returned to the bedroom, the morning light had reached the bed, and Ryder was propped up on the pillows, hands behind his head.

"Leaving?" he queried.

'I have an early start. I'm interviewing a visiting singer when his plane arrives at six-thirty. It's the only time he can fit in the press. And I'll have to go home and change first."

Ryder insisted on driving her. In the car, he took her hand at a red light and rubbed it against his cheek, then nuzzled her knuckles with his lips. "Thank you for last night, Natasha." Slanting her a grin, he said, "I was sorry I couldn't put Jeffrey up during his stay, since my apartment only has one bedroom. Now I'm grateful for it."

"He's stayed with you before?" Natasha asked.

Ryder relinquished her hand as the lights changed. "Only once. Usually he's only here for a few days. A hotel near the store was more convenient."

"How long does he plan to be here this time?"

"Nearly three weeks."

"Isn't that a long time for the CEO to be away from head office?"

"Gabe will cope, and there are faxes and telephones in emergencies."

"What sort of place does he live in himself?" Natasha asked idly, envisaging something totally different from Ryder's apartment.

"Jeffrey?" He cast a glance at her before returning his attention to the road. "He has a very comfortable home in London, but in the school holidays, Grace and the children generally went to Kemberly, their country home, and Jeffrey would come down at weekends. We always spent Christmas at Kemberly."

A country estate, Natasha thought, on top of everything else. "They're very wealthy, aren't they?"

"They are," Ryder acknowledged. "But they've never been extravagant. They use their wealth wisely, and often generously." He smiled, although he wasn't looking at her. "Jeffrey used to grumble about the cost of the estate at Kemberly, said it didn't pay its way, but Grace loves—loved the place. So did he, really. They spent most weekends there, and if Jeffrey couldn't join her, Grace sometimes went alone."

"Couldn't join her?" Natasha echoed. "Why not?"

Ryder shrugged. "Business pressures. Jeffrey has a large corporation to run."

But Grace had been his right-hand woman, Natasha remembered. "Is that why she left him? Because he put the business ahead of her—of their personal life?"

Ryder slowed and stopped for another traffic light. "I don't think so. Grace was just as dedicated to DeWilde's as he is."

"Then what happened to make her leave?" Natasha asked, puzzled. "Do you think she...had an affair?"

"Grace? *No*—I don't know!" he said almost angrily, his foot pressing on the accelerator as the light turned green. "I can't imagine either of them—but I don't have any idea what went wrong. Nobody does."

"Jeffrey wouldn't easily forgive a betrayal of trust, would he?" Natasha guessed.

"Probably not." Ryder's voice had cooled a little. "He certainly hasn't been making it easy for Grace."

"Wasn't there some suggestion of legal action over her use of his name?"

"The use of the DeWilde name to promote her own business," Ryder corrected her as he stopped for another traffic light. "Where did you hear that?"

"I don't remember exactly. Is it true?"

"It didn't come to that in the end."

"It hasn't been an amicable separation, has it?" Natasha mused.

"On a personal level I'm sure they both try to keep things as cordial as possible. But Jeffrey's determined to protect the family business. And Grace seems convinced he wants to punish her."

"For leaving him?"

"I suppose so. Although she says he was the one who decided the marriage was over."

Natasha didn't know Grace DeWilde, but everything she knew of Jeffrey indicated a man who wouldn't easily compromise. Perhaps he was capable of exacting reprisal for whatever wrong he felt his wife had done him. "Nick said that Jeffrey doesn't believe in half measures, that he'll pursue something to the end no matter what it costs."

"Nick Santos said that?"

"Would you agree?"

"I suppose I would," Ryder said slowly. He gave her an oddly searching look. "I've found Santos a fairly taciturn character myself."

"I'm trained to draw people out."

"Did you manage to winkle any secrets out of our resident P.I.?"

Natasha shook her head. "We were just making cocktail party small talk. P.I.?" she queried, turning to stare at him. "I thought he was a security guard."

"You didn't know he's a private investigator?"

A nasty knot of foreboding in her stomach, Natasha asked baldly, "What does Jeffrey want a private investigator for?"

"To look after the collection. Santos specializes in that sort of work, apparently."

Natasha swallowed. "Is that normal—to hire a private eye for guard duty?"

"It's not unusual to hire one for transporting valuables. Jeffrey's simply extended the job to include the time the collection is in Australia. Though I must say Santos seems to spend a good deal of time away from it."

"Doing what?"

"I've no idea. Sightseeing, for all I know," Ryder conjectured flippantly. "What he does has nothing to do with me. He's Jeffrey's employee, not mine."

He drew up outside her flat and turned to look at her rather thoughtfully. "Do you find Nick Santos attractive?"

"Attractive?" Natasha asked blankly.

"Rugged Latin machismo is supposed to turn women on, isn't it?"

"Some women, maybe," she said cautiously. Perhaps she might have found Nick attractive if she hadn't already met Ryder. But there was something impervious about the enigmatic American with his fathomless, too-perceptive eyes. She didn't think any woman would easily get close to him.

"But you're not one of them?" Ryder asked her softly.

"He's a bit . . . unapproachable. Not my type."

"I'm approachable," Ryder said invitingly. "Approach me any time you like."

Natasha laughed.

Ryder turned her to him, a deep, glittery smile in his eyes, and kissed her once, but thoroughly. Easing away from her at last, he said, "I've got a business thing on tonight that I can't get out of. Tomorrow I've promised to give Jeffrey dinner at my place. I'd like you to come, too."

"If he expects to be alone with you—"

"He won't mind. It's purely a social occasion. A change for him from hotel meals." His mouth looked momentarily wry. "Jeffrey and I have been making heavy weather lately of anything other than business."

"What time?" Natasha asked.

"Sevenish? I can fetch you."

"No, don't. I'll be there. If you're sure Jeffrey won't mind."

"He won't mind. And afterward, I hope *you* won't mind being alone with me."

Natasha shook her head. "I'll look forward to it."

"Good." He leaned over and kissed her forehead, then her mouth, with lingering sweetness. "Thank you."

CHAPTER NINE

JEFFREY OPENED THE DOOR to her when she arrived, a glass of something in his hand, and welcomed her with a smile that she involuntarily found herself returning. "Ryder's cooking," he explained. "Can I get you something to drink?"

"I'll have a gin and lemon, if there is any."

He got it for her, and as she took the glass from him, Ryder came through from the kitchen. "Sorry about that," he said. "I see Jeffrey's looking after you."

"Yes, thank you. Can I do anything to help?"

"You're a guest. Sit down."

He poured himself a drink and they talked for a while before a bell summoned him back to the kitchen. "Won't be long," he said.

"I didn't think he'd be cooking dinner himself," Natasha said to Jeffrey. "I thought he'd either buy something or have someone in to do it."

"Ryder enjoys cooking," Jeffrey told her. "Although he says he took it up in self-defense. I'm looking forward to sampling the results."

"Who cooks for you at home?"

"I have a housekeeper who's been with us for a good many years. The kitchen is her domain, and I don't think men are welcome there."

The phone trilled and Ryder called, "Jeffrey, can you get that, please? Tell whoever it is I'll be there in a minute."

Jeffrey put down his drink to go and answer the phone. "Ryder Blake's residence," he said.

Idly watching him, Natasha saw his face harden. "Yes," he said, his voice courteous and very even, "this is Jeffrey. How are you, Grace?" And then he added, "I'm in Sydney for DeWilde's first anniversary—you did? Ryder... I see. He's tied up in the kitchen temporarily, but he won't be long... here he is now."

Ryder had appeared, wiping his hands on a tea towel.

"It's Grace," Jeffrey said, looking positively arctic. "For you."

Ryder took the phone from him and tossed the tea towel onto the telephone table. "How are you, Grace?" His voice sounded warm, in direct contrast to Jeffrey's chill tones. "Yes, he is. No, that's okay, not a problem. I'm cooking, though. Hold on a minute." He put a hand over the mouthpiece. "Natasha, I have some potatoes under the grill—watch them for me, would you?" As she went to the kitchen, he said, "Okay, Grace. Where were we?"

The call was quite short, but Ryder didn't come back to the kitchen right away. Turning the potatoes with a pair of tongs she'd found on the counter, Natasha heard Jeffrey say, "You're in regular contact with Grace, then?"

"I don't know if you'd call it regular," Ryder replied. "We keep in touch."

"And you informed her I was going to be in Australia. Only she expected I'd be at my hotel. She sounded quite flustered at finding me here."

Although they weren't speaking loudly, Natasha could hear every word. She straightened and put down the tongs, but decided the men wouldn't thank her for barging into the middle of this conversation.

"I didn't think it was any secret that you were going to attend the celebrations," Ryder said.

"What else have you told her?" Jeffrey spoke almost idly, yet there was a thread of steel in his tone.

"We don't discuss business matters," Ryder replied in a hard voice, "if that's what worries you. I've passed on family news sometimes. She misses the twins, and they don't seem to have kept in touch very well."

"It was her choice to put the Atlantic between them. And to leave without even saying goodbye."

"I think she was too upset to talk. She wrote them letters, didn't she?"

"She told you that?"

"Actually, Gabe told me."

There was a short silence. Natasha bent and peeked at the potatoes. They were just beginning to brown.

Jeffrey said, "Gabriel is very fond of his mother."

"I know that," Ryder replied tersely. "But he might remember that she's fond of him, too."

"Grace has a valiant champion in you, Ryder." Jeffrey sounded half bitter, half amused.

"I owe her," Ryder said, adding, "I owe both of you."

The silence that followed had Natasha holding her breath, although she had tried not to eavesdrop. "We've put you in a difficult position," Jeffrey acknowledged. "I'm sorry."

"We're all sorry," Ryder said. Then he was in the doorway. "How are the spuds?"

"Coming along nicely," Natasha informed him, moving away to let him see for himself. "What else can I do?"

She dished up the vegetables while he carved the roast loin of pork. By the time the meal was over, any tension between the two men seemed to have dissipated.

"That was delicious," Natasha told Ryder as she and Jeffrey helped him clear up. "I'm impressed."

"That I can cook?"

"That you do it so well. Jeffrey said you learned in self-defense, whatever that means."

Ryder grinned. "In my student days, you have no idea the concoctions some of my flatmates served up and called food. I bought a cookbook and taught myself to turn out a decent meal.''

"He'll make some lucky girl a fine husband one day," Jeffrey said, "if she can catch him."

"Is he a good catch, then?" Natasha asked innocently, eyeing Ryder up and down.

His eyes, laughing into hers, promised retribution when they were alone.

But Jeffrey's mood seemed to have changed abruptly. "Very," he said. "A natural target for gold diggers."

A moving target? Natasha thought. Ryder was obviously very eligible, but so far he had evaded marriage. He'd obliquely warned her, after all, the first time he'd taken her out. Despite running a store that had made its reputation in bridal wear, he had yet to commit himself to wedlock.

Jeffrey returned to the living room while Natasha went into the kitchen to help Ryder make the coffee. When it was ready, they carried it out, along with a bowl of chocolate after-dinner mints.

Jeffrey was standing by a shelf full of videotapes, inspecting the titles.

"Not much to your taste there, I'm afraid," Ryder said.

"Mmm," Jeffrey agreed, sliding a tape back onto the shelf and taking the coffee Natasha handed him. "Mostly opera and educational tapes on management techniques. Don't you ever relax?"

Ryder laughed as he took a seat beside Natasha, who had sunk down on one of the couches. "I find opera quite relaxing, actually. More so than your *Rambo* and *Terminator* movies."

Jeffrey returned a faint smile as he sat at right angles to them and stirred his coffee. "Action movies take me out of my safe, sedentary world into a more exciting one—help me unwind after being stuck behind a desk all day."

"Jeffrey had the first video player I'd ever seen," Ryder told Natasha. "He pretended that the James Bond and Clint Eastwood movies he hired were for Gabe and me."

"Nonsense." But Jeffrey was looking, for him, remarkably sheepish.

Ryder grinned at him. "While we were soaking up culture at Covent Garden with Grace, you were secretly wallowing in *Goldfinger* and *Dirty Harry*."

The older man gave a reluctant chuckle. "You and Gabriel got to watch them the next day. And don't say you didn't enjoy them."

"Of course. Only I thought then that testosterone sagas were strictly teenage fare, something *you'd* have grown out of." His eyes dancing, Ryder added, "They're still your favorite viewing, admit it. I reckon you nurse a hidden ambition to right the wrongs of the world and kick the bad guys around a bit."

Jeffrey smiled. "As a boy I had the usual male fantasies of being a gunfighter or, more likely, a gumshoe detective. The combination of brain and brawn required had a distinct appeal."

Like Nick? Natasha thought, remembering the investigator's thorough appraisal of his employer's character, and his comment that they'd spent a lot of time together. Intrigued by this new side of Jeffrey DeWilde, Natasha tried to draw him out further, but he had reverted to his usual urbane, detached manner. Obviously he'd had long years of practice at holding a perfectly normal conversation while giving minimum information. Perhaps he had remembered that she was a journalist.

She learned very little about the family or the business that she had not already gleaned from her research or from Ryder, who had also been deliberately circumspect when it came to the DeWildes. Even a direct question about what had happened to the DeWilde jewelry between the earlier exhibition in the forties and the present one didn't garner much of a response.

"Most of them are locked up for safekeeping," Jeffrey answered, telling her nothing she couldn't have guessed.

But she persisted. "The two pieces you allowed me to wear during our interview were so lovely, it would be a shame to keep them locked up. Have they been used since the New York exhibition?"

"Some have been worn from time to time. Ryder, may I get myself some more coffee? Excuse me, Natasha."

As Jeffrey went to the kitchen, Ryder slid an arm along the sofa behind her and tugged gently at her hair. "Hey," he said quietly, "remember me?"

She turned her head to find him smiling rather quizzically at her. "I thought you wanted me to help entertain Jeffrey."

"I wanted you," he said.

He put a hand under her chin and his lips touched hers, softly caressing, exploring. She couldn't help responding, kissing him back, loving the feel of his mouth, the taste and scent of him. And then it was over. Jeffrey came back into the room and Ryder lifted his head without haste and withdrew his arm from her shoulders.

Jeffrey made no comment, but soon after he'd finished his second cup of coffee, he said he must be going.

Ryder offered to drive him to his hotel, but he insisted on taking a cab. "Can I drop you off somewhere?" he asked Natasha.

Before she could answer, Ryder said, "I'll take Natasha home."

Jeffrey didn't blink an eyelid. With a courteous goodnight to her, he turned and walked out the door Ryder held for him.

NATASHA STAYED TILL DAWN again. This time Ryder had fullfilled his promise, and by the time they fell asleep, there wasn't an inch of her body that he didn't know intimately. But when she vowed to return the favor, she had barely started before he grabbed her and pulled her down to him, smothering her protesting laughter with his kisses, his hands on her hips urging her to put him out of his agony.

The night had been filled with such passion and tenderness and shared, loving laughter that she ached at the knowledge that it might not last.

He was still asleep when she quietly retrieved her clothes and slid them on, but before leaving she couldn't resist bending over to touch her lips lightly to his beard-shadowed cheek.

Her hair brushed his skin, and his eyes snapped open. Natasha drew back, but his hand snared her wrist.

"Sneaking up on me, huh?" He grinned.

"Sneaking out," she retorted. "Sorry, I didn't mean to wake you."

"Give me five minutes and I'll drive you."

"There's no need. Sleep."

"Five minutes. I'll have a shower." He kicked back the covers and stood up, gloriously naked.

Natasha's eyes widened and then closed. She sank down to sit on the bed, fanning herself with her hand.

"A *cold* shower," Ryder promised, heading for the bathroom. He turned in the doorway. "Unless I can persuade you to join me?" One eyebrow lifted ever so slightly. "Water conservation. Save the planet."

Natasha looked at her watch, then back at him. "Five minutes?" She stood up. "Well, I hate waste."

HE DROVE HER HOME, and despite the brief time they'd spent in the shower, her lips were swollen with his kisses and her knees unsteady as she made her way toward her bedroom, trying not to wake her flatmate.

Flinging off her clothes and scrambling into fresh undies, jeans and a knit top, she assured herself that nothing had changed, really. Soon that other business would be all cleared up and Ryder need never know a thing about it.

Her conscience pricked her, and she placated it with the thought that what he didn't know couldn't possibly do him any harm. It had no bearing on their feelings for each other, and as long as nobody found out what she had done—or rather, intended to do—she had no worries.

IT WASN'T ONLY RYDER'S lovemaking that set her heart pounding and her blood singing, that made her feel more alive than at any other time in her life. It was the way he smiled at her across the crowd that had gathered when the team filmed him handing the winner of the birthday draw her prize; the way he'd shaken his hair from his eyes against the sea breeze when they went sailing again on the Mc-Kenzies' boat; his laughter at her description of the jet-lagged pop singer who hadn't known which country he was in and had answered all the journalists' questions in mono-syllables; his anxiety when he took her to the Blue Mountains, a two-hour drive from the city, and she slipped climbing a rock for a better view of the famous Three Sisters formation.

He had gently swabbed the small scrape on her knee with disinfectant and pressed a bandage over it from the first aid box in his car, expressing his chagrin that he hadn't caught her in time. *He* was the one who winced when he poured the stinging yellow liquid over the hurt. She had laughed at him, and then he had kissed her, hot and hungry, making her bones melt.

Away from him, she warned herself she was playing with fire in more ways than one. But when she was with him, she simply didn't care.

"I'M WORKING SOMETHING out," she assured her mother, crossing her fingers as she spoke into the receiver. "I think I can do it without anyone knowing."

"You're not going to take any risks, are you?"

"It isn't dangerous, don't worry. Is Gran all right?"

"The doctor says she should be fine if she takes things easy and doesn't get overstressed or have any nasty shocks. He's found some pills that seem to agree with her, thank goodness. She's almost like her old self, and she'll be even better once this business is finished, I'm sure."

"I'll let you know as soon as it's done. Give her my love," Natasha said, uncrossing her fingers as she put down the phone.

More than once she had been on the brink of pouring out the truth to Ryder, even enlisting his help. But she could hardly count on that.

Natasha was accustomed to standing back from her emotions, evaluating the facts.

Fact: Ryder owed both professional and personal allegiance to the DeWildes. Fact: if she confided in him he was likely to go straight to Jeffery DeWilde and tell him everything. Fact: even if he didn't do that, she would be putting a burden of divided loyalties on him, and he had enough such problems with the DeWildes' separation; she could see how it troubled and even grieved him. Fact: she was in love with Ryder, and love was notoriously apt to skew one's judgement. Fact: Jeffrey was unlikely to let the matter rest; he had a private investigator on the spot and would probably enlist Nick Santos to dig further. Fact: given the doctor's warning on her grandmother's precarious health, the consequences of a thorough investigation into Natasha's clandestine activities might be literally life and death. The risk was simply too great.

Natasha had thought that once Jeffrey DeWilde arrived, her problems would be over, or at least easily resolved. Instead, things had become even more complex. But there was one new factor that she might turn to good account—the pink pearl, emerald and diamond bracelet Jeffrey had brought with him from England. Perhaps it would provide the solution she so desperately sought.

ALL THE FILM for the DeWilde anniversary special had been shot except for the fashion show to be held on Saturday evening in the Skyroom. On Friday afternoon the raised catwalk and stage area were constructed and carpeted with amazing speed. Tables and chairs were arranged on either side so that the guests would have a good view. Carpenters were erecting a partition from the sides of the stage to the walls for the models' changing area, with a door for access from the floor.

"It won't be soundproof," Violetta said, worried. "We'll have to ask the backstage people to be as quiet as they can. Do you want interviews, Natasha?"

"No interviews, just action shots. The music will probably drown out everything else, anyway." In Natasha's experience this kind of event was bedlam, but the music was usually loud enough to cover any other noise. "We'll use whatever we get and edit it later."

"Do you still want to film the rehearsal?"

"It's expensive to bring the camera team in twice, and since you've told me they won't be using the jewelry for the rehearsal, we'll wait for the real thing." She'd been dismayed at the news, realizing that she now had only one chance. "We'll just have to get it right the first time." In more ways than one. "But I'll be here making notes at the rehearsal. Would it be okay for us to film from the steps that lead up to the microphones onstage?"

"I think so, once Ryder's done his introductory speech and gone back to the floor."

"Terry will have to move between front-of-house and backstage to get his footage. If you could ask the workmen to leave a clearway from there to the doorway into the dressing area, hardly anyone will notice the camera going back and forth." Everyone's eyes would be on the catwalk and the models, anyway, so the camera team could sneak along to the unobtrusive doorway near the end of the partition.

Nick Santos was prowling about, accompanied by the security chief and consulting at length with Violetta. When Natasha was passing later, he looked up. "Violetta says you want to film in the dressing room."

Natasha felt her nerves contract. He wasn't going to veto it, was he? "We want some backstage footage, and close-up shots of the jewels on the models."

After a moment Nick nodded. "Wear your security tags," he reminded her.

"Will the TV equipment set off the metal detector?" Violetta asked.

Natasha's heart seemed to stop. "Metal detector?" she repeated stupidly.

"They're going to have one at the dressing room door," Violetta explained. "Your equipment—"

Nick glanced from her to Natasha. "It might beep at the camera and stuff. Those are big and visible. Not a problem. It's designed to detect small metal objects that someone's trying to hide."

Natasha swallowed. "I'll tell the others."

Violetta smiled at her. "It's going to be a great evening. Everyone who's anyone in Sydney will be here, all dressed up to compete with the models."

"What are you wearing?" Natasha asked her.

"A DeWilde original," Violetta said. "And Jeffrey's chosen a wonderful pair of earrings for me to wear with it."

"From the collection?" Natasha asked.

"From the shop. I told him I didn't think I should wear the DeWilde jewels."

Then Jeffrey had suggested it. Natasha wondered if Ryder knew about that, and if he did, what his reaction had been.

Lee Bolton, a worried frown on his face, said, "Excuse me, Violetta, but—"

Natasha left Violetta in conversation with the publicity officer and dashed for the elevator, mentally reviewing her wardrobe. The black skirt and plain peasant-style blouse she had planned to wear wouldn't do. She'd have to work in some urgent shopping, as well as make a call at the bank.

THE DRESS REHEARSAL went without a hitch, the models apparently unfazed by the presence of carpenters and electricians and people racing around with clipboards and harried expressions.

Jeffrey was taken patiently through his part by Violetta, who was an island of calm in the midst of what looked like chaos.

Ryder made an appearance to rehearse his welcoming speech with the sound engineers, but Natasha was too preoccupied scribbling notes to do any more than wave at him across the room.

THE FOLLOWING EVENING Natasha chose a moss green taffeta skirt from her wardrobe to go with the black silk-velvet top she'd bought the day before at a secondhand store specializing in clothing of bygone eras. She had raced home and shortened the sleeves, then nipped in the waist with soft but firm elastic, giving a loose bloused effect and allowing the fabric to flare over her hips. The neckline, bordered with a gold-thread design, wasn't so low that the modestly cut black lace bra she wore underneath was in any danger of showing. A huge, heavily sequined butterfly with padded body decorated the front, its iridescent wings spreading across her breasts. Although scarcely worn, the garment probably dated back at least forty years.

She took a coin purse containing money, keys and her credit card out of her bag, then replaced the bag on the shelf in her wardrobe. Picking up her leather-covered folder, she checked that two pens occupied the sleeves made for them in the spine, and that the pad on which she'd typewritten a list of precisely ordered camera shots was secured by the big clip. Then she slipped her purse into the pocket on the opposite side of the folder and slid it close to the inside spine. It made the remainder of the pocket gape, but the folder still closed snugly.

Nearly ready. Before getting dressed, she'd placed a small suede drawstring bag on her dressing table. Until yesterday it had been in a safety deposit box at her bank. Taking a deep breath, she picked the bag up and carefully pulled it open.

CHAPTER TEN

"GET SOME AUDIENCE shots for cutaways before the show starts," Natasha told Terry, "and when the models come on I'll tell you which ones I want."

Beneath the chandeliers and the domed skylights, the Skyroom was abuzz with excited conversation and aglow with the flash and glitter of expensive evening wear and precious stones. The occasion was all that Ryder could have hoped for.

Natasha watched as he mounted the steps to the podium at one side of the catwalk and stood at the microphone. He looked devastating in his tuxedo, and the audience hushed expectantly as he launched into his brief welcome.

After introducing Violetta, he came back down the stairs and took a seat at a nearby table, close to the steps and not far from the temporary partition.

Violetta wore a midnight blue shot-silk gown with a huge flat bow on one shoulder. Diamond-and-sapphire pendants suspended from her ears sparkled under the bright lights. Jeffrey stood unobtrusively in the wings, waiting for his cue.

Natasha and Terry moved to the steps, and Terry set up his camera while the sound technician checked his levels. Ryder caught Natasha's eye and smiled at her. Then the introductory music that had been played at the rehearsal began, and a model swayed onto the catwalk. Amid applause and ripples of comment, Violetta's voice announced, "Our first gown . . ."

The camera whirred, and Natasha concentrated on her list, counting the outfits as they came and went. Just before the end of the evening-wear section, she whispered to Terry, "Time to go backstage."

He nodded, and they tiptoed along the partition wall to the doorway, skirting the edge of the audience.

At the entrance, a woman in uniform stood holding an electronic metal detector. Natasha had made a point of being friendly to the security staff, who had become accustomed to her walking into areas not open to the public, holding her folder or clipboard and making copious notes, and now they usually smiled, greeted her and, after a cursory glance at the ID tag, waved her through. But this woman was a stranger, probably hired from an outside firm for the occasion. Perhaps she came with the special equipment.

Natasha tried a smile and pointed at her ID badge, but the woman stepped forward and passed the metal wand over her, inches from her body. The machine beeped discreetly, and Natasha handed over her vinyl-covered folder with its large metal clip securing the notepad. When the device continued to beep, Natasha said, "It must be this top." She laughed apologetically. "It's vintage clothing, you see—the sequins are metal, not plastic like modern ones."

The guard unsmilingly requested her to step aside, then relayed a terse message into a radio.

"We don't have much time," Natasha protested.

Unmoved, the woman turned to check the camera operator and sound technician. The two men put down their gear while she used the detector on them and waved them on. Natasha glanced toward Ryder's table. She could see the back of his dark head, but as if he'd felt her gaze, he turned to look in her direction, and involuntarily she made a small movement of appeal.

Immediately he rose from his chair and came toward her. "Something wrong?" he asked.

"There seems to be a problem." She gestured at the security guard.

"The TV people have permission to enter the security area," he said to the woman.

"Our instructions—"

Natasha turned to Ryder. "We need to shoot some film in there and then get the camera back outside for the evening and bridal wear. You wouldn't want us to miss the finale. Violetta and Lee would be terribly disappointed." She glanced down ruefully at the glittering butterfly spread across her bosom. "I shouldn't have worn this top. That's what set the thing off."

"It's...spectacular." Turning to the security guard, he said, "Try again, okay?"

Again the metal rod beeped as it came close to her chest. "I told you," Natasha said plaintively.

Ryder laughed quietly. "Let her through."

The woman looked uncertain, and Natasha held her breath, hoping she wasn't going to argue.

"I'll take the responsibility," Ryder assured the guard.

At last the woman shrugged and stepped aside from the doorway.

"Thank you, Ryder." Weak with relief, Natasha walked past the guard and her colleague, standing just inside, into the midst of the models, dressers and security staff crowding the makeshift dressing room.

She looked around at the racks of clothes filling the shallow dais at the end of the room. Leggy young women in various stages of undress hissed questions and instructions as they were zipped and buttoned into garments pulled from the racks while a hairdresser with a comb in one hand, hair spray in the other, flitted among them. Security guards were stationed at the entrance to the catwalk and auditorium, and on the raised section at the other end of the dressing room, with a view of the entire crammed area.

A familiar metal case sat open on a baize-covered table, the DeWilde collection nestled into its individual compartments. Beside it a couple of velvet-lined trays held more jewelry from the store's stock. The jewelry manager—his name was Fynne, Natasha recalled—was at the table, along with the dresser, a woman in a plain black dress. Nick Santos stood nearby, back to the wall, his ever-vigilant dark eyes belying the lazy stance.

The models hurried one by one up the steps, disappeared into the brightly lit auditorium and came back on cue, frantically wriggling out of one garment and into another. A striking brunette in a silk evening suit paused by the table, and Mr. Fynne handed a brooch to the dresser, who pinned it to the suit's lapel.

"I want a panning shot around the room from here," Natasha said.

The models appeared oblivious to the camera crew and security people. The one wearing the suit came back, and the brooch was removed by the dresser and the manager replaced it in the tray.

As Mr. Fynne passed each piece of jewelry to the dresser, he checked it against a list on the table. Sometimes one compartment was empty, sometimes two, and for a short time three.

The Boucheron bracelet was slipped onto a slim wrist to complement black harem-style trousers and a sleeveless gold top. Natasha recognized a touch of genius in teaming the expensively casual outfit with the flamboyant, chunky rope of gold and costly stones. She motioned the cameraman closer. "Terry, zoom in on that?"

Nick stepped forward to watch. As the model sped off to the catwalk entrance, Natasha turned to her team. "Get on out there to where we were before. Give me a long shot before she comes back in, and then keep filming right to the end of the show."

"You're not coming?" Terry asked her.

She grinned. "The dragon on the door might not let me back in. I know I can trust you." He had a good eye for composition.

Jeffrey's deep voice chimed in after Violetta's, the cue for the DeWilde collection, and then was drowned out by the beat of the music. Terry and the sound technician returned to the auditorium almost running.

Two more evening outfits were shown, then wraps were taken off the bridal gowns, which were the finale. The models were hurried into them, veils and headdresses adjusted, flowers thrust into their hands. The jewelry manager produced the tiara Natasha had worn briefly when she'd interviewed Jeffrey, and it was fixed carefully on the designated model's elaborate hairstyle.

The next model had a tear-drop diamond pendant hung around her neck. Natasha stood by with her folder, occasionally making a mark on her pad.

The young woman who had modeled the Empress Eugénie tiara came back holding up the train of her satin wedding gown and bent her head for the removal of the priceless accessory. It caught in her upswept hair, and the dresser struggled to free it.

"Ow!" the model complained indignantly, and put a hand up to her hair.

"Don't touch it!" Mr. Fynne ordered. Natasha remembered that at the rehearsal the models had been told not to put on or take off the jewelry themselves. "Be careful," he added to the dresser. "That's a very valuable piece."

"So's my hair," the model muttered crossly.

"It's snagged on a hairpin," the dresser said.

"You mustn't damage it!" The jewelry manager stepped around the table and began anxiously trying to help.

A very blond model in a summery, broderie anglaise gown trimmed with tiny pink rosebuds rushed to the table and thrust out her wrist. "My bracelet!"

"Hold it there," the dresser told Mr. Fynne, lifting the troublesome headdress a couple of inches, "while I untangle it."

The blonde was shifting from one foot to the other. "I'm supposed to have a pink pearl bracelet! Hurry!"

"In a minute, dear," the dresser said in harried tones.

Natasha's ears buzzed. She suddenly realized how stuffy it was in the room. Her hands on the leather folder were damp as she clutched it to her.

Mr. Fynne, the precious tiara poised in both hands, turned his head. "Mr. Santos—the heart bracelet."

Nick moved over to the table; his hand hovered over the bracelet, then scooped it up.

"Come on!" The blond model was hopping with anxiety. "That's my cue!"

"Here." Nick stepped by Natasha and the dresser and, fumbling a little, fastened the bracelet onto the girl's slender wrist.

"Thanks!" she gasped, and, bunching her skirt up in her hands, darted away.

The tiara was at last freed, and with a sigh of relief, the manager put it reverently away.

Seconds ticked by. Natasha could hear Violetta's voice describing the "perfect dress for a young spring bride" and then Jeffrey talking about his grandmother's bracelet. Mr. Fynne retrieved a jeweled comb from the case for a dark-haired young woman wearing a Spanish-influenced gown in cream brocade embroidered with gold thread, and a gold lace mantilla.

The young blonde swept back into the room and headed for the racks of clothes. Nick ordered sharply, "Wait up there!"

"Oh!" she said. "I forgot."

"We want a shot of that before you take it off," Natasha told her quickly.

"Sure, okay." She stepped out of the way to allow room for the next model, a striking brunette holding up the train of a wonderfully romantic gown with a frothy layered crinoline skirt, the last item in the show.

"Mrs. Concetti said I was wearing something blue," she announced to the dresser.

Nick watched the jewelry manager hand a cascade of diamonds and sapphires, the Dancing Waters necklace, over to the dresser, drawing a gasp from the model.

"Oh, it's *fabulous!*" she cried.

"When you come back," Natasha said, "we'd like to film you."

"Yeah, okay." The model lifted the floating folds of the veil she wore, allowing the woman to fasten the necklace about her throat. Violetta's voice came clearly through the microphones. "And, ladies and gentlemen, we come to the end of our evening of fabulous fashion, with our very last magnificent bridal gown this evening, designed by—"

The dresser snapped the catch and hastily adjusted the veil, and the girl scooted across the floor to the steps.

Thunderous applause greeted her appearance on the catwalk. Natasha hoped Terry was getting a good shot of the necklace.

He came back even before the clapping and cheering for the finale had died, giving Natasha a thumbs-up signal. "Okay," he said, "what now?"

"A couple of close-ups," she told him. She took the last model by the arm. "If you could just stand there so we can get a nice plain background. Can you tilt down from her face, Terry, to a tight shot on the necklace?"

Terry grunted. "I need a focus puller," he complained, raising his head from the viewfinder. He looked around and appealed to Nick, who appeared to be standing around with nothing to do. "Help us out, mate?"

Natasha's lips parted and closed again, her mouth suddenly dry.

Nick hesitated. "Natasha can't do it?"

"She's directing—she needs to watch the shot. All you have to do is turn that ring there, okay?"

The camera was hardly a step away from the table. Nick sent the jewelry manager a wordless message that was answered by a reassuring nod, then moved to the camera.

They rehearsed the shot briefly, and Terry nodded, satisfied that Nick was a quick learner. Natasha stepped back to watch.

"What about me?" the model in the broderie dress asked.

"We'll want you in a minute." Natasha gave her a smile.

Terry was peering into the viewfinder, Nick concentrating on his low-voiced instructions.

"Fine." Terry lifted his head. "Thanks," he said to the model. "You want more?" he asked Natasha.

Natasha drew the other girl forward. "Same kind of shot, then closing on the bracelet for this one."

As the men rehearsed it, the dresser was removing the necklace, handing it to the jewelry manager. Natasha saw Nick's eyes turn in their direction. He wasn't letting the jewels out of his sight, but he stayed by the camera.

Natasha glanced down at her open folder. Every nerve was poised.

"Okay," Terry said. "That it?"

"Just a second." Natasha went toward the model. "Don't move, but just hold your arm up a bit." Her back to the camera, Natasha took the girl's wrist, lifting it, and with the open folder balanced on her other arm, she turned the bracelet.

Her fingers encountered the hidden catch, and suddenly the bracelet was sliding free, the model giving a startled, disbelieving gasp. Natasha bent and grabbed at it, the folder snapping shut in her other hand. She heard Nick's low, violent exclamation, felt his hand on her arm as he pulled her aside.

She said sharply, "Be careful, don't stand on it!"

Nick's hand released her arm as he looked down between their feet. A ribbon of palest pink studded with green fire lay on the carpet. She held tightly to her folder as Nick stooped and picked up the bracelet. "Sorry about that!" Natasha said. "The catch can't have been fastened properly."

She met his hard eyes with a guileless, wide-eyed stare, trying not to hold her breath.

He looked down at the bracelet, seemed to heft its weight in his hand, then switched his assessing gaze back to Natasha. After a moment he turned away and fastened the bracelet on the model's wrist, taking his time. "Okay?" he asked Natasha, his eyes unreadable.

She nodded, and held her breath while Terry completed filming. When they'd finished, Nick stepped forward and removed the bracelet himself from the girl's arm, then slowly laid the lovely thing on the velvet-covered tray, fitting it into place.

Natasha swallowed, feeling dizzy. "Are you okay, Nat?" Terry said in her ear. "You've gone pale."

"Have I?" Relief made her laugh. "It's hot in here. I don't know how the models look so cool and elegant, the way they've all been rushing about."

Violetta came in from the auditorium and made a short speech, thanking everyone for their part in the show. Nick was snapping the locks shut on the metal case and the jewelry manager appeared to be counting the items in his trays. Terry quietly folded his tripod and exchanged some low-voiced remarks with the sound operator. Everyone else's eyes were on Violetta. Natasha slid two fingers into her folder.

When Terry turned to her, she had a hand at the neckline of her velvet top. As Violetta finished speaking, he grinned at the brilliant butterfly and said, "That's something, isn't it?"

Natasha nodded. "You like it?"

"Yeah—uh—dramatic, eh?"

"It's a special occasion," Natasha said. "I thought I should dress up."

"Well, we're off, okay?" Terry said. "I guess you'll be staying for a while."

"Actually, I hadn't planned—"

But as she made to follow him, a firm hand caught at her arm. "Not leaving already, are you, Natasha?" Nick said.

"Well, I—"

His strong fingers didn't move from her arm. In his other hand he held the case full of jewelry shackled to his wrist. "Ryder would be disappointed if you were to rush off. I'm sure he expects you to stay."

Natasha's eyes turned to Terry in something like fright but he was giving her a knowing grin and hoisting his gear in his arms. "See you," he said casually.

Natasha tried to remove her arm unobtrusively from Nick's grasp, only to feel him tighten it a fraction—enough to give her a clear message that he wasn't going to let go. Terry was loping off, oblivious, with the sound man at his side.

There was a lot of noise now that the show was over—the models chatting as they donned street clothes, the dressers calling instructions to one another while they packed up, and a babble drifting in from the other side of the partition as people left. Glancing round in some desperation, Natasha saw Violetta handing over her earrings to the jewelry manager. Ryder wasn't anywhere to be seen.

Her mouth dry, she said, "Ryder will be busy, and it's quite late. I really think—"

"I'm sure he won't be long," Nick replied pleasantly.

The woman with the security wand was waving it cursorily over Terry. Natasha thought of calling him, and instantly discarded the idea. No doubt Nick was counting on her not wanting to make a fuss, and he was absolutely right. Her palms felt damp and cold.

Terry and the sound technician were waved on and soon disappeared.

Natasha turned toward the stage entrance and as if in a dream, or a nightmare, saw Ryder coming down the steps into the dressing room.

His eyes found her, standing so close to Nick, and he paused for an instant on the step; following him, Jeffrey almost bumped into his back. Then he was on the ground level and heading straight toward them, while Jeffrey walked over to where Violetta stood talking to the jewelry manager.

Nick said easily, "Ryder—Natasha and I are just going downstairs."

Ryder stared at him, then at Natasha, his eyes baffled and questioning. Natasha looked back at him dumbly, unable to think of anything to say.

"Perhaps you'd tell Jeffrey we'll be waiting for him in the jewelry department," Nick added.

"Natasha?" Ryder said.

"It's . . . all right," she told him, knowing it wasn't.

He looked momentarily incredulous, then spun on his heel and went toward Jeffrey, who was smiling down at Violetta.

"Let's go," Nick said.

They reached the security woman and he nodded at her. "Let me hold that," he offered, deftly whipping the folder from Natasha's hands. Natasha contemplated running, but she knew it was useless. As the wand beeped, she saw Nick flip open the folder and slip his fingers into the pocket.

The woman shrugged. "We know about that," she said to Nick, jerking her head at the sequined butterfly.

"Is that so?" he drawled, and moved toward Natasha. He handed her folder back and renewed his hold on her arm.

Turning her head to glance behind them, she saw Ryder standing by Jeffrey, looking impatient and unsettled.

NICK TOOK HER DOWN to the second floor, commandeering an elevator to themselves with a terse, "Sorry, security," to the knot of people waiting ahead of them.

A uniformed guard watched them alight, obviously recognizing Nick even without glancing at the ID card pinned to his jacket. Another guard stood at the closed entrance to the jewelry department. He punched in some numbers at the security lock and the grille lifted to let Nick and Natasha in.

"Shall I leave it open now?" the guard enquired.

"No," Nick said. "Let's not take any chances. But Mr. DeWilde will be along shortly."

Natasha shuddered as the grille descended again, shutting her in with this forbidding man, who only now released his grip on her arm.

Resisting an urge to rub it, she regarded him warily, the folder held like a shield in front of her.

Nick rocked back on his heels. "Okay... Natasha," he said softly. "Do you want to tell me?"

Her voice croaked. "Tell—" She cleared her throat. "Tell you what?" He was guessing; he must be. He'd put the bracelet in the metal case himself. He had nothing to go on. Made bolder by the thought, she added, "I don't know what you mean."

He didn't move, but the fierce speculation in his dark, intelligent eyes sent a shiver down her spine. Nick Santos wasn't a fool, and he wasn't a man to cross.

There was a crackling silence as she stared back at him, trying to look innocent and puzzled as well as indignant.

The grille rumbled up again, and her knees went weak with relief. Ryder entered shoulder to shoulder with Jeffrey, closely followed by the jewelry manager carrying his display trays, the chief of security at his elbow.

In the dim light, Ryder's perplexed gaze flickered from Natasha to Nick and back again. She took an involuntary step toward him and was stopped, partly by the sudden coldness in his face, partly by Nick's glance of cynical derision.

Her chin went up, and she found herself passing her tongue over her lips to moisten them. Ryder frowned, and the jewelry manager was looking bewildered.

Nick turned to him. "Can we go into your office?"

"Of course." The man shifted his burden to one arm, took out a key on a chain and inserted it into the lock.

"What's going on?" Ryder demanded.

Nick exchanged an enigmatic glance with Jeffrey, ignoring Ryder, then gestured for them to follow Mr. Fynne into his office. To the security chief he said, "Watch the door, okay?"

Then he was at her side, keeping her separated from Ryder. Feeling as though she were approaching her execution, Natasha walked into the other room. Ryder and Jeffrey followed, and the security manager closed the door behind them. She supposed he would remain standing on the other side of it to prevent anyone else entering—or leaving.

There were two chairs in the room, one behind the big desk and another, an armless leather chair, in front of it. "Sit down, Natasha," Nick said.

"No," she said. "I'd rather stand...thanks." This was a nightmare, but no one could prove she'd done anything wrong.

"Natasha?" Ryder touched her arm, trying to make her look at him. "What is this all about?"

She turned her head and shrugged. "Ask Nick. He said...he thought you'd expect me to stay."

Nick's wolfish grin was almost admiring. He wasn't taking his eyes from her. "That's right, isn't it, Ryder?" he said. "I didn't think you'd want her...sneaking off."

"Shall I put these away?" the jewelry manager asked, indicating his laden trays.

"Yeah, okay." Nick was still watching Natasha. "Why don't you help him, Ryder?"

Ryder wasn't touching her anymore, but Natasha felt him stiffen beside her. "He doesn't need help."

"No, no," Mr. Fynne said hastily. "Thank you. Er...are you going to put that in the safe, Mr. Santos?" He gestured to the metal case still fastened to Nick's wrist.

"Later." Nick didn't turn his head. Ryder was staring at the American, his mouth taut, his brows drawn together.

"What have you got, Nick?" Jeffrey asked. It struck Natasha that Jeffrey's eyes were brighter than usual, and his sallow cheeks had a hint of color. Even his bearing evinced tension, as though he were ready for some kind of action.

Nick swung the case onto the desk and freed his wrist from the handcuff, all the while scarcely glancing away from Natasha. "I'm not sure yet."

Ryder said, his voice harsh, "What the hell is going on?"

"Natasha?" Nick's eyes held hers, giving her a last chance.

"I don't know what you're talking about," she lied. With any luck, she thought, he had it all wrong, anyway, and her only—admittedly slim—chance was to bluff her way out.

"Sure you do, honey." Nick's voice was almost tender. Effortlessly he removed the big folder from her grip and tossed it onto the desk, while his eyes focused on the glittering front of her velvet top. "It's about what you've got inside your bra."

Ryder went rigid, and Jeffrey said in a low voice, "Nick, are you sure?"

"Positive." His voice was flat, confident, and Natasha felt a leaden lump of dread in her chest.

Battling on, her chin thrust forward, she said, "I find that very offensive."

"So do I!" Ryder said furiously. "Jeffrey, call off your damned hound. I'm taking Natasha home."

He put his arm about her and began walking with her to the door. But Nick, with the speed of a striking snake, stretched out a long arm and dipped his hand inside her top, his fingers briefly intruding before he withdrew them.

Natasha's breath escaped in an outraged gasp, and Ryder emitted a low growl and hurled himself at the investigator, grabbing his jacket collar and pushing him backward.

Nick didn't retaliate; he just raised his hand and dangled what it held in front of Ryder's angry eyes.

There was a moment of silence in which no one seemed to breathe. Then Ryder abruptly released Nick and stepped back. His face had gone pale and his mouth was clamped shut in a rigorously controlled line. Very slowly, he turned fully to face Natasha, his eyes blank with shock.

Unable to meet his gaze, she transferred hers to Nick Santos. "I could have you for assault!" she told him ferociously.

His teeth showed in a white smile. "And what could we have you for?" he countered, gently swinging the bracelet in his fingers, the overhead light reflecting off the emeralds and making the pearls gleam subtly. "Theft?" he suggested. "Fraud? False pretenses?"

Could they? Natasha wondered wildly. "You can't prove anything," she said. "I haven't committed any crime."

"I have witnesses to the fact that you had this on you," he pointed out. "Don't I?" He swept his eyes over the other men.

Jeffrey gave a curt nod, his clever face giving little away.

The jewelry manager, looking bewildered and fascinated, said unhappily, "Yes, indeed. I'm afraid so."

And Ryder said hoarsely, as though the word were dragged from him by torture, "*Yes*."

A tight fist seemed to squeeze Natasha's heart. "You can't say I stole it, Nick," she argued. "You have the bracelet in your case. Open it."

"I have *a* bracelet in there," Nick agreed. He went to the desk, activated the lock and flung open the case, flipping up the velvet cover on one side to reveal the jewels. Ryder took an involuntary step toward them, his eyes going from the jewels in the case to the glittering thing in Nick's fingers.

"You swapped them, didn't you," Nick said. He tossed the bracelet lightly in the air, caught it in his palm and closed his fist over it. "I almost missed it—you're a very smooth operator. But that catch didn't come apart accidentally. I put it on the model myself, remember? And I know it was secure. You undid it, dropped it into your folder, then later transferred it to your bra, so that when you left, the security device would beep at that very obvious display of metal on your chest. Just as it must have when you went into the changing area."

Ryder's voice was blurred, as though he'd had a blow on the head. "When she went *in?*"

"Yes," Nick told him. "She should have been at least pat-searched then." Switching his attention back to Natasha, he said, "I suppose the woman couldn't feel it under all that."

Ryder made a choked sound in his throat. "She wasn't searched," he said in clipped tones. "I told the security guard to let Natasha through. It's my responsibility."

Nick's brief glance at Ryder was almost pitying. "Clever. You must have been planning this for a long time," he said, returning to Natasha. "You got in with the duplicate bracelet in your bra, and at some stage when no one was looking, you let it drop inside your top. All you had to do then was tug the elastic at the waist of your blouse at the same time that you let the other bracelet fall into your folder. So the one I picked up off the floor wasn't the one the model dropped. That movement must have taken some practice."

Natasha swallowed, and closed her eyes. He had it all figured out, and three witnesses; there was no point in continuing to deny everything. She opened her eyes again. "Hours."

Nick's eyes lit briefly with satisfaction. "I nearly missed it," he admitted.

Before he could say any more, Ryder, who had been standing like a stone statue, turned on her with sudden, spine-chilling intensity. "You lying little thief! You mercenary little cheat!"

"Ryder!" she gasped. "I didn't mean—"

I didn't mean to involve you, she would have said, but he interrupted her.

"No," he said. "You didn't mean any of it, did you? I realize that now. My God, how could I have been such a bloody fool!"

Eyes blazing and fists clenched, he moved toward her, and Natasha stepped back, blundering against Jeffrey, who automatically steadied her. "Ryder—" he said quietly.

Ryder tore his gaze from her to Jeffrey's face. What he read there, Natasha didn't know, but after a moment he nodded, and Jeffrey's hand left her shoulder, allowing her to move hastily away from him.

Still looking at Jeffrey, his voice hard and excessively even, Ryder suggested, "Hadn't we better call the police?"

Mr. Fynne murmured, "That would seem to be best."

Natasha saw a swift glance pass between Jeffrey and Nick. She felt the hair on the nape of her neck stand up, and instincts that had stood her in good stead during her career as a reporter came to the fore, banishing some of her fear.

They know. The thought hit her like a blow. Of course they knew. Not Ryder, or the jewelry manager, but Jeffrey and Nick—they'd known all along. She said huskily, accusingly, "You set me up!"

"Don't try to make excuses for your greed," Ryder said coldly. "It won't help you."

"You don't understand!" she told him fiercely, anger keeping the grief and pain from her voice. She couldn't blame him for accepting the weight of the evidence, but that didn't stop his rejection from hurting. "The bracelet is a *fake!* And they know it." She glared at Jeffrey, then Nick.

A glimmer of something that might have been respect showed in Nick's face, but Ryder's expression merely turned derisive. "You had the fake on you when you went in, and you substituted it for the real one, the one you were caught with. You just admitted it."

"No, I didn't!" she argued. "I said I'd swapped them. *That's* the fake." She pointed to the one Nick still held in his hand. "I exchanged the real one for it, yes. And the real one is in the case now."

For a split second Ryder seemed to waver, then his expression turned cynical once again. "You don't expect us to swallow that? How you ever imagined you could get away with a stunt like this—"

"She very nearly did," Jeffrey reminded him mildly, his eyes thoughtful as they rested on Natasha. "Why?" he asked curiously.

Natasha swallowed. "I'm not a criminal."

Ryder laughed. "This being the first time doesn't make it any less a crime, *darling.*"

And Natasha, overwrought as she was, disappointed and frightened and hurt, launched herself at him, her closed fists beating against his hard chest. "Damn you! It's not *funny!*"

He caught her wrists and held her away from him, his grip tightening as she tried to free herself. She saw that he was reining in his own temper. "Not when the joke's on you?" he jeered. "Do you know I laughed when my security people said you'd been eyeing the Boucheron in the jewelry department? Too bulky to hide, was it? Is that why you decided to settle for the DeWilde Heart instead?"

"You've got it all wrong, Ryder! I never intended to steal anything!"

"You just told us you'd practiced the trick for hours. And you spent weeks softening me up. You must have known I didn't quite believe your cover story. But you're not as clever as you think. I'll see you in jail." He looked past her to Mr. Fynne, standing by the desk, and said, "Call the police."

"No." Jeffrey's voice rang with quiet command.

Ryder's grip slackened in surprise, and Natasha wrenched herself away.

"Not yet, Ryder." Almost gently, Jeffrey added, "Natasha, why don't you sit down?"

She needed to, actually. Her knees felt weak and watery, and her whole body trembled.

She groped numbly into the chair, and then wished she'd stayed standing. Even the jewelry manager, not a particularly big man, seemed formidable from this level. Jeffrey, though tall and thin, had an aura of power that came with inherited wealth and the long exercise of authority; Nick had the back streets of San Francisco written all over him; and Ryder, despite his expensive evening clothes and civilized veneer, was a fit, well-muscled man whose grip she could still feel on her wrists, and who right now looked more dangerous than the other three put together.

And all of them were staring at her with varying degrees of hostility and suspicion.

But Jeffrey had apparently decided that a softer approach might serve their purpose. He thrust his hands into his pockets, exposing a black satin cummerbund and pristine white evening shirt, and fixed Natasha with a deceptively kindly gaze. "Maybe we won't phone the police just yet," he suggested, "but perhaps you'd like to tell us the whole story?"

"I can't," she said, willing her voice steady.

"What story?" Ryder enquired sarcastically. "That she did it for her dying mother, perhaps? I suggest you stop playing detective, Jeffrey, and let the cops take over. It's their job."

"Yes, well..." Jeffrey bent his head, regarding his highly polished leather shoes before looking at the younger man. "You see, Ryder, it's not that simple."

Natasha, struck by inspiration, turned to the jewelry manager. "Mr. Fynne, are you a qualified assessor?"

"Of gems? Yes."

"Ask him," she said, glancing from Ryder to Nick and Jeffrey. "Give him the bracelet and ask him to tell you if it's real. It will only take about twenty minutes, won't it?"

Jeffrey cast her a piercing look, then nodded to Nick, who handed over the bracelet. The manager peered at it doubtfully. "I can't be sure without putting it under a microscope and doing some tests," he said. "If it's a fake, it's a very good one."

"Go on," Natasha urged defiantly. "Tell him to do it."

Jeffrey shook his head. "No," he said. "Let's assess the other one. The one in the case."

Ryder frowned. "What on earth for?"

"Because that's the real one," Natasha said, staring hard at Jeffrey. "The one I... returned to the collection."

Jeffrey shifted slightly, his eyes not leaving hers. "The real one?" he repeated. "Returned?" His expression was alert and calculating.

"I had it assessed. There's no doubt of its authenticity."

"For God's sake!" Ryder exploded. "How gullible do you think we are?"

Without looking at him, Natasha said, "You believe me, don't you, Jeffrey?"

"Why should he?" Ryder asked harshly.

"Because he knows the one in the collection was a fake!" Natasha flashed, rounding on Ryder. "You have the real one back," she said to Jeffrey. "Isn't that all that matters?"

"It's a pretty story," Ryder sneered. "But a tad far-fetched, surely?"

Jeffrey's eyes were fixed on Natasha. "Yes, it is," he agreed.

Natasha's mouth tightened, and momentarily she closed her eyes. He surely wasn't going to deny it? What good would that do?

"But," Jeffrey said slowly, "I do believe it."

Ryder made a sharp exclamation. *"What?* How can you swallow something like that?"

"The thing is, what she says is quite correct, I'm afraid. The bracelet we brought with us to Australia was a fake."

CHAPTER ELEVEN

NATASHA SHOULD HAVE BEEN triumphant at Jeffrey's admission, but instead she felt an empty sense of desolation.

Ryder was clearly stunned. "What are you talking about?" he demanded. "You brought fake jewels into my store? I don't believe it! You wouldn't do that to me!"

Jeffrey suddenly looked uncomfortable. "I'm sorry."

"He wanted to tell you," Nick said laconically. "But I told him I wouldn't take the job if anyone else knew."

Ryder flicked him a look of patent dislike. "Really," he said shortly, as though it made no difference at all.

Nick's mouth moved in a lopsided, rueful grimace.

Jeffrey turned to the jewelry manager, who was frankly gaping now. "All this is, of course, highly confidential," he said.

"Oh, yes—yes!" the man assented hurriedly. "Of course. In my work, it's understood—confidential information. Nothing said here will go outside this room, I assure you."

Natasha stood up. "If you don't mind, I'd like to go now."

"Not so fast," Nick said.

And Jeffrey actually stepped in front of her, his demeanor distinctly unyielding. "We haven't finished yet."

"You've got your bracelet," she said. "What more do you want?"

"Quite a lot, actually. Please sit down again, Natasha." He sounded patient but implacable.

"No." Natasha looked him straight in the eye. "I'm going home."

She made to walk around him, but he flung out his arm, not touching her but creating an effective barrier. "Don't force us to get heavy with you, Natasha," he said.

It was a direct threat. Her eyes went to Nick, and panic rose in her throat. He stared back at her without a flicker of expression.

Jeffrey said, "We could still call the police."

She didn't know if she was relieved or angry. Anger won as a momentary vision of being tied to a chair and tortured receded under a healthy dollop of common sense. "And tell them what?" she demanded. "That I was caught red-handed smuggling a priceless bracelet *into* the DeWilde collection?"

"What about receiving stolen goods, for a start?" he retorted coolly.

That stopped her for a second, her heart lurching in fright as she mentally reviewed the implications. But he must be bluffing. "You won't make that stick," she said with far more confidence than she felt, making her voice almost insolent. "The bracelet was never reported as stolen, was it?" The faintest change in Jeffrey's eyes told her she was right, and she pursued her advantage. "How long have the DeWildes known it was missing without contacting the police? Or your insurance company? Fifty years?"

If she hadn't been standing so close to him, she might have missed the way his pupils contracted and his brows momentarily twitched.

"Fraud?" she taunted, flinging his threats back in his face. "False pretenses? Ever heard of glass houses, Mr. DeWilde? There you were on stage tonight, telling all those hundreds of people about how your dear old grandmother cherished that bracelet, her anniversary present. And the tiara Empress Eugénie's supposed to have worn on her wedding day...?" She was drawing her bow at random now, but she saw the muscles of his face tense and knew she'd scored another hit. Hiding her own sense of dawning surprise, she asked scornfully, "Are they *all* fakes?"

"The tiara is genuine," he said, taking the wind out of her sails for a moment. But she knew he'd reacted to her accusation; what he wasn't saying was just as damning.

"But not all of them are genuine," she said, "are they?" Knowing he wouldn't answer, she didn't stop there. "How do you think DeWilde's wealthy clientele will like being told that they were duped tonight? That you stood there and lied to them all evening about what they were seeing? That maybe half of those jewels weren't what you said they were? And when it gets out that DeWilde's has hoodwinked and defrauded the public and maybe their insurance company for years—what will that do to the company's reputation?"

Jeffrey's eyes had narrowed, going coldly inimical. But she couldn't be intimidated now. "Your precious family firm is only just recovering from its last crisis, Mr. De-Wilde. Can it afford another?"

Jeffrey's mouth tightened, and a muscle twitched in his cheek.

Utterly reckless now, Natasha refused to let up. "Just why *did* your wife walk out on the business? Was it anything to do with this? Did she discover that the famous DeWilde collection wasn't what it was purported to be? The press will have a field day speculating once the story gets out. Has the family been selling off the collection over time to hide irregularities in the company finances? Is that what Grace DeWilde couldn't stomach?"

"That's enough!" Jeffrey whipped out.

It took Natasha all her courage not to shrink from the icy fury in his eyes, the bite in his voice. The words had been tumbling out, but now they caught in her throat. She swallowed but refused to back down. She couldn't afford to. She was fighting for her life—or, if not hers, her grandmother's. "You wouldn't risk opening that can of worms," she said, injecting all the confidence and satisfaction she could muster into her voice. "You daren't accuse me of receiving! So if you call the police, what are you going to tell them?"

There was a fraught, tense pause. Natasha broke it, making to walk past him.

"Perhaps," Jeffrey said slowly, his face taut with barely controlled anger, "that you were caught with a fake bracelet, intending to substitute it for the real one. Or—" he glanced toward the open case "—that you were found to have the real one in your possession."

Natasha gasped and halted in her tracks. From the corner of her eye she saw Ryder make an abrupt movement of protest, but he quickly checked it. "You know that's untrue!" Her voice rose. "You said you believed me!"

"As Ryder suggested, that was a naive belief."

"You admitted the bracelet you had was the fake!" Her eyes frantically sought out Ryder. His face had briefly reflected her own shock but was now totally wooden. He was watching Jeffrey intently.

She turned to the jewelry manager. "You heard him!"

The man looked appalled and avoided her eyes, clearing his throat.

"Mr. Fynne works for DeWilde's," Jeffrey reminded her. "You heard him say that anything said here tonight won't be repeated outside this room."

Natasha swung round again, her eyes finding Ryder's, blazing into his. His jaw was clenched so hard she could almost feel the muscles aching. *"Ryder!"* It was a cry for help.

But there was no help for her there, no compassion. She was on her own. "You *bastard!* Bastards!" she cried, her gaze sweeping wildly round the room. "All of you!"

Ryder seemed to come to life. "If your story is true," he said, taking a step toward her, "tell us where you got the bracelet."

"No!" She faced him. "It's none of your damned business!"

Ryder's eyebrows rose. "May I remind you—"

"Maybe I should remind *you,*" she shot back, "that I can still stir up a media frenzy about this! A TV reporter arrested at DeWilde's big night! Do you think you could keep that story under wraps? Reporters would be wearing a path to the jail to interview me—and believe me, I'd tell *them* all they want to know, and more. See, I was investigating this jewelry scam, and DeWilde's framed me to protect their corporate name—the media love a juicy big-name scandal. It'll probably finish the firm for good here in Sydney, and it won't do the other stores a power of good, either."

His face was stony as he stared down at her. "You bitch," he said quietly, deliberately, the barb going deep into her heart, more hurtful than if he'd hurled it at her in open anger. "What the hell makes you think you'd get away with that? You might derive some kind of poisonous satisfaction out of it, but you have damn-all evidence and you know it. Anyone who broadcast or printed those accusations would get slapped with a libel suit so fast they wouldn't have time to draw breath. And *you*—if you didn't go to jail for receiving stolen goods or even theft—would never work as a journalist again for any reputable employer. Besides, you'd be so busy defending yourself from lawsuits, you wouldn't have time to work. You'll end up owing more money than you'll see in your lifetime."

"So, take me to court!" she invited, turning to include Jeffrey in the challenge. But she knew that if they did, she wouldn't stand a chance. They could afford the best lawyers money could buy. "You'll win, but I'll go down fighting," she promised. "And I can bloody you, if not break you."

The slight spasm that crossed Jeffrey's face might have been distaste or possibly a reluctant acknowledgment of a worthy opponent. "All right, Miss Pallas," he said stiffly at last. "I don't like submitting to blackmail—"

"You started it!"

"But perhaps you're right. Neither of us will gain much by involving the police, and as you pointed out, we have the bracelet back. I'm . . . grateful for that."

"It's taken you a damned long time to admit it!"

Astonishingly, she realized with disbelief that the movement at the corner of his mouth restrained a smile this time. "I apologize."

"You *what?*" Ryder sounded disgusted.

Ignoring him, Jeffrey said almost humbly, for him, "I would be even more grateful if I knew just where it came from?"

Resolutely, Natasha shook her head. He was clever, this urbane, experienced and wily Englishman. He knew when to threaten and when to coax, even when to pretend humility or smile in that rare, though oddly familiar way. But he wasn't going to get anything out of her. "Sorry. I'm not at liberty to tell you."

"Hmm." Jeffrey looked thoughtful, but he seemed to realize it was no use pressing her any further. "Mr. Fynne," he said, "Nick and I need to talk to Ryder. May we borrow your office for a little longer?"

"Yes, of course," the man said instantly.

"Perhaps you might call a taxi for Miss Pallas and escort her out of the building."

"Certainly." The click of the phone buttons sounded unusually loud in the silence of the room. Natasha avoided meeting Ryder's eyes, but she could feel his tension almost as much as her own. Jeffrey continued to regard her with a considering, equivocal gaze, while Nick lounged against the jewelry manager's desk with arms folded, apparently gazing into space.

"Nick," Jeffrey suggested quietly, "perhaps it's time we put the collection away."

"What about this?" Nick held up the fake bracelet and Jeffrey took it from him, silently slipping it into his pocket.

Natasha was infinitely glad when the jewelry manager put down the phone and told her, "A cab will be at the front entrance in a few minutes."

Nick locked up the briefcase and handed it to the manager, who put it away in the safe before turning to accompany Natasha. He was looking faintly embarrassed and appeared to be avoiding direct eye contact with her.

Jeffrey opened the door for them. Ryder took a step toward Natasha and then stopped, his hands held rigidly at his sides.

"Good night, Natasha," Jeffrey said.

She glared at him with disdain. "Goodbye, Mr. De-Wilde." It was no use even trying to say good-night to Ryder. He wouldn't speak to her, she knew.

JEFFREY CLOSED THE DOOR behind Natasha and glanced at Ryder, then sighed sharply. "I know," he said. "We should have told you. I thought once Nick met you he'd agree to it. When we arrived I was prepared to insist on it, but—" he stopped and rubbed at his forehead "—somehow..."

Ryder thought he knew why he hadn't insisted. They'd been drinking coffee in Jeffrey's room when Ryder mentioned that he'd seen Grace, talked to her. And Jeffrey had decided he wasn't to be trusted, after all.

The hard knot of anger and pain that seemed to have settled in Ryder's midriff wasn't dispelled by Nick's laconic contribution to the discussion. "I wouldn't have agreed, anyway," the investigator announced.

Jeffrey glanced inquiringly at Nick, who continued, "It was obvious Natasha Pallas had him dancing to her tune—"

Ryder stiffened, but he could hardly argue with the cynical assessment.

"Although you'd told me," Nick added, "that he didn't trust her."

He *hadn't* entirely trusted her at first, Ryder recalled. He'd told Jeffrey she had a hidden agenda. But never in a million years would he have guessed what it was. He still didn't entirely understand....

And the minute he'd decided she was falling in love, he'd swept aside his doubts and fallen right along with her.

But it had all been a sham. She wasn't in love with him at all. She'd only pretended to be, leading up to that moment when she'd sent him a mute but unmistakable appeal: *Help me.* And he'd gone to her like a puppet on a string, waived his own rule not to interfere with his staff while they were doing their job. *You wouldn't want us to miss the finale,* she'd cajoled, beseeching him with those big, dark, innocent eyes. And he'd said, Let her through. Like the blind, besotted, gullible fool that he was.

Acid bile rose from his stomach. "So what," he asked Jeffrey abrasively, jerking his head toward Nick, "is your tame private investigator really here for?" And as the older man hesitated, he added with barely controlled rage, "If I don't get told—*now*—what this is all about, DeWilde's Sydney can find itself another general manager."

Nick gave him a look of unwilling respect, then turned to Jeffrey and shrugged.

Jeffrey said, "You *are* DeWilde's Sydney, Ryder. I can only apologize again—"

"I don't want apologies," Ryder said harshly. "I want answers. For instance, how many of those jewels we've been guarding so carefully, the jewels that thousands of my customers and other people have come here to admire, are fakes? And why in God's name would Natasha want to steal one and replace it with the genuine article? If that's what it is!"

"I don't doubt that it is," Jeffrey said. "And I have no idea how Natasha came into this, but I'll tell you the whole story as far as I know it."

Not before time, Ryder thought. Aloud he said grimly, "This had better be good."

"You've heard the family talk about my Uncle Dirk," Jeffrey began.

"Rarely," Ryder said. "I thought he was dead."

"He disappeared in 1948, just after the DeWilde collection had been exhibited in the New York store, which he was in charge of at the time."

"Disappeared? What does that have to do with what happened here tonight?"

"That's what Nick is trying to find out. You asked me why he was here," Jeffrey reminded him. "About the time that my Uncle Dirk left the New York store, half a dozen pieces of the family jewelry also vanished."

For a couple of seconds, Ryder was silenced. "He took them?"

Jeffrey said cautiously, "There are other possibilities, but the family strongly suspected that Dirk was responsible."

"Could he have been the victim of some kind of foul play?"

"He left a letter. Not particularly informative, but it did reassure his staff and the family that he was leaving of his own free will. A second letter was posted from Hong Kong, saying he was well and happy. Father hired a Pinkerton's detective to locate Uncle Dirk, but no trace of him was found, and eventually the search was called off."

"So instead they covered up the theft," Ryder said slowly, "and substituted copies to avoid a family scandal."

"*Someone* substituted copies. My father didn't find that out for some time. The assumption was that Dirk was responsible. But Henry, by all accounts, idolized Dirk and might have covered up for him."

Ryder frowned. "Didn't the insurance company have them inspected over the years?"

"My father changed the policy to another company as soon as the theft was discovered. He simply excluded the...suspect...pieces from the list."

"Then why include them in this exhibition?" Ryder asked, his voice cool.

"For a good reason."

"Good enough to excuse you making me your stooge?"

Jeffrey cast him a troubled look but didn't apologize again. "Earlier this year, the Empress Eugénie tiara turned up in New York and was recognized by a very surprised dealer, who discreetly contacted me. That was the first sign we'd had of any of the missing pieces. We had assumed they'd been broken up years ago, but if one was still intact, perhaps the others might be. I hired Nick to find out where it had come from."

"And...?" Ryder involuntarily turned his gaze to the dark, silent man who was once again leaning on the desk, his arms folded as if the conversation were boring him.

"And," Nick said, "it came from here."

"Here?"

"Australia," he clarified. "I traced it to a jewelry store in Sydney, which sold it to an American buyer last year."

"So, who sold it to the jewelry store?" Ryder demanded.

"I wasn't able to find that out." Nick shook his head regretfully.

"Why not?" Ryder shot back. "You're supposed to be a detective, aren't you?"

The American stiffened, just a small flexing of his broad shoulders, and his eyes narrowed. Ryder tensed in anticipation, adrenaline running thick and hot in his veins. He'd never been a violent man, and he probably didn't stand a chance against a streetwise, experienced type like Nick Santos, but he was in the mood to fight someone, and if Santos would just make the move, Ryder was willing and eager to give it a go.

But Nick didn't stir from his position. "The shop had been burned down a few months back," he explained patiently, the tension in him gradually receding. "All the records went up in smoke. The cops thought it might be arson—the proprietor was planning to retire at the time— but in the end they figured he might have been responsible though it probably wasn't deliberate. The old guy suffers from Alzheimer's disease—that's why he was retiring. He got much worse after the fire, his wife told me."

"So he didn't remember who sold him the tiara."

"His memory isn't totally gone, part of the time he's quite lucid, but all he could tell me was that the woman was—"

"Woman?" Ryder interrupted.

"He thought the tiara was brought to his shop by a woman. A middle-aged Australian woman."

Not Natasha, then.

"There might have been a man with her, but he couldn't describe him."

"It wasn't much to go on," Jeffrey said. "When Nick returned from his last trip to Sydney with the news that he'd run into a dead end, we came up with a plan, a long shot."

"To show the fake jewelry?" Ryder guessed. "What exactly was that supposed to accomplish?" he asked, not hiding his sarcasm.

"The possibility of driving something—or someone—out of the woodwork. Advertising that we still had the missing pieces might prompt anyone holding them—very possibly in all innocence—to come forward. If they thought they had a replica, it might worry them, and if they knew theirs was the genuine article, then possibly they'd be anxious to prove it. We had the tiara, but five pieces were still missing. Four now."

"If the bracelet is the real one."

"We'll have it checked, of course, but I'm sure we'll find that it is. I want the collection complete again. Someone must know something that will help us to recover the other pieces."

"Natasha," Ryder said dully. "She knew the tiara was a fake."

"Actually, that's not so, as I told her. Since we got the real one back, we replaced it in the collection."

"She *thought* it was a fake," Ryder insisted.

"Yes," Jeffrey mused. "She did seem to know there had been a fake. So she probably knows about the others, too."

"Maybe you could find out, Ryder," Nick suggested. "You're close to her."

Ryder clenched his fists. "*I* don't make my living peeking into bedrooms and rifling through other people's dirty linen."

Nick gave a short laugh. "I was thinking of pillow talk," he said. "But if you're giving me the go-ahead to try it myself with the lovely Natasha, I must say it could be a tasty assignment—" He straightened quickly as Ryder lunged toward him.

Jeffrey intervened, reeling backward as Ryder plowed into him.

"Get out of my way, Jeffrey!" Ryder said with gritted teeth.

"No. Calm down." Jeffrey put a hand on Ryder's chest and pushed with surprising force, making him step back. "I know you're raring for a fight, Ryder, and I know you'd like to hit *me* if my venerable age wasn't stopping you. But hitting Nick instead won't help matters. And, Nick," he said, turning to the other man, "I don't pay you to bait my manager. It would help if both of you would stop acting like a couple of scrappy schoolboys trying to determine who's cock-of-the-walk."

Knowing deep down that Jeffrey was right didn't make Ryder feel any more kindly disposed toward the American, but with an effort he tamped down his feelings, shoving his hands into his pockets.

"*Would* you talk to Natasha?" Jeffrey asked him. "She may be willing to confide in you."

"What makes you think that?" Ryder said bitterly. "She's had all she wanted from me." *And all she's going to get,* he added to himself.

"I know how you feel," Jeffrey said, "believe me. It isn't pleasant to discover that someone you're close to was simply out for what she could get."

Nick added nonchalantly, "She used you, man. Think about it. You could give it right back to her. Get her to trust you and maybe she'll let something slip."

Ryder looked at him with loathing. The very thought made him feel sick. He hoped he would never see Natasha again. If he did, he was afraid of what he might do.

"After all," Jeffrey put in, "she was probably telling the truth about not being a criminal. We just want to find out exactly what she *is*. And why she wanted to replace the bracelet."

What she is, Ryder thought, *is a liar and an opportunist, at the very least.* But he couldn't bring himself to say it aloud. Even now he wanted to protect her—at the same time that he wanted to strangle her with his bare hands.

Jeffrey put a hand on his arm. "Sleep on it," he counseled. "See how you feel about things in the morning."

CHAPTER TWELVE

IT WAS ALL NATASHA could do not to weep as she accompanied Mr. Fynne in numbed silence through the rows of ghostly white-clad mannequins in the dimly lit bridal department.

Once she'd indulged in a foolish, romantic dream about walking at Ryder's side wearing one of these fabulous gowns. That dream now lay in shards about her leaden feet. It would never happen. He wasn't going to forgive her for this. Not ever.

She directed the waiting cab to the studio, where she started editing some clips of the show for the Sunday news programs. It was one of the hardest things she had ever done, examining frame after frame of wonderful clothes, spectacular jewelry and beautiful models, reliving the evening. She was profoundly thankful that she'd told Terry not to shoot footage of the opening speeches. At least she didn't have to look at Ryder's face. She didn't think her precarious composure would have stood it.

By the time she got home, it was too late to phone New Zealand, so she had to wait until the following day.

When she did call, the phone rang five times before the receiver was picked up. A tentative, elderly voice said, "Yes?"

"Gran? It's Natasha. How are you?"

"I'm fine, dear. Your mother's just dressing to go to church. Are you getting on all right?"

Tears threatened to spill over at the loving concern in her grandmother's voice. "Yes," she lied. "I . . . I have some good news for you." She swallowed. "You can stop worrying, Gran. It's done."

There was a long silence, and Natasha said anxiously, "Gran, are you there? Did you hear me? I've done it. The bracelet's back where it belongs."

"I heard you, dear." Sara Freeman's voice wavered, and Natasha realized that she was weeping. "Oh, you are a darling girl! I've been so anxious, you know. If anyone found out—"

"Yes, I do know," Natasha said gently. "It's all right, no one will ever find out now. I promise."

She had made the promise for the first time months ago, never imagining what keeping it would cost her. But since last night, she was more than ever determined to protect her grandmother from Jeffrey and his henchman. They weren't getting a chance to bully Sara the way they'd attempted to bully her. The memory was still fresh in her mind; just thinking about it raised gooseflesh on her arms. "Give my love to Mum," she said, keeping her voice determinedly steady. "I have to go now. Bye, Gran."

Her hand hovered over the phone but she didn't quite dare lift the receiver again and call Ryder.

She spent the day at the studio. All the footage they'd shot over the past several weeks had to be edited down to an hour-long program. Some rough-cutting had already been done, of course, but there were still days of work ahead.

Every frame reminded her of Ryder, even if he didn't directly appear in it. Surely when he thought things over, he would realize she hadn't done anything criminal, merely returned the bracelet to its rightful owners. He'd be willing to accept she'd had her reasons for secrecy, wouldn't he?

Maybe he was waiting for her to contact him, explain and apologize. She owed him that much, didn't she? Before leaving, she picked up the phone and dialed his number.

It rang and rang. No answer. Just as she was about to give up, the receiver at the other end was lifted and Ryder's peremptory voice said, "Yes?"

"I'm sorry," she said. "Is this a bad time?"

There was a lengthy pause, and she crossed her fingers, willing him not to hang up. Finally he said, "I just got in. What do you want, Natasha?"

"To talk to you," she said quickly. "Please."

Again he didn't answer at first. And when he did, his voice sounded terse and unfriendly. "About what?"

She needed to see his face. Was it as uncompromising as his voice? "It's difficult on the phone," she said. "Can I come over?"

This time she thought the silence indicated astonishment. It stretched unbearably. Was he going to turn her down?

But at last he said indifferently, "If you like. I'll be home all evening." And then he put down the phone.

It was a start, she told herself, chilled by his abruptness. At least he hadn't turned her down flat.

She flew to the door, then stopped, looking down at her jeans and loose shirt. She'd go home first and change into something more ... well, less casual. She needed armor.

In her bedroom, she averted her eyes from the skirt and sequined top she had worn last night. She would never wear them again. She dragged out a dress that Ryder had once said he liked, a cream-colored cotton sprigged with small pink flowers. Six tiny buttons fastened the bodice below a round, scooped neckline, and it was fitted under the bust and loosely skimmed her waist before flaring into a graceful skirt. She wore high-heeled sandals, recalling vividly how vulnerable she had felt with Ryder and the other men towering over her. The heels wouldn't bring her up to his height, but at least they would minimize the difference.

Wanting to look her best, she used a smidgeon of eye shadow, and even mascara, which she seldom wore, then outlined her mouth with a lip pencil before smoothing on pink lipstick. She brushed her hair to a silky sheen and left it loose, as Ryder preferred it.

In case it grew cooler, she took a light jacket and slipped her coin purse into the pocket. Draping the jacket over her arm, she left the flat.

WHEN RYDER OPENED the door, she could see he hadn't gone to any bother on her account. His hair was less groomed than usual, and his shirt unbuttoned halfway, the sleeves carelessly pushed up, one higher than the other. And the shadow on his cheeks indicated that he hadn't shaved recently. Ryder's job didn't lend itself to designer stubble, and she knew he always shaved if he was going out in the evening.

He swept a glance over her, and his mouth turned down disparagingly at one corner. Immediately she knew she'd made a mistake.

"May I come in?" she asked.

Wordlessly he stepped back, inviting her in with an exaggerated wave of his hand. "Should I have dressed up?" he asked.

Natasha flushed. "I'm not dressed up," she protested.

"No?" He inspected her again, more thoroughly and with chillingly clinical eyes. "Well, you look . . . luscious."

"Thank you," she said stiffly, not at all sure it was meant as a compliment.

"Have you eaten?"

"Yes. I . . . had a sandwich. Are you . . . am I too early? Were you having dinner?"

"Not at all." Even his politeness was impregnable. "I'm not hungry, anyway. Why don't you sit down?"

"If *you* will." Again she remembered her discomfort last night, sitting in a chair while the men all stood.

He raised his brows, then shrugged. "Okay." He indicated the sofa facing the windows, and as she dropped her jacket over the back and seated herself, he settled at the end of another, about as far from her as he could get. He lounged back with his legs extended, ankles crossed. "You wanted to talk. To tell me all about what you were playing at last night?"

Natasha shook her head. "I can only tell you that I'm truly sorry it was necessary to...deceive you, but I had a very good reason. I...hope you'll trust me on that."

"Trust you?" He gave a crack of laughter. "You don't ask much, do you? After playing me for weeks like a fish on a line—"

"It wasn't like that!"

"Just how stupid do you think I am?" he asked with dangerous softness. "I knew the first time you looked at me with those big, artless eyes that you weren't as innocent as you seemed, that you had something up your sleeve I didn't know about. That's why I asked you to lunch that day."

"You knew?" Natasha felt numbed. "All along?"

"That you were hiding something, yes. Later I made the mistake of almost forgetting it...of letting you use me."

"I told you, it wasn't like that. And if you only asked me out to find out what I had up my sleeve, then aren't you calling the kettle black?"

"I wasn't lying to you," he said harshly. "I wasn't using you for my own ends."

"Ryder, I didn't—"

"You persuaded me to let you have the run of the store," he said, "against my first, better judgment. You even got me to introduce Jeffrey to you—"

"That was his idea!" she protested.

"After I'd sung your praises to him. You didn't miss a trick, did you? Hanging on his every word, sitting beside him—right where you are now. What were you hoping for? To get even closer to the real money? You surely didn't imagine you could replace Grace, did you?" He laughed unkindly. "I'm afraid Jeffrey's grown out of the ingenue type."

Confused by the absurdity of his insinuation, she said, "I never thought of Jeffrey that way—you must know that! I only wanted—"

"Yes?" His eyes burned into hers. "What did you want, Natasha?"

Baldly, Natasha played her one, desperate card. "I wanted . . . you."

It seemed at first that he wasn't going to respond. He might have been a wooden statue. Then, unexpectedly, he flung back his head and laughed, a caustic sound that sent a shiver down her spine. "That's good," he said finally, his mouth still curled in derision. "Try another one."

She said, almost whispering, "It's true."

His eyes narrowed on her, studying her for a long, long moment as if she were something wriggling on the end of a pin. "Prove it."

The blood roared in her ears. She closed her eyes, thinking that if she fainted it would be just too Victorian altogether. When she opened them again, he was still staring at her, his expression wary, challenging.

She caught her lower lip in her teeth, released it, took a quick, agitated breath.

Ryder drawled, "You just said you want me. So prove it."

She could do nothing at first but stare at him, her heart hammering, her shocked eyes locked with his. Then she stood up, her hands clenched.

Her legs trembled as she walked toward him. It seemed to take an age, everything happening in slow motion. Ryder drew his legs in so they didn't block her, but otherwise he remained still.

She halted before him. Something flared in his eyes, but he didn't move.

His cool gaze dropped to the front of her dress. "You could start," he suggested, "by undoing those buttons."

Sudden heat seared her cheeks. She swallowed, willing her voice to be steady. It came out low and uneven. ''No,'' she said, feeling her heart break within her. It couldn't possibly make things any better, not when he could look at her with nothing in his eyes but that angry, oddly cold lust.

She made to step back, but the coffee table allowed her only a few inches. ''I'm no sacrificial virgin, Ryder. I won't let you make love to me for some kind of revenge.''

She turned to leave, but he shot out a hand and captured her wrist, jerking her to a stop. ''No, you're not, are you?'' he queried softly. ''Just the opposite, I guess.''

''That's unfair!'' She had to force out the words, her throat raw.

''Yes, maybe it is. If I'd picked up a woman off the streets, she would at least have been honest about what she wanted, and what she was prepared to give for it.''

''I wasn't dishonest with you!''

''You were, Natasha—every time you put your arms round me, opened your sweet, lying mouth for my tongue. When I felt your breasts bud and blossom under my hands, when you kissed me back and pressed yourself close to me until you could feel me wanting you, when your thighs fitted so snugly around mine. And when you lay in my bed and...loved me, as I thought. But I was a means to an end, and I never realized it.''

There was a huge, painful lump in her throat, but she was determined not to cry, not to let the tears fall in front of him. ''It wasn't at all like that,'' she said huskily. ''You don't understand.''

''Make me understand,'' he said, harsh challenge in his voice. ''Tell me why.''

She looked at him with futile longing. ''Why can't you take my word?'' she asked him sadly. ''I've done nothing wrong. I didn't mean to use you. But I can't tell you why I did it. I can't.''

His face didn't change, and she turned away, trying to pull her imprisoned wrist from his grasp. He wouldn't let her; instead he tightened his grip and twisted, yanking her off balance and down across his lap, holding her there with hard hands, his eyes ablaze now with sullen desire. And then he kissed her.

It was unlike any kiss he'd given her before. He took her mouth, her poor bruised heart, her very soul, slaking a blind, bitter passion.

She wouldn't give in to that. He had practically called her a whore, and the sting couldn't be soothed by passion without affection. She closed her teeth warningly on his lower lip, and he drew back, laughing low in his throat. He nipped gently at her own lip in retaliation, then nibbled the same spot with his lips, touched his tongue to it as if to heal the hurt that was no hurt at all. His arms were strong, holding her against him, and his lips left hers and grazed down the taut, resistant line of her throat. She felt his mouth on the smooth rise of her breasts above her neckline, his fingers tugging at the disputed buttons, and a rush of heat licked through her body, heat compounded of an extraordinary mixture of outrage, dread and—appallingly—primitive, naked desire such as she had never known.

The bodice parted, and his other hand lowered the zipper and unclipped her bra. He eased her dress and the thin bra strap underneath from one shoulder, his mouth moving on her breast, half-bared to him.

Warmth invaded her body, made her limbs weightless. Feeling her diminishing resistance, Ryder laughed again softly and pushed the flimsy fabric of her dress farther down, his fingers finding the yearning bud at the center of her breast.

The laughter had brought Natasha to her senses. *"No!"* she gasped. Struggling to free her hands from his embrace, she grabbed at his wrist.

"No?" he queried, his eyes traveling slowly over the flushed, exposed skin to her face. "Then what does this mean?" His fingers and thumb moved meaningfully, sending a shaft of pure pleasure straight to her groin, so that she had to grit her teeth to prevent herself from moaning.

"It means," she said, making a supreme effort, "that I'll fight you every inch of the way."

His hand stilled, lying warm and heavy against the swell of her breast. *"Why?"* he demanded with furious incredulity. "You've convinced me this is one thing you were telling the truth about. *You want me.*"

"Not enough," she said. Too much, if the truth were known. But she didn't want just sex, and certainly not sex marred by distrust and contempt. "Not enough," she reiterated, "to let you treat me like this."

"Was I too rough for you?" he inquired, sounding genuinely contrite. "Sorry." He bent his head, feathering the lightest of kisses across her breast, a teasing, insistent caress that made her catch her breath.

Hearing her do so, he raised his head. "Better?" he asked, a brilliant glitter in his eyes.

"Stop it, Ryder!" She had to convince him—this could be her last chance before the insidiousness of his lovemaking overcame all her fragile defenses. And this wasn't the way it should be—all mixed up with resentment and distrust. She held her body rigid, her hands shoving against him, her eyes defiant. "I said *no.*"

She saw the surprise in his face, followed by speculation, and knew he was debating with his better self the possibility of overcoming her resistance with a combination of strength and his experience at arousing a response in a woman . . . in her.

His jaw locked, and she could see the tension under the taut skin of his cheeks. Gradually the fire died from his eyes. "All right," he said at last.

He stood up, bringing her with him, and she hastily re-arranged her clothing. Once she'd finished, his hand cupped her chin, and he examined her face with a fierce, probing gaze. "Top marks for self-control," he said, "to both of us. Tell me something. Was the game you played—whatever it was—worth the candle?"

"Yes," she whispered miserably. She'd achieved her goal, hadn't she? And set her grandmother's mind at rest. That had to be worth something. But in the process she'd created an unbridgeable distance between her and the man she was horribly afraid she was going to love all her life.

Tell him, a small, insidious voice inside her brain urged. *Tell him, and maybe he'll forgive you.*

But reason reminded her there was no guarantee that he would. He knew she hadn't stolen the real bracelet, and it hadn't made any difference; he still blamed her for deceiving him, using him, abusing his trust in her. That was what he couldn't forgive. That had nothing to do with whether or not she was a thief or what her motives had been.

And he was too close to the DeWildes. Jeffrey hadn't fooled her last night; he wasn't giving up on finding out where she'd got the bracelet, he was just biding his time. Jeffrey DeWilde was a very determined man, with a dangerous amount of money and power. And influence over Ryder. She had no right to gamble with her grandmother's life.

"Why did you come here tonight?" Ryder asked.

"I...wanted to say I'm sorry. I didn't set out to use you."

"Sure," he said.

"Last night, I hadn't planned to involve you. Only they wouldn't let me in and...you were there."

"Yeah, and I came running right on cue. Fortuitous, wasn't it?"

"I know you don't believe me, but..."

"You're right," he said, "I don't."

"Well, anyway," she said hopelessly, "I owe you an apology. That's…why I came." *And to see if there was any hope that you'd trust me after all, if there could be any kind of future for us.* "I'm sorry," she said. "I'd better go now."

She felt his fingers contract as though he would have detained her longer, then abruptly he released her. "Yes," he said, and turned to pick up her jacket and hand it to her. "You'd better, before I lose what little is left of my temper—and my willpower. How did you get here?"

"By bus."

"I'll call you a taxi." He went to the phone and dialed, spoke briefly and told her, "Five minutes."

"Thank you."

"I'll walk you down to the street."

"Please—no."

"I'm not leaving you hanging about the street on your own at night."

He walked with her to the door and flung it open for her. She paused on the threshold, trying to think of something to say, but nothing came to mind. In the end, defeated, she hung her head and walked past him.

In the elevator they didn't even try to talk. There was nothing more to say.

The cab was there in a mercifully short time, and when he opened the door for her, she lingered for a moment, saying, "Good night, Ryder."

"Goodbye, Natasha," he said, sounding woundingly indifferent.

"You comin', darlin'?" the driver inquired.

"Yes." Natasha climbed in and heard the door close with a snap behind her. The final humiliation was seeing Ryder lean in and hand the cab driver a note with the curt instruction to keep the change.

CHAPTER THIRTEEN

RYDER DROVE JEFFREY to the airport. The security man from London and a member of Ryder's own security staff sat in the back seat with the precious metal case, but Nick Santos was absent.

"I don't suppose," Ryder said, "you'd care to tell me what your P.I.'s plans are now?"

Jeffrey glanced over his shoulder to the stolid pair behind them. "I'll tell you all you want to know before I get on the plane."

"That'll be a change," Ryder muttered.

Jeffrey said mildly, "You have been avoiding me since Saturday night."

That was true, but Ryder wasn't prepared to concede it. Instead he said, "I thought you were spending the time with Violetta. After the show you said you'd see her later."

"I had lunch with her and her family on Sunday. Very traditional and Italian. And enjoyable."

"I'm glad you had a good time."

Jeffrey studied Ryder for a moment. "Did you see Natasha?"

"No." Ryder's hands tightened on the steering wheel. The night she'd come to see him didn't count, though the memory of it made his stomach turn with anger and self-disgust. What Jeffrey really meant was had he found out anything about the missing DeWilde jewels.

As if reading his mind, Jeffrey said, "I understand your

reluctance. You're right, it's not your job to play detective. You...er...haven't really known her very long, have you?''

In other words, *How close are you?* ''Not long.'' Ryder made his voice casual, uncaring. ''And not that well.'' That was true; if he'd known her half as well as he'd thought, she wouldn't have been able to pull the wool over his eyes the way she had.

If the denial surprised the older man, he didn't show it. He cast a glance over his shoulder at the other two men, then lapsed into silence.

When Jeffrey had checked in his baggage, he said, ''Come and have a drink with me,'' and led Ryder to a bar, where the two security men sat at a separate table.

Gently rotating a glass of whiskey between his hands, Jeffrey said quietly, ''Nick is trying to locate the rest of the missing jewels and trace my uncle. It seems that Dirk may have immigrated here when he left New York.'' He paused. ''Natasha is our only lead now. Nick will be keeping her under surveillance. He...didn't want me to tell you.''

Ryder remained silent. Jeffrey was trying to make up for not having apprised him of their plans before, but the wounds were still too new and raw for him to meet the older man halfway.

''I hope,'' Jeffrey said, ''that you will give him every assistance you can in his investigations.''

Ryder stared broodingly at his chilled, foaming beer, erasing all expression from his face before looking up. ''I'll keep that in mind...sir.''

Jeffrey's lips momentarily thinned. ''It's a request, Ryder, not an order.''

''Sure.'' Ryder raised his glass to his lips and swallowed deeply. ''Okay. Give my regards to Gabe when you see him.'' He put the glass down on the table. ''Did he know about all this?'' Since Grace's defection from the family and his own elopement, Gabe had been less inclined to phone

Ryder just to chat and catch up, but it was hard to believe that his old friend would have condoned deceiving him.

Jeffrey sipped his whiskey. "Gabe knows about the theft. He never saw the list of pieces to be included in the Sydney exhibition."

The tight knot of resentment inside Ryder's chest eased a little. At least Gabe hadn't been a party to the subterfuge.

"Was that girl important to you?" Jeffrey asked.

"Important?" Ryder kept his gaze blank, making his lips curve in simulated amusement. "I told you she was lovely to look at. But remember, I also told you that I thought she was up to something, and that I'd be keeping tabs on her. Only I was thinking in terms of her job—that she could be after a story other than the one she'd told us about. I assumed the metal detector was to keep out people carrying weapons, and keep *in* people smuggling out jewelry, so I was caught off guard there. Just as she planned."

"I thought you were going to punch Nick on the nose when he found the bracelet on her."

"My public school education," Ryder said wryly. "Always protect a lady's honor. But I couldn't argue with the evidence."

"You and she seemed . . . close."

"We were sleeping together for a time," Ryder admitted casually. "In that sense, we were close. But...you could say her heart wasn't in it. Nor mine."

Jeffrey eased back in his chair, his dark eyes regarding the younger man attentively. "I wouldn't like to see you hurt, Ryder."

It was on the tip of Ryder's tongue to ask Jeffrey what the hell he'd thought he was doing, then? Instead he drawled, injecting amusement into his voice, "You may have noticed—Natasha Pallas isn't the only pretty girl in Sydney."

Jeffrey gave him a rather troubled smile and didn't press the point. Grace would have known infallibly that he was covering up, but Jeffrey, astute though he was in the business world, didn't have her intuitive insight on a personal level.

Perhaps she had also curbed Jeffrey's ruthless streak. She wouldn't have countenanced for an instant threatening Natasha with a false accusation, or let Ryder be an unwitting party to a fraud on his customers.

Or maybe Jeffrey had grown thick-skinned because of his failed marriage and his obvious disillusion with Grace. Ryder couldn't imagine Grace being unfaithful, but what else could have made Jeffrey so bitter toward her?

Jeffrey finished his drink, scanned the overhead screen showing arrivals and departures, and said, "It looks as though my flight is boarding. I'll say goodbye to you here. Finish your drink."

He got to his feet, slinging his flight bag onto his shoulder. The two men at the adjacent table began to move, too.

Ryder stood up as Jeffrey held out a hand to him. He clasped it firmly, and Jeffrey's other hand came up to hold Ryder's between his palms. "I'm truly sorry, Ryder. Take care, now."

"Yes," Ryder said as Jeffrey released his hand. "You, too."

NATASHA BUMPED INTO Nick Santos as she was entering a self-service lunch bar a week after her last disastrous encounter with Ryder.

"Hi, there," the investigator greeted her. "Mind if I join you?"

Natasha was too surprised to object. "I thought you'd have left with Jeffrey by now. Aren't you supposed to be looking after the jewels?"

"He made other arrangements for the return journey." Nick picked up a tray and put two plates on it. "I thought I'd stay on for a while, have a summer Christmas for a change."

Natasha insisted on paying for her own lunch, but she could hardly refuse to share a table without making a fuss. She didn't believe for a minute that Nick no longer worked for the DeWildes, and she braced herself for questions. Instead she found herself enjoying his self-deprecating stories of the lighter moments of detective work, while he grinned at her in a totally disarming fashion.

"You must have some fun in your work, too," he said.

Sharing carefully chosen anecdotes was safer than trying to field questions. Nick listened to her, laughing aloud.

"We should do this again," he suggested.

But Natasha shook her head. "I don't often have time for a proper lunch."

"That's too bad." He cocked an eyebrow at her. "Dinner?"

"No, I'm afraid not."

He nodded understandingly. "Still carrying a torch for Ryder?" he asked, making her flush. "Or you just don't like me?"

Strangely, she had very nearly liked him today, as far as one could like a man who was a threat to you and yours. "How are your investigations for the DeWildes going?"

His eyes acknowledged the accuracy of her guess. "Not that good," he admitted. "You wouldn't care to help me out a little?"

She had to admire his gall. "I would if I could."

"Oh, I think you could," Nick argued, "if you wanted to. Who were *you* working for, Natasha?"

"No comment," she said crisply. "Now I have to get back to work."

IT WASN'T THE LAST she saw of Nick Santos. He was in the small crowd that gathered when she interviewed an aboriginal protest group in Hyde Park. He was at Bondi, obviously not caring that she saw him, when she went to a surfing carnival with her flatmate, and at a nearby table in the pub where she had a drink with her colleagues one night after work. He was even waiting outside her local supermarket when she emerged with two plastic bags laden with groceries the following Saturday morning.

"Here, let me carry those." He was removing them from her hands before she had time to resist. "You don't have a car, do you?"

"You know I don't," she said. "And this is harassment."

"Carrying your groceries? You one of those radical feminists who want to send a guy to jail for opening a door?"

"You've been following me."

"Of course," he agreed easily. "Come on, it's this way, isn't it?"

She followed him down the street, fuming. It must have been dead easy for him to find out where she lived. What else did he know about her?

Before unlocking the door of the flat, she took the bags from him. "Thanks," she said curtly.

"You wouldn't invite me in?"

"Dream on." She glanced down at the bulging grocery bags. "I'll let you know when I'm throwing out the empty containers. The rubbish bin is at the back door."

Nick laughed. "Thanks, but I think I'll pass on that." He touched her cheek with his knuckles, still grinning. "See ya, Nat."

"SHE'S A TOUGH NUT to crack, your girl," Nick said. Leaning back in the chair opposite Ryder's, he folded his hands behind his head and rested his feet in their well-worn loafers on the big desk, one ankle crossed over the other.

"Natasha Pallas is not my girl." Ryder debated asking the American to remove his feet from the desk, and decided that was just what Nick was after.

"No?" Nick raised his black brows.

"No! I haven't seen her for...since...I can't even remember."

"Since she came to visit you the evening after the show," Nick told him.

Ryder involuntarily pushed back his wheeled chair, quelling an urge to leap from it and grab Nick's throat. "You were watching her."

"Yep. She didn't stay long. Had a fight, did you?"

"No." He was damned if he was going to say any more. What had passed between him and Natasha was no one else's business. It certainly wouldn't help Nick to find the missing DeWilde jewels. "What do you want, Santos? I have work to do."

"So do I. That's why I'm here. Tell me about Natasha."

Ryder flashed him a look of disgust, but Nick seemed impervious. "I don't mean bedroom secrets," the investigator said. "Did she say anything to you about her family? Where they live?"

Ryder shrugged. "Somewhere in New Zealand."

"North Island, South—where?"

"I don't know. But she worked in Auckland before coming here," he said reluctantly.

"I know that," Nick said dismissively. "Did she ever talk about her parents? Sisters, brothers?"

"Half brothers," Ryder supplied automatically.

"Her father's children or her mother's?"

"Father's." After a moment Ryder added, "One of them lives in Queensland." He owed Natasha nothing, he reminded himself. It wasn't as though Nick intended her any harm.

Nick nodded. "He shouldn't be difficult to find. Is her father alive?"

"He drowned when she was a child."

Nick remained unmoved. "When?"

"I don't know! She was eight, I think."

"She never mentioned her mother's maiden name?"

"Why should she?" Ryder asked irritably, torn between Jeffrey's request for him to cooperate with Nick and an irrational feeling of disloyalty to Natasha. "You're the detective. Why don't you ask her bank? That's the kind of question they put on their forms, isn't it?"

Nick grinned. "They won't tell me," he said. "And New Zealand's got a privacy law that makes it hard to get information out of anyone."

"Tough." Ryder couldn't find it in his heart to pity the other man.

"It's a challenge." Nick stood up. "If she's not your girl, you won't mind if I take up where you left off."

Ryder felt his teeth clamp shut with an audible snap. "Would it have stopped you?"

Nick actually laughed. "Maybe not. Do you think I stand a chance with her?"

"No." Ryder was fighting to maintain a calm facade to conceal the rage boiling inside him. "One thing she's not is stupid. She wouldn't pass the time of day with you."

"You reckon not?" Nick seemed to be enjoying himself. "Did she ever tell you the story about the nun on the flying trapeze? Or the time she had to interview a politician who'd left his fly undone?"

Ryder was sure he'd just felt his stomach drop two feet. He clenched his jaw so viciously his teeth ached. What the *hell* was Natasha doing, hobnobbing with Nick Santos? Didn't she know he was being paid by Jeffrey to find out whatever secret it was she'd been hiding? Was she crazy? "You've been seeing her?" he heard himself say, his voice hoarse, unrecognizable.

"Coupla times. If you remember any more," Nick said, "let me know."

He sauntered out, gently closing the door, and Ryder found himself reaching for the phone and dialing Natasha's work number and her private extension before he'd even thought about it.

He almost hung up immediately, but she lifted the phone after the first ring. "Hello, Natasha Pallas."

"Nick Santos is still working for the DeWildes," Ryder said.

There was a breathless silence. Then she asked coolly, "Is this an anonymous call?"

Damn her sarcasm. She must know his voice, just as he'd known hers from the first syllable. His hand tightened on the receiver, slippery with sweat. "You've been seeing him," he growled.

"Seeing him?" She sounded blank. If he hadn't known better, he'd have thought she didn't know what he was talking about. She was so *good* at acting the innocent. Then she said uncertainly, "Yes, I have seen a lot of him lately. He's been fo—"

Ryder didn't let her complete the sentence. Rage overtook him. "If you imagine you can wrap him round your little finger the way you did me," he snarled, "you should think again. He'll take whatever's on offer, but all he's really interested in is what he can get out of you." The two of them thoroughly deserved each other; he didn't know why he was doing this.

She was probably going to hang up. He was contemplating being the first to do so when she said, "Thank you for your concern. My mother gave me that warning, about men in general, along with my first bra. I should have remembered it when I met you."

She did get in first. Hearing the click in his ear, Ryder slammed down the phone. He was incensed. If anyone had been using anyone, it was *her.* How dare she suggest that . . . that . . .

He'd been in love with her, damn it! Gut-wrenching pain gripped him, reminding him that he still was in love with her, despite everything. His feelings had refused to die even though he knew now that she had lied to him, cheated him, used him.

Hold on to that, he told himself grimly. Remember that when she was kissing you, clinging to you, sighing and crying out beneath you, she was thinking about how she was going to worm her way into your confidence, hoping you'd make it easy for her to carry out her plan.

He scowled. The plan was the strangest scam he'd ever heard of. If she'd wanted to return the bracelet to the DeWildes, why the hell hadn't she just handed it over to Jeffrey? Or had it delivered, if she wanted to remain anonymous? Any security firm would have done it. *Why* cook up that elaborate, hair-brained scheme?

She may be willing to confide in you, Jeffrey had said. *I wish you'd give it some thought.*

And Nick Santos. *She used you . . . you could give it right back to her.*

Well, he hadn't even tried. And later, Jeffrey had more or less told him to forget it, leave the matter with Nick.

Now Nick was out to gain her confidence, hoping she would "let something slip" to him. Good luck to him, Ryder thought sourly.

But that evening, after warring with himself all day, and finally discarding the dinner he had made himself cook but had no appetite for, he flung himself into his car and drove to Natasha's flat.

WHEN NATASHA OPENED the door to Ryder, she had to hold on to the doorknob to steady herself.

His mouth was hard and his jaw thrust forward, but his eyes were almost sullen, and his face looked thinner, hollowed beneath the cheekbones. The first thing he said was, "Are you alone?"

"Roberta's home."

Something that might have been relief crossed his face. "We need to talk," he said.

"I don't think there's anything left to say, Ryder."

"I could start by apologizing." He offered it almost carelessly, but an underlying harshness in his voice hinted at what it cost him.

She hesitated. Then, cursing herself for her weakness where he was concerned, she stepped back and tacitly invited him in.

Roberta was watching a television sitcom. She looked up and waved at Ryder. "Hi, there."

"We can talk in the kitchen," Natasha said, and led him through. "Coffee?"

He said yes and sat at the small table, watching her as she reached for the coffee jar, spooned instant powder into the cups and poured hot water and milk.

"Want a biscuit?" she asked.

He shook his head, and she sat opposite him, curling her hand about her cup so that he wouldn't notice how it trembled. She fixed her eyes on the steam rising from her coffee, not daring to meet his gaze. "If you're here about the bracelet," she said, "I have nothing to tell anyone."

"Weren't you listening?" he asked almost irritably. "I said I want to apologize."

Want was probably too strong a word, Natasha thought. He seemed to feel some compulsion, forcing out the words.

"For what?" Last time they'd met, she'd been apologizing to *him,* and a lot of good it had done her.

"First, for the things I said when Nick...found the bracelet that night." His gaze was oddly bleak. "I should have known you're not a thief."

"I don't blame you for that," she said fairly, although at the time she had been mortally hurt. "The evidence was pretty powerful."

"And for...the way I treated you when you came to see me. I've never behaved like that in my life. I guess I was still pretty raw at the knowledge that you'd been using me." His eyes flashed briefly at her, and he failed to keep a note of accusation from his tone.

"I told you," Natasha said with some difficulty, "I hadn't intended to."

"But it just worked out that way." Ryder studied her for a moment. More calmly, he said, "I guess you had your reasons for deceiving me. Maybe one day you'll tell me—"

She looked up at that, giving a faint shake of her head, and then returned her gaze to the coffee cup in her hands.

"But it doesn't matter. What matters is how we feel about each other." He paused as if expecting her to say something, but she couldn't. She was too busy controlling her emotions, her expression. Finally, he said starkly, "I want you back, Natasha—I want us back together."

Hope flared and died. Natasha remained silent, aching inside. She longed to reach out to him, tell him that was what she wanted, too, but ... "There's no way back," she said sadly.

As if she hadn't spoken, he went on doggedly, "All day I've been thinking about you ... about us. We had something special. Very special." His eyes fixed almost painfully on her face, as if he were trying to read it. "You weren't putting on an act all the time, were you?" he challenged her. "Some of it was real!"

Natasha closed her eyes. She ought to deny it, tell him she hadn't meant any of it. That he'd been a means to an end. But she couldn't. He'd been hurt enough lately.

She saw the abyss that yawned between them, the impossibility of any ongoing relationship with a man so closely involved with the DeWildes.

"I'm sorry," she whispered, lifting tragic eyes to Ryder's face.

"*Sorry?*" The word was a challenge, a denial.

Unwillingly, Natasha spelled it out for him. Picking her way through the minefield, she said, "I did ... feel something for you, but it's over, Ryder. Time to ... to move on." She was sure she could feel her heart tearing slowly, agonizingly, in two.

The initial disbelief in his eyes gave way to the anger that she'd sensed simmering beneath the surface. "Then," he said raspingly, "you *were* just using me!"

"*No*." Natasha choked on the word, knowing she should have left it unsaid.

"*Yes*." His jaw was rigid. "Damn you!"

Her own temper flared a little. "All right, I wanted to get close to you, to Jeffrey if I could—I needed access to the DeWilde collection. That's all I was after. Now are you satisfied?"

"No," he said flatly, and she saw he was fighting hard to control his emotions. "Even if that was true initially, in the end you got caught in your own net, didn't you?"

"*No*." She had to throw the lie in his face.

"No?" He looked like a tiger closing in for the kill, his eyes narrowed and brilliant. "Why did you come to me the way you did—asking me to understand, to forgive you?"

Natasha stared at him, feeling that her heart was about to burst through the wall of her chest.

She should have kept away from Ryder after the awful evening of the fashion show. He had written her off as a cheat, if not a thief, and she ought to have had the sense to leave it at that, instead of stupidly hoping he'd accept that she'd had no choice, wanting him not to think badly of her. Trying to have her cake, even knowing damned well she couldn't eat it.

She clamped her lips together to stop them from trembling, stop herself from digging a hole deeper than the one she was in already.

He said roughly, "Natasha, you could have stolen the bloody crown jewels for all I care! *I love you*. And I think you love me."

A pain centered right in the middle of her chest. For just an instant she savored the three simple words, but they were bittersweet now.

He shot out a hand and took one of hers in a hard clasp. "You can't turn your back on it. I won't let you."

If only she'd been less clumsy, or Nick Santos less clever at his job. If she'd got away with replacing the bracelet, none of this would have happened.

She shouldn't answer him, but silence would condemn her as much as defense. Casting about, she said, "You're an attractive man—I thought so the very first time we met." Acting for all she was worth, she added regretfully, "But you're not the only man in the world, you know. I enjoyed . . . being with you. Any normal woman would, and you were a very . . . exciting lover."

She saw his knuckles whiten as his grip on the coffee cup tightened, but his voice was even as he answered. "As exciting as Nick Santos?"

Natasha blinked, momentarily outraged, then strangely grieved as she realized why Ryder was here now, trying to win her back with this odd mixture of anger, resentment and desire.

Did he really think she and Nick were lovers? It made no sense; he was waiting for her to deny it. But that was what had spurred him to visit her tonight, she was sure of it. Not love, or tenderness, or a deep conviction that he'd wronged her, that she couldn't be the treacherous being he'd thought her. It was simple sexual jealousy. And that wasn't enough, would never be enough, to overcome her caution, loyalty, her self-respect.

As she sat dumb before him, he said, "It's not the same, is it? You're still in love with me."

The flat arrogance of the statement took her breath away, even though he was right. She scrabbled about in her mind for something suitably crushing to say, knowing that it would probably come to her hours later, in the middle of the night.

"Natasha?"

Before she could stop them, hot tears welled in her eyes, and she jumped up from the table, trying to hide them, turning away to dash her hand across her cheeks, intending to flee to her bedroom. "You'd better go—"

He grabbed at her shoulder as she got to the door, and reached past her to push it shut. Natasha pulled away, her back coming up against the wood, and his hands slammed down on either side of her, trapping her.

She quelled a sob in her throat and scrubbed at the tears with her palms, saying shakily, "Leave me alone!"

"Why are you crying?"

"I'm not." She looked at him defiantly.

She thought he very nearly smiled, but the fierce, questioning light in his eyes barely abated. Then one hand was in her hair, tipping her head back, while his mouth descended on hers with unerring precision and passion, driving the breath from her body.

She knew she ought not to be responding to him, but at the first touch she ignited, erupting in flames of desire that made her lips open like a desert flower eager for the scorching sun, her arms curve about his waist and her hands crawl up his back, her whole body shivering with wanting him, needing him.

When at last he relinquished her mouth, he put his forehead against hers, his breathing harsh and uneven. "You can't send me away, not when you kiss me like that."

Natasha swallowed. This was insane. She was sure he could feel her heart going like a jackhammer against his chest. Her mind scurried frantically for a way out and found none. She had to be brave and end this. "Kissing isn't everything," she said huskily.

"I know that!"

"But it's all we had, really, isn't it? Sex." *May lightning strike me,* she thought, her heart providing the requisite thunder. It might be true for him, although she didn't entirely believe that, but it certainly hadn't been for her.

Everything in him went still, the muscles of his body contracting; she could feel it.

His arms dropped away from her, but a hand closed about her chin, compelling her to look up into his blazing, baffled eyes. "Say that again," he invited her, his voice so quiet that she scarcely heard the words, yet with a thread of iron running through it.

"You're almost right—I was ready to forgive you for thinking me a thief and backing up Jeffrey's threats, because I still thought I was in love with you. But when I came to you that night—expecting you to understand, to listen to me, what did I get? Threats and insults."

He said swiftly, "I'll regret till my dying day what I said...what I did to you—"

"I know, I accept your apology. But whatever I felt for you, you killed it that night. I guess it wasn't really love, after all. Maybe it wouldn't have lasted much longer, anyway. I'm sorry it's over—quite sad, really, but...that's life. No hard feelings?"

Shock washed the anger from his expression, and he dropped his hand as though her skin had burned him. His face was sallow and he was breathing hard, his nostrils pinched. She must have finally convinced him. His eyes were suddenly lifeless, without expression, and she had to clench her fists hard to stop herself from reaching out to him, assuring him she hadn't meant it, it was all lies.

He took her arm, moved her almost gently to one side, and flung open the door. Then he slammed it behind him and left her staring at the painted wood, holding her arms about herself and trying to control her shuddering body.

CHAPTER FOURTEEN

WHEN NATASHA TOLD her mother that she might not make it home for Christmas after all, Lucille Pallas said, "Well, if you have to work it can't be helped, only Gran was so looking forward to it. She's been saying she doesn't know how many more Christmases she'll have."

"She's not ill again?"

Lucille hesitated. "She rallied amazingly after you phoned with the good news about the bracelet, and she's been much more cheerful ever since. But she's not strong, you know."

"I'll be there," Natasha decided rashly. She hadn't seen Nick Santos for days. He must have stopped shadowing her—perhaps found another trail to follow. Besides, she'd booked her air ticket ages ago, before he arrived in Sydney. There should be no danger.

All the same, she kept her eyes open at the airport, and once on the plane made a point of checking out her fellow passengers on her way to the washroom. Nick Santos wasn't among them.

She left the plane feeling lighter than she had for weeks. Nick, Ryder, DeWilde's and Australia were behind her across the Tasman Sea, and she was going home. She had two weeks' holiday, and maybe when that was over she would have regained some equilibrium. At least that was what she kept telling herself.

There was a crowd of people in the public area waiting for friends and relatives, but her mother wasn't among them.

She hadn't wanted to leave Natasha's grandmother alone, and if the plane had been delayed, waiting around the airport would have been too tiring for the old lady. "I'll take a bus into the city," Natasha had told her mother, "and catch another out to Parahiku."

The busy little town where her grandmother had lived all her life was less than an hour from Auckland, and Natasha would be there before dinnertime.

Her lips curved with anticipation as she skirted a woman being engulfed by hugs and kisses from a family she obviously hadn't seen for ages.

She almost cannoned into someone coming toward her. Sidestepping him, she murmured, "Sorry," and made to pass on, but he put a hand on her arm and said, "Natasha."

Her heart stopped beating. *It can't be,* she tried to assure herself. Ryder was in Australia. This must be a hallucination. But she would have known his voice anywhere. In a hundred years' time his name on her lips would have the same electric effect. "Ryder," she whispered, and turned huge, disbelieving eyes to his face. "What are you doing here?"

"Meeting you." He smiled as if it hurt. "I have a car outside."

"No." She realized he was still holding her, and wrenched away with much more force than necessary, panic succeeding shock. "No! You can't do this."

"Natasha—" As she made to flee, he stepped in front of her again. "This isn't a kidnap. I only want to take you home."

Natasha was frantic. A nasty suspicion that had nagged like a tiny prickle festering under the skin since she'd last seen him now erupted into heart-shattering certainty.

Jeffrey had sent him, she knew it. Ryder could have contacted her anytime without following her to New Zealand. "Do you really think I'm stupid enough to direct you to my home?'' she demanded. She made to move around him. She'd have to find some way of shaking him off, making sure he didn't tail her. She couldn't risk leading him to her grandmother.

"You live at a place called Parahiku,'' Ryder said, and recited the street address. "At least, it's where your mother and grandmother live. They'll be waiting for you. Come on.'' He touched her arm again. "Why don't we—''

"My mother...'' Horrified, she glared up at him, feeling the blood seep away from her cheeks. "What have you *done?*''

Ryder stared back at her for a moment, apparently puzzled, then raised his eyes briefly to the ceiling as if in exasperated enlightenment. "Only pulled out her fingernails one by one and forced your grandmother to reveal where the rest of the jewels are hidden.'' He took her shoulders and shook her gently. "Don't be silly, darling! I haven't even met her yet. Let me take you to her and I'll explain on the way.''

"I have a bus ticket,'' she said, stubborn with shock. "And I'm not your darling!'' she added irrelevantly.

He gave her a crooked, oddly sad smile. "We'll argue about that later. You'll be there much more quickly if I drive you. Give me your bag.'' He released her and bent to remove it from her slackened grasp.

She let him lead her to the hired car. There didn't seem much point in arguing now. He unlocked the door for her and put her case on the back seat. Natasha fastened her safety belt and sat in seething silence while he got in and started the car, paid his parking fee and left the car park.

She couldn't resist watching his hands on the wheel, remembering the feel of them on her skin, the way he touched her as though she were precious to him.

Last time they'd met, she'd had to stop herself from throwing aside all caution and sense and flinging herself into his arms. Just as well she hadn't. He'd probably been under Jeffrey's orders then, too, hoping she'd confide in him.

He'd said he loved her. But it was a lie. Perhaps he'd felt justified in deceiving her as he believed she had deceived him.

Along the road she was momentarily distracted from her turbulent thoughts by a familiar rush of pleasure and pride in the green paddocks with their wire fences confining contentedly grazing cattle, the clear summer air and the almost painful blueness of the sky, with a drift of white cloud lazing across it. But the pleasure failed to kill her increasing sense of dread.

"How did you know to meet me?" she asked.

"Nick Santos," he told her. "He ferreted out your address in New Zealand and planned to fly over here and talk to your family." As Natasha drew in a sharp breath, he said, "I persuaded Jeffrey to let me come instead."

Suspicion hardened to leaden certainty. He had instructions from Jeffrey to discover how she had come to have the bracelet. He was, after all, an employee of DeWilde's, no matter how many shares or whatever he held in the company. In fact, that probably made it more imperative that he protect the family's interests.

"You mean," she said, fighting a hollow feeling in her stomach, "you convinced him that you'd have more chance of getting the information they want."

"It isn't quite like that. Actually I—"

"Jeffrey's little errand boy," she said cruelly.

He shot a hard glance at her. "I'm no one's—"

But Natasha wasn't listening. "*How* did Nick find out the address?" A thought struck her. "*Did he bug my phone?*" That should have occurred to her much earlier, she realized, frantically trying to review all her recent telephone conversations. She thought of Nick Santos gaining entry to her flat, perhaps in the dead of night, and her skin crawled.

"Good God, no! Not to my knowledge." Ryder frowned, slowing the car to a stop before swinging into a right turn. "It's his job to find things out. Apparently it wasn't too difficult. I . . . told him you had a brother in Queensland.'' He sounded almost apologetic.

"I see." Her voice was brittle. "And he took it from there."

"I'm not sure. Maybe it helped—but Pallas isn't a common name."

He was right, of course. A look through a set of telephone directories and a methodical process of elimination would eventually have found the right one—she had done exactly that a couple of times when researching a program. Only she'd thought herself safe, because at home the telephone was in her grandmother's name. But acting on Ryder's information, all Nick would have had to do was phone every number in Queensland under the name Pallas and ask confidently for Natasha. Her half brother might have been surprised, but she hadn't thought to warn him not to divulge information about her. And once Nick had found her brother, on some pretext or other he could have got her grandmother's address, or at least the phone number.

Her mother or grandmother would have said, in all innocence, "Natasha's in Australia," and quite likely have added helpfully, "but we expect her home for Christmas." He would have prepared some plausible story in case they asked questions, and they'd have no reason to deny all knowledge of her.

"I suppose," she said bitterly, "it wasn't too difficult to get my flight number, either."

"Apparently not. I couldn't get a seat on the same flight, though."

"I should have stayed in Sydney."

"It would have made no difference. Nick would have tracked down your family somehow."

Warning bells clanged in Natasha's mind. How much did they know? She'd assumed they were just following *her*, hoping for a lead to where the bracelet had come from, and that if she hadn't come home, Nick wouldn't have bothered her mother and grandmother. She said sharply, "What does my family have to do with anything?"

"You told me once that the two things you were passionate about were your work and your family. Nick uncovered no link between the DeWilde collection and the Kiwi Connection or anyone you work with. That leaves family."

And of course he'd shared his knowledge with Jeffrey and the private investigator. *Traitor,* she thought unfairly, looking out blindly at the luxury motels they were passing. Hadn't she always known where Ryder's loyalties lay? It was why she had abandoned any idea of being close to him. Wisely, as it turned out, but he was dangerously close to the truth, all the same. A pulse hammering at her temple, she said, "It's an interesting theory, but you're on a wild goose chase, I'm afraid."

It was a brave attempt, only she could see he didn't believe her. He cast her a look of tolerant understanding that set her teeth on edge.

"Do we go straight ahead here?" He slowed for some traffic signals. "I'm not familiar with the route yet."

"Yes," she said. Blocks of unpretentious shops were succeeded by painted houses sitting in small squares of grass and garden. They passed a park where some children were kicking a ball about, then stopped briefly to allow a party of Pacific Islanders in colourful shirts and flower-garlanded hats to walk in leisurely fashion over a pedestrian crossing.

As Ryder accelerated again, Natasha burst out, "I returned the damned bracelet! What the hell more does Jeffrey want? Did he have it appraised?"

"Yes. It's the real thing—the one that's been missing since before you were born."

"So you know I wasn't stealing it!"

"No one thinks that, Natasha."

"Then why are you still hassling me?"

He sighed sharply. "I'm *trying* to protect you. Would you rather have had Nick Santos arrive on your grandmother's doorstep without warning?"

She wouldn't, of course. She could still break out in a sick sweat recalling that moment in Mr. Fynne's office when she'd thought Jeffrey was about to set Nick on her physically. She wasn't going to risk having her grandmother subjected to a similar fright.

Ryder said, "That bracelet wasn't the only piece missing from the collection, as I think you know."

Stunned, Natasha turned her head to stare at him. "You mean they *are* fakes? *All* of them?" Her voice rose in disbelief.

The glance he threw at her seemed to hold extreme skepticism. "Of course not all of them," he said curtly. "Are you trying to tell me that you didn't know?"

"Only about the bracelet! And I only found that out when Jeffrey produced it on camera."

"The Empress Eugénie tiara," he reminded her. "You mentioned that."

"I was *guessing!* And anyway, Jeffrey said it was genuine."

"But until recently it had been missing for a long time... like the bracelet. If you didn't know about it, why did you suggest the tiara was a fake?"

"I suggested a lot of things." She'd been scared stiff and using indiscriminately whatever ammunition came to mind. "I had no idea I was so close to the target." She swallowed, feeling sick. "How... how many pieces *are* missing?"

He seemed to debate whether to answer. Then he said, "Four, now that the bracelet and tiara have been recovered."

So that was why they were still pursuing her. If someone had told her earlier they might have saved themselves the trouble. "That's what you meant by 'the rest of the jewels'?" She'd thought it was just a twisted sarcastic joke.

"If *you* don't know what happened to the other pieces, perhaps your mother or grandmother—"

She felt her hands go clammy, the skin at the back of her neck prickling. "They don't know any—*Look out!*"

A car had shot by them, cutting dangerously close in front, and Ryder swore and hit the brake, jerking her forward against her seat belt.

"Sorry about that," he said. "Are you all right?" When she nodded, he asked, "Where do we turn?"

She directed him to the motorway and then covertly studied his profile. He was frowning slightly, casting frequent glances into his rearview and side mirrors, driving with smooth competence but showing the strain of handling an unfamiliar car in a foreign country. The Christmas traffic was heavy, and no doubt some drivers had begun celebrating the season already.

Natasha bit her tongue on the questions and accusations that hovered on it. This was no time to get involved in an argument. Negotiating the traffic needed all his attention.

Soon after hitting the motorway, they left the suburbs behind for paddocks of grazing cattle and rolling hills shorn to a smooth green sward by woolly white sheep, except in the hollows where patches of native bush survived.

The summer sun had faded the grass a little, but even so, the landscape was noticeably greener than in Australia. There the relentless season had parched the grass to straw. Its smaller neighbor was lush and gentler—at least in the North Island. Natasha loved both countries, but New Zealand, after all, was home.

After a while Ryder said without looking at her, "Thanks for sending the cassette. The program was everything you promised it would be, and the staff are all thrilled."

"We just did our job," she said stiffly. "I told you there was nothing to worry about."

"Yes," he said dryly. "When you were so eager to convince me that your reasons for wanting to film DeWilde's were all in our favor."

She turned on him, her eyes flashing. "We delivered exactly what I promised you—good publicity." The documentary had been bought by both "Inside Story," who planned to show it in the New Year, and an Australian channel.

He spared her a glance, then returned his eyes to the road ahead. "True. And more than I'd bargained on," he added.

When she didn't answer, Ryder said in a reasoned tone, "Believe me, Natasha, I'm not here for Jeffrey's sake."

"You said that you persuaded Jeffrey you could get more out of me—"

"*You* said that. I told you it wasn't that way—"

"Not *exactly*, you said." Her voice held a measure of sarcasm.

Ryder spared her a glance. "I don't give a stuff what you've done or what your motives were. But Jeffrey wants to know where the other pieces of the DeWilde collection are, and you're his strongest lead. I managed to force a promise from him that he'd give me until the New Year before he sends Nick Santos over here. And Nick's good. If you won't tell him what he wants to know, he'll start digging."

So she was caught between a rock and a hard place, Natasha thought. Tell Ryder all she knew, or wait for Nick to arrive....

It wasn't much of a choice. "I was right, then, wasn't I? You're here for Jeffrey and the DeWildes."

Ryder passed a hand through his hair. "I'm here for *you*," he insisted. "Look, it was all I could think of. To get here first and warn you. DeWildes don't ever give up, and since his marriage ended, Jeffrey's become rather... inflexible. It isn't just the jewels, you know...I think he really wants to trace his uncle. Family has always been important to the DeWildes. I imagine you'd understand that," he added, casting her a sideways glance.

That was clever. Natasha lapsed into silence, her mind a jumble of disconnected thoughts. If Ryder was telling the truth regarding his motives, then he cared about her. But the DeWildes were the only real family he had; his livelihood and his ambitions for the future, his life, past and present, were all inextricably tied in with them. Would he lie to her for their sake? Would he try to gain her confidence, only to betray it?

Her heart told her he wasn't like that, but her head reminded her that feelings weren't always the best measure of fact. In any case, promises weren't made to be broken, and other people's confidences weren't hers to give away....

Ryder left her to her thoughts, and she was so immersed in trying to sort them from her emotions that she almost missed the turnoff to Parahiku.

It was a good road but less busy than the motorway. Macrocarpa trees leaned from the paddocks over the road, creating patches of shadow. A flock of sheep grazing close to a fence suddenly took fright, galloping off across the shorn grass.

"Is there someplace we can talk?" Ryder asked. "Have a cup of coffee or a drink?"

"There's a pub, but it's Christmas Eve. The place will be crowded."

He looked at her briefly, questioning, and she said, "They have a lounge bar. We could have a drink there."

THE HOTEL CAR PARK was almost full, but although a hubbub of talk and laughter emanated from the overcrowded public bar, they found a window corner in the less busy lounge bar, which looked out at a pond with a couple of ducks floating serenely on murky green water.

Ryder ordered a beer, which came frosted and foaming, and Natasha opted for a long, cool gin and lime with soda and lots of ice.

She took a couple of sips, and then sat stirring the drink absently with a plastic straw.

Ryder drank half of his beer before he said quietly, "I didn't tell Nick—or Jeffrey—everything."

"What do you mean?"

"Nick asked me if you'd mentioned your mother's maiden name, and I said no. Later I remembered you talking about your grandfather. Sometime after that I remembered his name. Derrick Freeman."

"Well, it didn't make any difference in the end, did it," Natasha said. "Nick didn't need it."

Ryder hesitated. "He might, in order to piece together the whole story. But I warn you, he knows your grandmother's name, and it won't take him long to figure it all out."

Natasha moved uneasily on her chair. "What whole story?" she demanded. "Figure what out?"

Ryder clutched his glass and drew a small, wet circle with it on the table. "Did your grandfather make a deathbed confession, ask you to return the stolen jewelry? What happened to the rest?"

Natasha's heart lurched. "No, he didn't! And I've no idea what happened to the rest of it. We only had . . ."

"You only had the bracelet?" he said, finishing her sentence for her. "He must have got rid of the rest earlier."

Despite the warm day, her face felt cold and pale. "Did you make this up all by yourself?"

"Nearly fifty years ago," Ryder began with deliberation, "Dirk DeWilde absconded from the New York store with part of the family jewelry collection."

"So?" Natasha shrugged.

Watching her carefully, Ryder continued, "He made his way to New Zealand eventually and married your grandmother."

"My grandfather was Derrick Freeman!"

"He changed his name."

Natasha gaped at him. Her mind whirled in all directions. "That's crazy!"

"Is it? Dirk...Derrick. They're very close. And what better name than Freeman for a man starting a new life?" He paused, then asked incredulously, "You didn't know?"

"It's not true. It can't be!" But even to herself she sounded unconvincing. It made sense of so many things.

"Did you ever see his birth certificate?"

Dumbly, Natasha shook her head.

"You said he spoke fluent French. Dirk would have spent his early years in France, before going to New York. He enlisted from there during the Second World War. You said you thought your grandfather served in the American armed forces but there was no record of him. It all fits."

Did he remember everything she'd ever said to him? Natasha looked down, moistening her lips. She felt almost dizzy, her mind whirling. Was it possible that he was right, that her grandfather had been Dirk DeWilde? "And what," she asked him, "does Jeffrey think of your...theory?"

"I haven't told him."

"You wanted to check it out before you presented him with the proof?"

Ryder shook his head. "I'll swear on a stack of Bibles never to breathe a word to him or anyone else, if you want me to."

She looked at him suspiciously. "Why should you do that?"

"Because maybe then you'll believe that I love you, and admit you love me—"

Natasha flung her head back, her cheeks flushing. "You're taking a lot for granted!"

He reached for her hand. "I'm not stupid. Well...I have been monumentally so sometimes, like the night you came to me and tried to explain and apologize. I was still furious and confused and smarting—not only because of you, but at discovering that Jeffrey had been keeping me in the dark, too. But that's no excuse. The way I treated you, by rights you should have loathed me forever."

"How do you know I don't?"

"I know because, despite that, despite...everything, when I kissed you the last time, in your flat, you couldn't help kissing me back. And because you cried. Why should you cry if you didn't give a damn about me?"

She couldn't answer that. She pulled her hand away from him, afraid that his touch would crumble her frail defenses, muddle her brain still further.

He leaned forward, saying quietly with intensity, "I'll fight Nick Santos and Jeffrey and the entire DeWilde establishment to the death for you, but I can't promise it will make much difference in the long run. Jeffrey's very determined . . . and maybe he has a right to know what happened to his uncle. Maybe," he added, "you have a right to know who your grandfather really was."

She wanted to repudiate the idea, but her job had trained her to keep an open mind, to weigh evidence and make logical conclusions. "If . . . if Dirk took the jewels," she said slowly, "was it really theft? I mean, he was a member of the family. Wouldn't he have been entitled to a share?"

"Morally, maybe. The note he left apparently didn't mention the jewels, but it did say something about renouncing any future claims to the DeWilde fortune."

"So he never intended to go back?"

"It seems not."

"Why would he want to disappear?" Fearful of the answer, she asked, "Was there . . . had there been some problems with the books at the New York store or something?"

"Jeffrey didn't suggest anything like that. But there was some sort of scandal when he left, involving another man's wife."

Natasha's eyes widened. "Who was she?"

"They don't know. Jeffrey's father confided the story to Jeffrey before he died, but as for the lady's name, his lips were sealed. A gentleman of the old school, Charles was."

"Jeffrey told you all this?"

"Eventually," Ryder said grimly. "The night of the fashion show I told him I'd resign if he didn't let me in on what the hell he and Nick were after. I got most of the story then."

"Give up your store? Leave DeWilde's? You can't have meant it!"

"Every last word. A while later I tried to find out what Nick was up to—apart from hunting down every jewelry dealer in Australia—and he said he reported to Jeffrey, not me. I burned up the telephone wires to England, threatened I'd go public with an apology for exhibiting imitation DeWilde jewels if Jeffrey didn't instruct Nick right then that he was to tell me every damn thing he knew. He knew I meant it, too. Among other things, that would have thrown doubt on the authenticity of the entire collection."

Startled, she looked up at him. "Why did you do that?"

"Because I'd finally figured out that you lied to me that night you sent me away. At the time I believed you when you said you'd fallen out of love with me—heaven knows I deserved it. But I kept remembering the way you kissed me, and there was only one explanation for it. For some reason you still loved me. Only you didn't dare get too close to me because of this deep, dark secret over the bracelet. So I had to discover what that was."

Natasha looked at him with misgiving, almost suspicion.

Ryder leaned forward. "There's no point anymore in you keeping me at arm's length. I'm not interested in where the bracelet came from or where the blasted jewels have been all these years, but I had to find out so I could tell you that I know it all, that you've nothing more to hide from me. It was the only way I could free you to love me."

CHAPTER FIFTEEN

NATASHA THOUGHT HER VERY breath had stopped. When it started again, she felt light-headed. Was she free to love Ryder? Could it be possible after all?

"I won't push you for an answer," he said. "I know you don't quite dare to trust me." His smile was a little crooked. "Well, I guess it's fair for the boot to be on the other foot. I can't *prove* I'm not here as Jeffrey's spy. I can only ask you to take my word for it."

A group of people entered the bar, all laughing and talking at once. Ryder glanced over at them impatiently as they pulled out chairs and sat around the next table. "Do you want the rest of that drink?"

Still speechless, Natasha shook her head.

"Let's go," he said. "I'll take you home."

WHEN RYDER PARKED THE CAR in the driveway of her old home and she got out, the front door of the sprawling weatherboard house opened and her mother hurried toward her. "It's so good to see you!"

Natasha hugged her. "It's great to be here. You look good, too." There were signs of recent strain about her mother's eyes and mouth, and perhaps a few extra gray strands in the short brown hair that curled gently around her face.

A white-haired woman appeared in the doorway. "Gran!" Natasha hurried to her grandmother and kissed her lined cheek. "How are you? You look heaps better!"

Sara Freeman beamed at her and patted her arm. "I'm fine, dear," she said, but her voice was thin. "Now that you're here, we're going to have a wonderful Christmas. And who's this young man?"

Natasha introduced Ryder. "He gave me a lift."

"Thank you for bringing our darling home!" Sara gave him her hand and he took it carefully in his. "You must stay for a cup of tea or some sherry."

"Thank you, I'd like that." He had Natasha's bag in his hand and made not the slightest move to relinquish it to her outstretched hand. "Just show me where to put it."

Her room was at the end of the wide passageway; Ryder followed her and placed her suitcase gently on the white cotton bedspread that covered the brass bed.

He ran an admiring finger over the golden patina of the old kauri dressing table. "Very nice."

"Gran inherited beautiful antique furniture from her family. The Mulvaneys were pioneers, one of the first European families in the district. Town founders and all that."

He turned away, pausing by the shelves that held books from her schooldays. *"Huckleberry Finn,"* he said, reaching out to touch the illustrated version that her grandfather had bought for her one day when they'd been waiting for Sara on a shopping expedition in Auckland. "I used to own a copy of that when I was a kid," Ryder said. "Read it over and over. I wonder what happened to it?"

"Grandpa gave me that." Natasha picked up a hairbrush from the dressing table and passed it quickly through her hair. "It was one of his favorite books." She put down the brush and turned to him, bundling her hair into a clasp. Going to her suitcase, she unlocked it and rummaged for two parcels wrapped in Christmas paper, her presents for Lucille and Sara to be placed under the tree. Ryder waited for her in the doorway.

When they walked into the big living room with its comfortable old-fashioned furniture and the modest but real pine Christmas tree standing in the bay window, her mother said, "We're having sherry." Lucille's smile conveyed both amusement and resignation to her daughter, with a hint of apology. Sara considered sherry a suitable drink for afternoon, but it was only conferred on special guests.

Ryder had probably never drunk sherry in all his life, Natasha supposed, and he'd hardly be aware that it was a privilege to be offered it. But he accepted a glass with good grace and seemed quite contented, smiling and talking to her grandmother.

Natasha tried to avoid looking at him, because every time he caught her eye she felt a warm, melting sensation somewhere inside that threatened to cut off her breathing. She blamed the sherry.

Ryder glanced about the room and got up to take a closer look at a photograph on the mantelpiece. "Is this your husband?" he asked Sara.

"In his mayoral robes," Sara confirmed.

"You didn't tell me that your grandfather had been mayor," Ryder said to Natasha. "May I?" he queried Sara, and picked up the photo to examine it closely.

"He was mayor for ten years," Sara said proudly. "He was a fine man, very highly respected in this town. Natasha, fetch my photo album, dear—the red one—and show Ryder..."

Natasha went to the dining room sideboard and pulled out the big, leather-covered album.

Sara and Ryder were both on the sofa when she got back. "Sit over there, dear," Sara instructed her, pointing to Ryder's other side.

The first pages of the album held old, decal-edged photographs of Sara as a solemn, overdressed child among other Mulvaney children, and of the imposing two-story house they had lived in. "My brother sold it when he inherited the place." Sara snorted genteelly. "His wife wanted a modern house in Auckland. Our home was converted to a boarding house. But it's in private ownership now. They call it a historic home."

She turned to a picture where she appeared as a pretty young woman, dressed in white and holding a posy.

"That was taken for my debutante party," she said. "Even though it was wartime, my mother insisted I should be presented to the bishop. It was a wonderful evening. We danced all night."

Next came a picture of her wearing a rather severe wartime suit and a pillbox hat, smiling on the arm of a smooth-faced young man in American army uniform.

"Is this your husband?" Ryder asked.

"No, that's the man I would have married, only he was killed in battle in the Pacific. My parents never really approved of Americans, though of course they were very sorry for me when the telegram came. I met Derrick quite a long time afterward." She turned a couple more pages. "That's our wedding picture."

Natasha looked down at the familiar photo. Her grandmother had worn an empire line dress and a small hat without a veil. Her grandfather was upright and handsome with his thick black mustache, but looked rather solemn.

"And did your parents approve of him?" Ryder asked.

"Oh dear, no! It was many years before they acknowledged that Derrick was good enough to marry a Mulvaney. He never said much about his background, but I'm sure he came of good family. You can always tell."

Natasha hid a smile. The snobbery Sara had inherited from her ultraconservative family had never worn off. Derrick the adventurer must have swept the staid Sara right off her feet. She'd spent the rest of their lives trying to tame him. Natasha suspected it was his wife's insistent prodding that had led her grandfather into his modest political career. Sara had certainly played a part in the menswear business he had operated in the town. She had been determined that her family and community should be made to recognize her husband's worth.

"And I've kept all the press cuttings of his public life. Although there aren't many, really. He didn't especially like having his picture taken."

She turned the remaining pages, pausing now and then to expand on a particular item, and then Ryder handed the book back to Natasha, saying, "Thank you, Mrs. Freeman. That was very interesting."

"Would you like to see some pictures of Natasha?" Sara asked.

"No, Gran!" Natasha protested.

Ryder grinned at her. "Why not? I'd love to."

Natasha fetched another album, and then escaped to the kitchen, where her mother was preparing a roast chicken that they would eat cold on Christmas Day.

"Your grandmother's taken a fancy to Ryder," Lucille said, a smiling question in her eyes.

"He met me at the airport. I wasn't expecting him."

Lucille's brows rose. "A surprise? Not an unwelcome one, I take it, or you wouldn't have allowed him to bring you home."

"Well . . . we had things to talk about. Is there anything you want me to do?"

"Peel some potatoes if you like, for tonight. Better do some extra . . . I have a feeling your grandmother is going to invite Ryder to stay for dinner."

Sara did more than that. Over dinner she pressed Ryder about his plans for the night and, discovering he had no hotel booked, decreed, "At Christmas? You'll have terrible trouble! You must stay here! Lucille, he can have the boys' old room."

Ryder looked at Natasha, and she gave a tiny shrug. It was Sara's house; she could invite whomever she liked. Lucille looked at her questioningly, too, before saying, "Of course. Natasha, can you make up a bed?"

At midnight they all went to church. Ryder drove them, carefully ensconcing Sara in the front seat. He stood next to Natasha during the service, and as they sang carols, she was aware of his strong baritone mingling with her clear though unexceptional soprano.

Before they left the church she offered up a heartfelt, wordless prayer that held all her longing and confusion, despair and hope.

Back home, Sara and Lucille went straight to bed. "If you'd like a hot drink," Lucille said to Ryder, "I'm sure Natasha won't mind making it."

"It's been a long day," Ryder said. "I expect Natasha's tired." Natasha didn't argue. She had a lot to think about, and her head was buzzing with all that had happened today, not least Ryder's extraordinary theory about her grandfather.

She climbed into bed wearing a cool, jade green satin nightshirt, the house fallen silent around her. With her hand on the switch of the bedside lamp, she hesitated. As she looked around the room, her eyes lit on the bookcase. Quietly she left the bed, padded over to the shelves and took out *Huckleberry Finn*.

At the back of her wardrobe she found some Christmas paper and labels left over from last year, and a roll of sticky tape, and quickly wrapped the book.

She opened her door and crept down the passageway to the living room. She had slipped into the room before she realized that the light filtering under the door hadn't been only from the decorative bulbs on the tree. Ryder had switched on the lamp behind her grandfather's chair, and he looked up almost guiltily from studying the photograph album he had open on his lap.

"What are you doing?" she whispered, and then hastily shut the door behind her, advancing into the room. "What are you doing?" she asked again. "I thought you'd gone to bed."

For a moment his eyes seemed to glaze over as they took in the nightshirt falling softly over her breasts and stopping well short of her knees. He swallowed, then returned his gaze quickly to her face before standing up. "Come and look at this," he said, holding the open album toward her.

Slowly she walked over to him and stood peering at a photograph that she'd seen dozens of times. Her grandfather was smiling into the camera, his mustache graying but still dapper on his upper lip. He must have been in his fifties when it was taken.

"Doesn't he remind you of someone?"

The photograph was so familiar, she didn't know what to look for. She shook her head.

"Try to imagine him without the mustache."

Natasha frowned. Her grandfather had always had a mustache. "I don't—" Something teased at the edge of her consciousness. Someone smiling at her and evoking an odd feeling of familiarity. She leaned closer. *"Jeffrey?"*

"You do see it—and you've only met one member of the family. But I know several of them, and I've seen their old photographs. I'm right, Natasha. Your grandfather was a DeWilde!" He sounded elated.

Natasha swallowed. "Supposing you are right," she said. "He deliberately cut himself off from the DeWildes, and personally I don't blame him. I can't say the idea of being related to Jeffrey exactly thrills me."

Ryder smothered a startled laugh. "Jeffrey's not some Mafia godfather."

"Well, he sure comes close!"

"Be reasonable—"

"Tell *him* that!"

"You can't blame him for wanting to know what happened to his uncle, not to mention some very valuable jewelry."

"I can blame him for his methods," Natasha argued. "That night in Mr. Fynne's office I really thought he was going to have Nick beat me up to make me talk."

Ryder blinked, closing the album with a snap. "You're not *serious?* You must have known I'd never have let any harm come to you, even if Jeffrey had any such intention!"

"You looked likely to kill me yourself—grabbing me, calling me names—"

Ryder winced and dropped the album onto the chair. "You were frightened?"

Natasha gaped. "What do you *think,* with all you men standing over me, deliberately intimidating me? Wasn't that the whole idea? To scare me into talking?"

"But no one in that room would have really hurt you. Not even Santos."

"I wasn't to know that, was I?"

He said slowly, visibly upset, "I suppose not. I had no idea.... You didn't seem scared, just fighting mad."

"That, too. I know you think the sun rises and sets on the DeWildes, but you said yourself that Jeffrey's ruthless. He's not above threats and coercion."

Ryder gave a reluctant nod, as though just understanding something. "Is that why you're so determined to protect your grandmother from him?"

Suddenly wary, Natasha stepped back from him, clutching the wrapped book against her chest. "My grandmother?"

Ryder looked momentarily impatient. "It's perfectly obvious. When your grandfather died, your grandmother decided it was time to return the bracelet to the DeWildes. *She* must have known who he was, even if you didn't."

Natasha shook her head. "You're wrong! She had no . . . she had nothing to do with it."

Ryder's face went taut. "I thought when you agreed to my staying that you'd decided to trust me."

"It's Gran's house. She didn't ask my opinion."

"You know I would have gone if you'd wanted me to."

Instead she'd signaled her acquiescence with a shrug, with acceptance in her eyes. Because her heart had said, *Trust him.*

"I do trust you," she said slowly, her heart in her eyes. "I want to."

Ryder nodded, his own eyes kindling into lambent fire as he looked at her. "Then why are you holding that—" he indicated the parcel in her hands "—like a shield against me?"

She'd forgotten about it. Glancing down, she said, "It's a present. I was going to put it under the tree for you."

Ryder smiled with surprise. "You didn't know I would be here for Christmas."

"No, but . . . I hope you'll like it." She held it out to him and he took it from her, looking at the inscription on the label.

Merry Christmas, Ryder, was all it said, *from Natasha.*

"And my love," she said softly, with deliberation.

His head jerked up, his eyes blazing now. Hoarsely he demanded, "Say that again."

This was bridge burning, she knew. But she wouldn't back down now. "I said I love you. Open your present," she added shakily, but the words were hardly out before his hand tangled in the hair that tumbled round her shoulders, curved warm and hard about her nape and dragged her to him, his mouth finding hers in a long, sweet, starving kiss.

When they surfaced for air, he said thickly, "I was afraid I'd never hear you say it." His eyes, darkened with passion, swept her face, then he wrapped his arms about her and pulled her close. "God, I love you!"

She turned her lips to his cheek and kissed it, whispering, "You haven't opened your parcel."

He laughed and picked her up in his arms, going to the sofa, where he sat with her on his knee and tore open the wrapping. "Thank you," he said. "This one I'll keep forever."

"There's an inscription inside," she said. "You...you wouldn't know Dirk DeWilde's handwriting?"

Ryder shook his head, opening the cover to read the loving message her grandfather had inscribed for her. "Jeffrey might."

"I suppose so," she said shortly.

He smiled and kissed her again, a light kiss that became something quite different, until the book thudded to the carpet and they were both lying full-length on the wide, old-fashioned sofa. Natasha looped her arms about his neck, and Ryder's hand rested on the naked curve of her hip where the satin nightshirt had ridden up to reveal a pair of matching bikini briefs trimmed with lace.

He lifted his head and his gaze swept over her, lingering, his hand stroking her thigh. "The first time I saw you, I remember wondering what your legs were like." His hand made another foray up her thigh and then slipped across the nightshirt to the buttons that closed the garment across her breasts. Slowly he undid them, one by one, watching the rise and fall of her rapid breathing, while her eyes, heavy with desire, remained on his face.

"I've missed you," he said.

"I missed you, too." Her eyes closed as he bent forward and his lips settled between her breasts.

He touched her with shaking hands, his fingers drifting across her skin like cool fire, until her breasts peaked into aching desire, and she had to bite her lip to stop herself from crying out. As he undid the last button and pushed aside the satin, she heard a door open along the passageway, and another close. Her grandmother visiting the bathroom. Stiffening in his arms, she managed to whisper, "Ryder?"

"Yes?" His eyes met hers, and she almost forgot what she was going to say at the look of love and wanting in them.

"Gran..." she said quickly. "We're in her house, and I wouldn't be comfortable doing something she wouldn't approve of."

Ryder looked down at her and groaned, "Oh, hell!"

The look in his eyes was like pain, but he nodded jerkily and sat up, pulling her upright with him. He kept his arms wrapped about her, his face against her hair as he fumbled with her nightshirt, clumsily refastening the buttons.

Natasha heard her grandmother return to her room, but neither of them moved. After a while Ryder said, "I have a present for you, too. I was afraid to give it to you."

"Afraid?" Natasha repeated, puzzled.

He released her to dig into his pocket, his hand emerging with a small leather box wrapped in silver paper with *DeWilde's* printed on it in flowing script. "I didn't dare put it under the tree, in case you threw it back at me."

She undid the wrapping, and he took the box from her and removed the tiny circlet with its gleaming stone. "Jeffrey said you should wear opals," he told her, "but they're for another time. This...is forever. Like my love." He slipped the diamond solitaire onto her finger. "If you don't like it, I'll buy you something else."

"Of course I like it!" She would have loved it if it had been a bit of colored glass. Even the fit was perfect. "It's beautiful."

"It doesn't hold a candle to you."

Natasha laughed. "That's nonsense, but it's a lovely thing to say."

"I have lots of lovely things to say to you." He murmured some of them into her ear, and she laughed again, then flushed all over, and finally turned to hush him, only to have him capture her lips in a warm, languorous, persuasive kiss.

Natasha kissed him back, until he withdrew with a sigh. "I want to marry you tomorrow," he whispered.

She laughed softly. "No one gets married on Christmas Day. Anyway, we need a license."

"Damn." He lifted his head. "And I suppose your grandmother will insist on your having a proper wedding, too."

"Mmm-hmm." She smiled, resting her cheek against his shoulder. Suddenly she sat away from him. "Will you want the DeWildes there?"

"Try and keep them away. Of course, we could take a leaf from Gabe's book and elope. It wouldn't make us popular with the family, though. Or yours, I imagine."

"If you want them," Natasha said, trying to overcome her reluctance, "then I guess I can stand it."

"That's very generous of you. I want you to meet Gabe and the rest of them."

"I know they mean a lot to you. They're the perfect family you never had, aren't they?"

"I suppose that's true," he said slowly. "Although recently..."

"Recently you've discovered their feet of clay. The perfect family split in half, and... you didn't like the idea of Jeffrey being interested in Violetta. It unsettled you."

He looked down at her in surprise and she thought he was about to deny it. "I guess it did," he acknowledged. "I'm having as much trouble accepting the breakup as Gabe and the rest of his family. And it really isn't any of my business. But if you knew Grace—"

"Nobody's perfect, Ryder."

Ryder regarded her thoughtfully. "Yes, I know. You're right. I've idealized the DeWildes ever since I met them. But they're only human, after all."

"Like your real parents."

He looked defensive at that, and she touched his lips with her finger. "You've never forgiven them, have you? Do you really think they don't care?"

Frowning over her shoulder, he said, "I don't know. My father seems completely wrapped up in his new family. My mother . . . sometimes when I was younger, I thought she wanted to talk, try to explain. But I choked her off. I guess I was scared of my own feelings. As a teenager I was mortally afraid of bursting into tears. And when I wasn't trying not to cry, I was angry."

"Why don't you phone her tomorrow?" Natasha suggested diffidently. "It's Christmas."

"Maybe I will." He smiled at her, his hand stroking her hair. "Maybe. Natasha?"

"Mmm?"

"If I've been a bit shortsighted about the DeWildes and their virtues, don't you think you're possibly biased in the other direction? Not without some reason, I know," he added, as she looked about to argue. "But I've known Jeffrey for a long time. He would never have charged you with something he knew wasn't true. He was bluffing. Believe me, he might be hard sometimes, but he's a very principled man. He and your grandmother would probably understand each other perfectly."

"You promised—"

Ryder put his fingers gently over her mouth. "I'll keep your family's secret to the grave, if necessary. But . . . if her husband was Jeffrey's uncle, don't you realize you have nothing to worry about? The DeWildes certainly won't be telling people about the skeletons in their closet."

Of course, Natasha thought dazedly. He was right. If her grandfather had been Dirk DeWilde, and he had stolen the jewels from his family, they weren't going to be looking for retribution—or publicity. That would be the last thing Jeffrey wanted. She said slowly, "The DeWildes don't want anyone to know who took the missing jewels any more than . . ."

"Than you do? Or your grandmother? No, darling, of course they don't."

CHAPTER SIXTEEN

NATASHA AND RYDER FLEW back to Sydney together a few days after the new year began. When Natasha queried how Ryder could stay away from the store so long, he'd told her his assistant manager was competent, and he'd kept in touch by phone. He was not going to be the kind of husband who neglected his wife for his work, and he might as well start practicing now. So for ten days they'd been, as Ryder said somewhat ruefully, "courting" under Sara's benign but vigilant eye, while Lucille looked on with sympathetic amusement.

There had been one memorable day when they'd driven to a beach and found a secluded hollow sheltered by sword-leaved flax bushes and overhanging manuka, overlooking the sea. For a few precious hours they'd been alone with the blue sky, the hush and shush of the waves on the beach below, and each other. And one night after they'd been out to dinner, Ryder had driven down a lonely road and found a patch of bush, where he'd spread a rug under a tree and taken Natasha into his arms, with no witness but a nearby morepork invisibly calling its name to the stars.

RYDER HAD ARRANGED for a company car with a driver to pick them both up from the airport. "We'll take Miss Pallas home first," he told the man, helping to put their bags into the luggage compartment.

"Uh...Mr. Blake," the man said, "Mr. DeWilde is waiting to see you."

"*Jeffrey* DeWilde? He's back in Sydney?"

"Arrived this morning. Your secretary said to tell you. He's at the store now."

Natasha said, "I'll find my own way home—"

"No. Why don't you come with me?" Ryder asked.

Natasha swallowed, hesitating. "Yes, all right." She'd have to meet Jeffrey face-to-face again sometime.

"MR. DEWILDE SAID HE'D BE in the bridal department," Ryder's secretary told him. "Shall I ring down and get them to tell him you've arrived?"

"No," Ryder said. "We'll meet him there."

Natasha looked at him rather anxiously as they rode the elevator down to the second floor, Violetta's domain. Was she the reason Jeffrey had unexpectedly returned?

The door slid open and Ryder put his hand on her waist, a light touch that she was nevertheless acutely conscious of as he guided her through the frozen bridal tableaux toward Violetta and Jeffrey, who were at the far end of the department, along with one of Violetta's assistants. The two women were putting the finishing touches to a new display while Jeffrey watched appreciatively.

He turned as Ryder and Natasha approached, and Natasha felt Ryder's arm tighten about her.

"Jeffrey," Ryder said. "We didn't expect you back so soon." His eyes moved to Violetta and he gave her a warm, friendly smile.

"Unfinished business," Jeffrey said briefly. "Hello, Natasha." His eyes moved back to Ryder. "You have something to tell me?" he asked with veiled curiosity.

"*I* have something to tell you, Mr. DeWilde," Natasha said. "Ryder wasn't going to, but...I know how much your family means to him." She felt Ryder's hand move to her shoulder, gripping it, and she looked around them, seeking somewhere private.

"My office is free," Violetta said, quickly understanding her dilemma. "Please use it if you want to." Concealing her own curiosity, she turned back to helping her assistant.

"Shall we?" Jeffrey motioned Ryder and Natasha to accompany him.

The workroom was in its usual state of orderly shambles, and in the center a mannequin stood splendidly gowned in lace and satin and shrouded in a long veil.

Ryder pushed open the door of Violetta's office, allowing Natasha to precede him.

Moving away from his protective arm, she turned to face Jeffrey.

"I want to tell you why I had to swap the bracelets," she said baldly, and took a deep breath. "You see, last year my grandfather died, and my grandmother had a mild stroke with the shock. While she was in hospital, my mother and I sorted through Grandpa's things, to save her the stress of having to do it herself. And..."

"You found the bracelet," Jeffrey guessed.

"We didn't know where it had come from. When we mentioned it to Gran, she said Grandpa used to call it their 'insurance,' and told her if anything happened to him and she needed money, she was to sell it. But then she got very agitated and said she knew it was stolen. After she got home she kept fretting about it, insisting that Grandpa had told her he'd 'taken' it."

"Did he say where from?"

"He never told her that. I didn't really believe the gems could be real, but I said I'd get the bracelet valued. That upset Gran even more—dangerously so. She was afraid it would be traced, and if the story got out, Grandpa's reputation would be ruined."

"But you did find out where it came from," Jeffrey said.

"She agreed finally that I could get the appraisal done in Australia, by someone I could trust not to talk about it."

"You know some interesting people," Jeffrey commented dryly.

"You meet them in my job," Natasha said briefly. "I was stunned when I found out how much it was worth. The jeweler was pretty surprised, too. He looked through a lot of old reference books and told me where he thought it had come from, and a computer check confirmed it. I told Gran I'd write to the DeWildes and explain, but she nearly had another stroke at the idea. I mean, literally. We had to call the doctor to come. She was afraid the press would have a field day with the story if they found out, and Grandpa wasn't here any more to defend himself or explain. She was even convinced the DeWildes might send her to jail."

Jeffrey raised his brows. "How old is your grandmother? What did you imagine we might charge her with?"

"Seventy-eight. And she thought she might be charged with receiving stolen goods." Natasha stared at Jeffrey accusingly. "I wouldn't say her fears were entirely groundless."

"Hmm." Jeffrey had the grace to allow a hint of embarrassment to flicker across his face. "Why didn't you just send me the bracelet anonymously?"

"I intended to. Not by post, of course. At first I hoped that I might be able to return it to the family through the store, especially if I got access to restricted areas." She cast Ryder a look of apology. "Maybe secretly deposit it in the jewelry department or something. Or even put it into the display dome with the Boucheron bracelet when no one was about. But the security seemed watertight, and I could hardly just leave anything that valuable on someone's desk. Then Lee told me the collection was coming to the store, and I thought there had to be some way I could slip it in with the rest."

"You surely didn't imagine we wouldn't notice?"

"No, of course not. What mattered was that you couldn't figure out where it had come from. When I learned *you* were to be in Sydney with the collection, I thought I'd hire a security firm to deliver it to you personally. But then I found out . . ."

"Found out what?" Jeffrey asked as she paused in her recital.

"That there were two bracelets. And that you had a private investigator with you. A security firm would be traceable, and he might ferret out who'd asked them to deliver it. Until then I'd assumed the bracelet had just disappeared. It had never occurred to me that there was a duplicate. When I discovered that, I figured that if the DeWildes didn't know the one they had wasn't the original, and I simply replaced it with the real one, they'd never be any the wiser. So no one would come looking, and Gran would have nothing to worry about."

"You thought we didn't know?" Jeffrey queried in surprise.

"I had no way of finding that out, did I? All I wanted was to get the bracelet back where it belonged and set my grandmother's mind at rest. Even if you did know, it might have been ages before the swap was discovered, and the trail would be cold. And why should you bother when you had the real one back again?"

"I'd like to meet your grandmother."

Natasha's eyes widened in alarm. "You keep away from her! She gave me permission to tell you about this because I assured her that the DeWildes don't want publicity any more than she does. And I *promised* no one would harass her."

"Natasha is convinced that you're a cross between Al Capone and Attila the Hun," Ryder observed.

Jeffrey looked taken aback. "I was only thinking of asking the lady a few questions."

"Well, you can think again!" Natasha said curtly. "We can't help you recover the other pieces Ryder tells me are missing. My grandfather had one bracelet. That's all she ever knew about.''

"You're certain of that?" Jeffrey asked.

"Totally."

"And how do you think he'd come by it?"

Natasha looked at Ryder, but he remained silent. "Ryder believes my grandfather was Dirk DeWilde," she announced.

"Does he?" Jeffrey's eyes swiveled to Ryder.

"He called himself Derrick Freeman," Ryder said, "but he looked like a DeWilde. I'm sure he was your uncle. Without his mustache, he might almost have been you."

Turning back to Natasha, Jeffrey asked, "How long ago did he die?"

"Last year," she told him, her voice lowered and her eyes stinging with tears.

"As recently as that? I'm sorry." Jeffrey's regret seemed genuine. "I would have liked to have met him again."

"You knew him?" It hadn't really occurred to her before. Somehow that made a difference. Ryder was right— Jeffrey did have a right to know what had happened to his uncle. And if he had been her grandfather...

"Childhood recollections," Jeffrey was saying. "I was very young, but he was a memorable visitor, very dashing in his uniform, and even when he returned to civilian life, Uncle Dirk always seemed rather larger than life. He used to bring wonderful presents and luxury foods from America when we still had rationing in England, and he'd tell me stories." A thought seemed to strike him. "If he was your grandfather, then you," he said slowly, "are my...first cousin once removed, I think?"

Natasha stiffened. "Nothing's proven."

"But it seems likely. As a matter of fact, Nick has come up with a very similar theory. The name Freeman wasn't lost on him, and your grandmother, it seems, still goes by her husband's initials?"

"Yes." After his death, Sara, who had taken pride in being Mrs. Derrick Freeman, had insisted on observing the outdated custom of her generation that a widow retained her husband's name and initials as a form of address. "It's all I have left of Derrick," she'd said. Any bills inscribed to "Mrs. S. Freeman" were promptly returned unopened to the senders.

"Nick traced my uncle's arrival in Australia under that name and is trying to discover how long he remained here and what he did before settling in New Zealand. Your grandmother wasn't with him then."

"Definitely not," Natasha confirmed. "So there's no point in Nick interviewing her."

"You know," Jeffrey said, his eyes suddenly amused, "you remind me of my Aunt Marie-Claire! There's a definite resemblance."

Ryder grinned. "Like it or not, darling, you're a De-Wilde descendant."

"I'm sorry if you don't like it," Jeffrey said quite diffidently. He looked quizzically at Ryder. "Darling?" he repeated, his glance going back to Natasha.

"Natasha is going to marry me," Ryder explained.

Jeffrey turned his interested gaze to Natasha, and she was startled to see the warmth in his eyes. "As you're obviously aware, Ryder is very special to us," he said, "to the family. I'm glad his children will have DeWilde blood."

She didn't share his sentiments, but she bit her tongue and said nothing.

His eyes almost fierce, Jeffrey added, "I hope you truly love him."

"I do." She returned the penetrating gaze unflinchingly. This was weird, she thought. She could imagine her grandfather acting exactly the same if he'd been around to question Ryder's intentions toward her.

Ryder's arms slid about her, pulling her back against him as he dropped a kiss on her cheek. "Will you say that again for me, soon?"

"Have you set a date?" Jeffrey asked.

"Not yet. Natasha's mother and grandmother want her to have a 'proper' wedding," Ryder said ruefully.

"Naturally," Jeffrey agreed. "And we'll insist on it."

"We?" Ryder questioned warily.

"The family. Gabe and Lianne have already cheated us out of one wedding." He turned to Natasha. "You must talk to Violetta about your gown."

"I can't afford a DeWilde gown."

"Don't worry about that. We'll take care of it."

"But—"

"My dear girl, this will be a DeWilde occasion. Apart from your own apparent . . . connection, Ryder is manager of a store that specializes in weddings. It will be a great opportunity to enhance our image in Australia."

Natasha snorted. "The hell with your image, Mr. De-Wilde. It's *my* wedding—ours," she amended, and turned to the man at her side, appealing to him. *"Ryder—"*

"Natasha will have exactly what she wants, Jeffrey." Ryder held the other man's eyes. "Whatever that is."

Jeffrey drew himself up, then suddenly relaxed. "Of course. Forgive me, Natasha." He smiled, and she felt a tiny ache inside, because she knew now why his smile had always tugged at her heart, why it had seemed familiar. Ruefully, he added, "I owe you other apologies, too."

"For threatening to send me to jail on a trumped-up charge?" Indignation colored her cheeks and flashed in her eyes.

"I admit that was going too far."

Ryder's hand caressed her shoulder. "She thought she was going to get beaten up."

Jeffrey looked shocked, almost swaying back on his heels. *"Beaten up?"*

"What did you expect me to think?" she challenged him. "With the four of you standing about looking menacing and making threats?"

"I ... I hadn't looked at it from your point of view," he admitted. Surprisingly, she saw a slight flush on his cheekbones. "I'm *very* sorry. If you were frightened, you hid it well—and gave as good as you got. You hit back hard," he recalled, grimly rueful.

"In true DeWilde fashion," Ryder said. "A chip off the old block, I'd say."

Recalling some of the speculations she'd flung at Jeffrey in the heat of the moment, particularly about the sensitive subject of his marriage, Natasha admitted, "I said some things that maybe I shouldn't have. I pictured you using the same tactics on my grandmother, and—"

"I don't go around scaring old ladies," Jeffrey protested. "Maybe we all got a bit carried away that night. I'm afraid finding the jewels and bringing them home has become something of an obsession. It takes my mind off ... certain other things." He cleared his throat as if he'd embarrassed himself. "Believe me, I'm not a thug—nor do I hire them. You seem to have forgiven Ryder for his part in that evening." He looked at her rather quizzically. "Can you find it in your heart to extend it to me?"

He held out his hands, and she hesitantly put hers into them. "I suppose so. Yes." For Ryder's sake, if not for Jeffrey's.

"Welcome to the family," he said, and bent to kiss her cheek. Stepping back, he regarded her with interest. "You know, I think there is a likeness."

"If I'm a member of the family," Natasha said, "will you take my word as a DeWilde that my grandmother knows nothing about the other jewels—and keep Nick away from her?"

He actually laughed aloud, then glanced at Ryder. "I have no more doubts! All right. In any case, Nick's talking of returning to New York to track down the Mrs. Freeman who seemingly arrived in Australia with Dirk.''

"He had a wife here?" Natasha's eyes widened.

"They were probably not legally married."

"Ryder said he was involved with someone else's wife."

"In New York, yes. It looks as though they ran away together. We seem to have solved the mystery of where Uncle Dirk ended his life. But there's a piece of the puzzle we haven't found yet. Nick hopes to find out who the woman was, and pick up the trail from there. There are other possible leads, too. If Dirk didn't have all the missing jewels, perhaps he should follow some of them up."

"I hope you find them . . . Jeffrey," Natasha said sincerely.

He smiled at her again. "Thank you. Now, I'll go and finish my talk with Violetta and leave you two alone to plan your wedding. May I spread the good news?"

"Sure," Ryder said. "The more people who know, the harder it is for Natasha to back out."

As Jeffrey made his way toward the door, Ryder called his name and he turned inquiringly.

"Violetta's a very nice woman," Ryder said. "It's over a year since she lost her husband."

Jeffrey looked extremely pensive. "Violetta and I have both experienced the loss of a marriage. We understand each other, and hope to remain . . . very good friends. Nothing more." He quickly walked out the door and through the workroom.

"I won't back out," Natasha said softly to Ryder. "Jeffrey's right, isn't he? Your wedding should live up to the image of your store."

"I don't care a brass razoo about that. All I'm worried about is that you marry me somehow, and not too far in the future." He kissed her lingeringly, and as they wandered into the workroom, their arms about each other, he stopped to eye the mannequin glassily smiling through the mists of veiling. "I suppose your grandmother would love us to have a lavish affair with all the trimmings?" He smiled. "I have to admit I share a little of Jeffrey's chagrin about Gabe and Lianne running out on *their* wedding and cheating me of a chance to be best man. I haven't even met his new wife yet. We'll have to invite them. Maybe we *should* show Gabe how it's done. And perhaps," he added thoughtfully, "we might persuade Grace to attend."

"And your mother?" Ryder had talked to his mother briefly on Christmas morning, and so had Natasha. She had sounded excited and a little tearful, and told Natasha she'd asked Ryder to bring his fiancée to see her. "I'd like to meet her."

"She wants to meet you, too. Is a DeWilde wedding what you'd like?"

"What's your preference?" she countered. "Do you want me to marry you wearing a DeWilde gown?"

"It'd make no difference to me if you were in sackcloth and barefoot. You'd still be ravishing. Tell me what *you* truly want."

Natasha laughed, and confessed, "I've been dreaming of a real DeWilde wedding ever since I first walked into the bridal department with you."

"You have?" Ryder smiled and kissed her again, under the benign stare of the plastic bride in her cloudy veil. "Then it's settled," he said, raising his head at last to smile at his love. "If a DeWilde wedding is what you want, then a DeWilde wedding is what you shall have."

"Only if you're sure it's what *you* want, too."

"I want you," he said, lifting her hands to kiss each one in turn. "I thought I'd made that plain. Only you, to have and to hold and be mine, as I am yours, for the rest of our lives. After all, even a DeWilde wedding is just a beginning."

WEDDINGS BY DeWILDE

continues with

A BRIDE FOR DADDY

by Leandra Logan

Available in August

Here's a preview!

A BRIDE FOR DADDY

STEVEN COULDN'T HELP but admire her chutzpah. She'd expected to just waltz in here and finagle the matrimonial package out of him! It hadn't been his style in recent years to confide his real feelings to anyone, but he didn't know any other way to put the brakes on this captivating steamroller.

He studied his blunt fingernails, avoiding her vivid green eyes. "As you've no doubt gathered by the essay, I was widowed relatively young."

"Yes. I'm as sorry as I can be about that."

"My wife had a weak heart, caused by a bout of rheumatic fever as a child. She was barely thirty at the time. It was all very hard to take, and I'm very set on remaining single. It's my goal to convince the kids that they can lead a happy life without a replacement mother."

"This isn't a real-life commitment," she protested. "It's just a few days out of your life!"

"I'm thinking especially of Natalie and Nick and their attachment to you. It would be devastating for them to lose you when the week was up. It seems best to me if you leave now, before they return."

Tessa sighed as she thought of the bubbly pair. "And never see them again? They adore me. They think I belong to them."

"But you don't," he argued. "Your hanging around would just encourage more false hope. And I'm hoping this mix-up will cure my mother's meddling once and for all," he confided with a wicked gleam. "She can explain to the press and everyone else that it was all a mistake."

"Can't you cure her next time?"

"No. She might not make the papers next time."

Tessa sighed doubtfully. "It just might put an end to Millicent's games for good. But I must warn you that those children are still going to want a new mum."

Steven smiled tightly, fuming at her nerve. "You speak like a parent with experience, Miss Jones."

"No, I'm a child with experience, Steven. One who lost her mum quite young in a light plane crash over the Greek Islands. My father never remarried, you see, and it was a tough go. I still...well, I still search out mother figures. Hard as I've tried to get over it, there's a tiny little girl inside me who wants that kind of affection. There's a uniqueness to the bond."

Steven could tell the admission was a tough one for her. He appreciated her honesty, but it scared him all the more. They'd barely met and yet were opening up the way people do when they're instantly attracted to each other. He simply had to get rid of her fast. "I'm sorry you were dragged into our affairs, but I think a clean break is the best," he said evenly. "You make amends to your employer and I'll take care of my family. Though, if you like, I could speak to your boss," he said as an afterthought. "Explain about my mother..."

"He already got a good dose of Millicent," Tessa cut in sharply. "That's doing a whole lot of nothing."

"I apologize. Good—" Steven whisked open the door, only to find his family on the other side, carrying sacks from a variety of shops.

"How nice!" Millicent greeted the startled couple. "Everybody's been shopping for what they need today, it seems."

Nicky's and Natalie's small mouths opened wide at the sight of their father with the mother of their dreams.

"She's here," Nicky breathed reverently.

Natalie's shiny eyes shifted to her father. "Isn't she perfect for us, Daddy? She even comes with her own dress and party shoes and everything!"

HARLEQUIN®

Don't miss these Harlequin favorites by some of our most
distinguished authors!
And now, you can receive a discount by ordering two or more titles!

HT #25663	THE LAWMAN by Vicki Lewis Thompson	$3.25 U.S.☐/$3.75 CAN. ☐
HP #11788	THE SISTER SWAP by Susan Napier	$3.25 U.S.☐/$3.75 CAN. ☐
HR #03293	THE MAN WHO CAME FOR CHRISTMAS by Bethany Campbell	$2.99 U.S.☐/$3.50 CAN. ☐
HS #70667	FATHERS & OTHER STRANGERS by Evelyn Crowe	$3.75 U.S.☐/$4.25 CAN. ☐
HI #22198	MURDER BY THE BOOK by Margaret St. George	$2.89 ☐
HAR #16520	THE ADVENTURESS by M.J. Rodgers	$3.50 U.S.☐/$3.99 CAN. ☐
HH #28885	DESERT ROGUE by Erin Yorke	$4.50 U.S.☐/$4.99 CAN. ☐

(limited quantities available on certain titles)

	AMOUNT	$
DEDUCT:	10% DISCOUNT FOR 2+ BOOKS	$
ADD:	POSTAGE & HANDLING	$
	($1.00 for one book, 50¢ for each additional)	
	APPLICABLE TAXES**	$_____
	TOTAL PAYABLE	$_____
	(check or money order—please do not send cash)	

To order, complete this form and send it, along with a check or money order for the
total above, payable to Harlequin Books, to: **In the U.S.:** 3010 Walden Avenue,
P.O. Box 9047, Buffalo, NY 14269-9047; **In Canada:** P.O. Box 613, Fort Erie, Ontario,
L2A 5X3.

Name: _____

Address: _____ City: _____

State/Prov.: _____ Zip/Postal Code: _____

**New York residents remit applicable sales taxes.
  Canadian residents remit applicable GST and provincial taxes.   HBACK-JS3

Look us up on-line at: http://www.romance.net

SILHOUETTE... Where Passion Lives

Order these Silhouette favorites today!
Now you can receive a discount by ordering two or more titles!

SD#05890	TWO HEARTS, SLIGHTLY USED		
	by Dixie Browning	$2.99 U.S. ☐	/$3.50 CAN. ☐
SD#05899	DARK INTENTIONS		
	by Carole Buck	$2.99 U.S. ☐	/$3.50 CAN. ☐
IM#07604	FUGITIVE FATHER		
	by Carla Cassidy	$3.50 U.S. ☐	/$3.99 CAN. ☐
IM#07673	THE LONER		
	by Linda Turner	$3.75 U.S. ☐	/$4.25 CAN. ☐
SSE#09934	THE ADVENTURER		
	by Diana Whitney	$3.50 U.S. ☐	/$3.99 CAN. ☐
SSE#09867	WHEN STARS COLLIDE		
	by Patricia Coughlin	$3.50 U.S. ☐	
SR#19079	THIS MAN AND THIS WOMAN		
	by Lucy Gordon	$2.99 U.S. ☐	/$3.50 CAN. ☐
SR#19060	FATHER IN THE MIDDLE		
	by Phyllis Halldorson	$2.99 U.S. ☐	/$3.50 CAN. ☐
YT#52001	WANTED: PERFECT PARTNER		
	by Debbie Macomber	$3.50 U.S. ☐	/$3.99 CAN. ☐
YT#52008	HUSBANDS DON'T GROW ON TREES		
	by Kasey Michaels	$3.50 U.S. ☐	/$3.99 CAN. ☐

(Limited quantities available on certain titles.)

TOTAL AMOUNT	$ _____
DEDUCT: 10% DISCOUNT FOR 2+ BOOKS	$ _____
POSTAGE & HANDLING	$ _____
($1.00 for one book, 50¢ for each additional)	
APPLICABLE TAXES*	$ _____
TOTAL PAYABLE	$ _____
(check or money order—please do not send cash)	

To order, complete this form and send it, along with a check or money order
for the total above, payable to Silhouette Books, to: In the U.S.: 3010 Walden
Avenue, P.O. Box 9077, Buffalo, NY 14269-9077; In Canada: P.O. Box 636,
Fort Erie, Ontario, L2A 5X3.

Name: _____

Address: _____ City: _____

State/Prov.: _____ Zip/Postal Code: _____

*New York residents remit applicable sales taxes.
 Canadian residents remit applicable GST and provincial taxes.

Silhouette®

SBACK-SN3

Harlequin Romance ®

Delightful
Affectionate
Romantic
Emotional
Tender
Original
Daring
Riveting
Enchanting
Adventurous
Moving

Harlequin Romance—the
series that has it all!

HROM-G

Harlequin® Historical

If you're a serious fan of historical romance,
then you're in luck!

Harlequin Historicals brings you
stories by bestselling authors, rising new stars
and talented first-timers.

Ruth Langan & Theresa Michaels
Mary McBride & Cheryl St. John
Margaret Moore & Merline Lovelace
Julie Tetel & Nina Beaumont
Susan Amarillas & Ana Seymour
Deborah Simmons & Linda Castle
Cassandra Austin & Emily French
Miranda Jarrett & Suzanne Barclay
DeLoras Scott & Laurie Grant...

You'll never run out of favorites.

Harlequin Historicals...they're too good to miss!

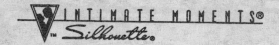

SPECIAL EDITION

Stories of love and life, these powerful novels are tales that you can identify with—romances with "something special" added in!

Fall in love with the stories of authors such as **Nora Roberts, Diana Palmer, Ginna Gray** and many more of your special favorites—as well as wonderful new voices!

Special Edition brings you entertainment for the heart!